BOBBY'S WAR

RKF ADAMS

Cover Design RKF Adams

Printed in the United States of America

Plainfield, Indiana

ISBN: 978-1-7354755-0-9

Library of Congress Control Number: 2020913961

This is a work of fiction. Names, characters, places, locales, and incidents are the product of the author's imagination unless otherwise attributed.

The Uniform Code of Military Justice is the governing code for the Armed Forces. Chapter 47, Subchapter 10, Section 918, Article 118 specifically refers to Murder.

UNCOMMON VALOR WAS A COMMON VIRTUE
~Admiral Nimitz

(29) AND YE SHALL EAT THE FLESH OF YOUR SONS, AND THE FLESH OF YOUR DAUGHTERS SHALL YE EAT.

(30) AND I WILL DESTROY YOUR HIGH PLACES, AND CUT DOWN YOUR IMAGES, AND CAST YOUR CARCASSES UPON THE CARCASSES OF YOUR IDOLS, AND MY SOUL SHALL ABHOR YOU.

(31) AND I WILL MAKE YOUR CITIES WASTE, AND BRING YOUR SANCTUARIES UNTO DESOLATION, AND I WILL NOT SMELL THE SAVOR OF YOUR SWEET ODOURS.

~ LEVITICUS 26

01 TROPICAL DEPRESSION

The truck skidded sideways through the intersection, rear end swinging back and forth until it decided to stay where it belonged, behind me. Windshield wipers at maximum as useless as the brakes, which were recently shoed. I plowed through three inches of standing water, turned on the emergency blinkers, exhaled, and backed off the accelerator.

Red starbursts filled the rear view mirrors. Whoop of multiple sirens rose over the noise of the pounding rain. I eased into the right lane searching for an opening into any unoccupied space. The vehicles were on top of me. I coasted through the river running down the turn lane. One, then a second green and white county prowler barreled into the intersection and skidded west onto Navy, followed by three marked Pensacola police cruisers, slipping and spinning on the wet pavement. A fire truck, then an ambulance followed at a more sedate speed, entering the intersection at less than sixty miles an hour, safely turning left due solely to their weight. Few visitors vacationed in the armpit of the continental United States during rainy season, which greatly reduced fatalities and near misses during a parade of power rangers on a mission. Goddam cowboys.

I detoured through an empty filling station, crossed the east bound lanes and turned west when a big black Chevy suburban bounced through the intersection against the light. I pumped the brakes and spun the wheel to the left, using the sideways skid to avoid ramming his back end. No lights, no siren. I let loose on the driver's maternal parentage, took a deep breath, and crossed the center line to re-enter the west bound lane.

Journey's end on such a dreary day was Port Bryant, rescued from bankruptcy by Michael Robert "Bear" Bryant, who was in the process of refurbishing the deep water marina complete with marine terminal services and access to intermodal storage and shipping. I had no idea what any of those terms meant, but I didn't need to. I owed him manual labor, unpaid and plentiful in exchange for all his help with my own fledgling tourist trap.

Although my very own personal tropical depression had not lessened, the early November rain slackened enough to provide a generous fifteen foot visibility zone in case more emergency response vehicles magically appeared out of the gloom. Damn Bear, I had a million things to do this morning, but I'd made a promise. The man had figured out a way to pull his pension and build boats for people who carried out amphibious assaults. Most of his clients consisted of military industrial complex types and rock stars. We'd made a few unscheduled amphibious landings as Marines. He served his time with distinction, learned a trade, and mustered out. I eventually earned my wings, but refused to become a dancing monkey for the wonders of gender inclusion in combat aviation. I had worked too damn hard and too damn long and I made it known I would never trade my stick nor my self-respect for a microphone. At that point I became a liability. Uncle Sam's angry diversity minions made me an offer I couldn't refuse. Unfortunately for me, breaking shit and killing people had left me ill prepared for the surreal world of civilian life. After a false start, I returned to the city of my youth, settled into a sedate life of selling little trees in little pots to unsuspecting tourists, and performing manual labor for my few friends.

I drove down the gravel drive missing few chuckholes. Couldn't see them under three inches of fast running rain water. The road curved away from the waterfront before gaining the marina, blocking my line of sight into the facility. Bear liked seclusion, and this place was the end of the line past four other marinas of varying sizes and financial states, including a recycling plant and a vinyl manufactory.

Emergency vehicle lights rippled the sodden view through my windshield. Two county prowler cars blocked the open gate. What fresh hell awaited our intrepid hero? Thoughts flew to my dusky, dusty, fusty, marble-muscled Jiminy Cricket, and camp philosophizer. So used was I to his low growl asking the questions that held universal meaning such as: "Letting this guy live gains us what exactly?"

I drifted to the right and rolled to a stop twenty feet behind the patrol cars, well out of their way. I stepped into the heavy mist and flicked away my unfinished cigarette. A black utility truck, its backdoors open, blocked the south west corner of the warehouse. No doubt one of the SWAT vehicles that nearly ended my morning commute. Three city squad cars, the fire truck, and an ambulance were scattered about the parking lot like Tonka toys. Small clots of response actors in proper costumes stood around without creating much movement other than shifting about and fiddling with equipment.

Bear normally parked his truck inside the west loading bay, and left the door open unless he was creating top secret toys. The bay was large enough to accommodate a C-130 transport. The hanger door stood open, and men in an assortment of gear milled about inside the warehouse. I spotted Bear's empty truck, but no Bear.

A county deputy clad in plastic rain gear exited his cruiser and approached me, hand on his holstered firearm. "Stop. You can't go in there." A male voice, young and nervous, far too loud this early in the morning. He was twelve feet away. Maybe he thought I was hard of hearing.

I held my hands aloft, fingers splayed. "I work here. I've got I.D. What the hell's going on?"

Another deputy, unaware of my hearing problem, exited the second car and approached. "You work here? Put your hands down. Let's see the I.D." A fierce scowl under the brim of his hat gave me pause. Older, male, baritone, with a hint of twang. His voice scratched at a soggy memory.

I slowly reached around to my back pocket and pulled out a little metal box that passed as a wallet, hoping to avoid mentioning the .38 tucked in a holster tacked to the back of my belt. Bear insisted that I never, ever venture down his road

3

without a weapon. Not all of the indigenous wildlife appeared on the endangered species list, but all of it was to be considered hostile.

I tossed the wallet to the scowling officer. He popped it open and shook his head at the glamor shot posted on my license. The youthful patrolman yelled, "We got a situation here, ma'am, you need to turn around and go home."

"Shut up, Sam," The officer ruffled through the few pieces of plastic in my wallet including a charge card, a library card, and a concealed weapon permit bearing a mugshot similar to the driver's license.

"You carrying?" He returned the pieces of plastic to the case.

I nodded.

"She's got a gun." The younger man struggled with his sidearm. The maneuver was complicated because he hadn't unsnapped the safety strap. His face scrunched up in anger. He finally freed his sidearm and aimed it at my midsection.

"For the love of God, kid, stow your weapon or I will relieve you of duty. Now." The older officer's scowl softened into exasperation. Sam stared wide eyed at his superior, mouth in an Oh of shock, "but, but –"

"No buts. Get in your car. Now."

Sam the younger stared at me with his most menacing glare. He tried to holster his weapon, missing the first time, and then stomped back to his patrol car. The familiar officer tossed my wallet back. "Just what is it you do here, Mrs. Archer?"

That voice. A spark flickered in the back of my skull. I couldn't see the face under the rain brim of his patrol hat. He'd pulled it down too low for me to get a good look. I recognized that voice, though.

"I'm helping my friend get the marina up and running. I have some skills."

4

"Like pulling out in front of tactical vehicles, and popping up at crime scenes."

"You all pulled out in front of me."

He cracked a smile, pushed back the brim of his hat, and stuck a foot up on my front bumper. "Driver got on the radio bitching about a brown and tan Chevy pulling out in front of him. Heroically, he saved both trucks and the lives of the townsfolk."

"Your driver was running with no lights, but I managed to get my truck out of the way."

"SWAT doesn't run lights. The point is stealth, not advertising. And anyway, they are –" His radio crackled. He pinched the mic pinned to his jacket and held up a hand for silence. I caught sight of his name plate. Moreno. I liked Officer Moreno, but I was getting a little tired of standing in the rain. And I couldn't remember who the hell he was. I avoided meeting law enforcement on a professional basis whenever possible.

He mumbled a response and signed off. "What I was saying was that they refer to themselves as Emergency Response. It's kinder and gentler. I gotta say, Archer, two crime scenes I meet you at. Neither one with a criminal in sight. Gotta be a record of some kind. Anyway, city's in charge, not me, so you go right on in, you being an employee and all. This oughta be good." Moreno banged on the hood of the rookie patrolman's Crown Vic and motioned him to move back. A white Ford Econoline rumbled through the open gate. No lights or sirens, a discreet green five pointed star identified the big brute as a county meat wagon. It passed me slowly. I walked in its dismal wake studying the patch on the bumper. A black skull impaled with the medical caduceus and flanked by the scales of justice and a handgun. Gruesome yet accurate. Coroner whimsy.

My phone rang with the electronic sounds of techno-salsa. I flipped it open. Bear asked, "You here?"

"Thirty yards out, following the coroner." Silence ticked. "Talk to me, what the hell is going on in there?"

"Don't need any ambulance. They're all dead in here."

I stepped aside to let a second ambulance rumble past. "Another wagon is coming in." I shut the phone and fell behind the truck, trudging toward the blazing yellow of high powered kliegs, glare bouncing off pools of water. The sprinklers had engaged at some point. The air inside looked smoky, like bars used to be, but it smelled, oh hell, the closer I drew, the unmistakable aroma of cooked meat gained strength.

I stopped inside the gate and scanned the hanger, finally spotting Bear, his head bowed as if in prayer, standing alone among the law enforcement types. I started toward my friend, but was stopped by a city officer. "You got no business here."

"Escambia Deputy at the gate sent me in. Survey damage to the property."

"Thought some big guy was the owner." The officer's eyes were red and wet as if he'd been in the smoke.

"I'm an employee. You been in?"

He swallowed visibly. "Not, not all the way, the smell's enough. I'm supposed to keep out the gawkers."

Bear approached, sniffing into a white handkerchief. He held it out toward me. Without question I jammed two fingers of the linen inside my nose. Deep breath. Bad smells coming. I could taste the fuel. Showing up for work today seemed like a bad idea. Gasoline in the nose was the only defense against the sweet corruption of rotting flesh. Or worse. And this was going to be worse.

I jammed the rag up my nose a second time. Coffee from breakfast tried to escape, but I refused to contaminate the crime scene or whatever was left of it after the sprinklers deployed, and all the law enforcement players tromped around. Medics huddled together away from the subject of the intense lighting. County

6

and local cops milled at the exits near the fresher air. SWAT crew had departed as there was nobody to kill and nobody to save.

Bear waited until I'd gotten my stomach under control, and twitched his head for me to follow him inside the building, toward the reason for this morning's parade of power rangers.

My brain shut down the feelings side and told the math side to take notes. Bodies stacked, maybe three, maybe four. Not much recognizable to determine sex or age. Glimpse of limb, upper portions charred down to wet blackened tissue. Darkened areas either clothing or skin where the fats and fluids ruptured the dermis. Ovoid skulls. Classroom voice of long forgotten professor describing what happened to the body in fire whether human or animal. Oh fuck oh fuck oh fuck. My brain began to process the images providing the data, and I no longer wanted to know. The fuel in my nose did not dampen the remembered stench of death by fire.

Bear leaned in close. "Fire was out when I got here, the sprinklers done their job. Could smell it soon as I got close. The bay door was shut when I arrived. I hit the remote, pulled in, parked, honked the horn a couple times. Nobody came running out. Spotted the puddles. Tank musta run dry. Enough to put out the fire at least."

Staring into the blackened pyre, I mumbled "Jesus wept."

"Ain't no Jesus here, sweetheart, he done gone to lunch."

He and I had traveled far and long, stood witness to crimes of the twentieth century, plus a bunch in the new millennium. Pits dug with backhoes, bodies tumbled in, doused with gasoline, and then torched. Anyone attempting escape got a bullet in the gut so they were alive when they went into the hole.

"This is some serious tribal shit, Bear. As in south of the border crazy. But here? This isn't some socialist paradiso. You know of any locals doing shit like this?"

"Cops might know, but they ain't talking. This looks personal. Piled up for what reason?"

"Honor? Insult? Hiding something?"

Bear shrugged. "Local news readers got the natives all het up about roving gangs of dangerous brown ruffians. Sanctuary cities bleeding out, yeah, but this ain't no sanctuary city. The hillbillies bag a lot of illegal drug runners, territory poachers, but I never seen this shit in-country. This don't look local. This is evil, eighth circle of hell shit."

"Seventh. Burning river of blood."

"Isn't that interesting, you knowing something like that." He twitched his head to the right. "Got another one. All by his lonesome." Bear led me farther into the hanger, lit like a grade B movie set. We stopped short at the pool of water surrounding a lone body, untouched by fire. A young man, early twenties, on his back, eyes open and unfocused. Harsh light shadowing the pits of acne scars. I squatted down, avoiding the puddle. This man died alone, away from the others. Skin dusty gray from blood loss, thick dark hair longish, teeth untouched by braces or western medicine, mostly intact from what I could see. His fingernails short, dirty, two fingers misshapen, likely old breaks badly set. Above the midline of his throat, ear to ear, someone had severed veins, arteries, muscle. Strength went into making that wound, cutting clean and deep with no hesitation. The man bled out quickly. The downpour from the sprinklers washed the wound clean. I stood and put a hand on my friend for balance, breakfast climbed to the top of my throat.

"Maybe he tried to run away from the fire, got caught," I suggested.

"Maybe somebody is making a statement about them, but not this man, hell, he's practically a kid."

"Maybe he's a kid here in the land of milk and honey, but I don't think he's from here." The smell was piling up inside my head. I tore my eyes from the dead man, and looked up at Bear.

His eyes as shiny as mine felt. He took my arm, and circumnavigated the burn pile, aiming for the open door and rain freshened air.

Limbs tightened, fats rendered, a successful burn left behind charred bone, ash, occasional teeth or shrapnel. This was not a successful burn. Temperatures necessary to reduce the human form to ash were impossible outside of an oven. This was someone making a statement. This was a funeral pyre, but not to honor these dead.

I prayed for their souls. I prayed they had been unconscious when set alight. Sidestepping puddles accumulated from the sprinklers, we made it outside as the yips and yaks started. I leaned against the front end of an ambulance and bent over, panting, pulling in oxygen and trying not to throw up. Unbidden, the baby floated into my mind.

Swaddled in dirty burlap, she had been tossed into the brush, thereby escaping the wholesale slaughter of her mother and traveling companions. A trench had been dug, the peasants shoved in alive, doused with fuel, then set afire, attempts at escape were met with lead as evidenced by the amount of spent shells surrounding the ditch. The stench of kerosene still strong, the rot of corruption made worse in the South American climate. The baby was inexplicably undisturbed by wildlife when I spotted her. She had succumbed to dehydration and exposure. I tucked the coarse fabric around the frail body and cradled her in my arms. Tears tracked through the dirt on my face and darkened her shroud. Without a word, the child was taken from me as tenderly as if she were alive. My people, my brothers, they provided a proper burial for the nameless infant. Her people were gone, her village burned. The child had been a dark shadow in my memories for decades.

My stomach lurched upon reentry to the here and now. I blinked tears from my eyes and slowed my breathing. Another of Pensacola's finest approached. "Hey, what the hell are you doing here? Who are you?" He pointed at Bear and demanded, "On whose authority is she in here?"

"Mine. Who the hell are you?"

"I don't have to – "

Bear interrupted. "Yes, you do. Jurisdiction with Escambia County Sheriff's department."

Still bent over, I told the officer, "Some guy said PPD's in charge. I personally do not care who is. You two duke it out. I am going home."

"No, you're not. I want identification right now."

The deputy's outdoor voice hurt my head. I stood upright slowly, rubbed the tears out of my eyes, turned left, seeking escape, and ran into a wall of dark blue windbreakers. The ocean roared in my ears drowning out all the voices. Deputy Moreno, the officer formerly with SWAT had entered the melee, and his voice broke the din. "You boys got here awful fast."

Another male voice among the blue jackets, even louder than Moreno yelled. "We can't afford to have the scene fucked up by a bunch of locals."

Not a fainter by nature, but my knees had lost strength. Bear got a massive arm around my waist and propped me up. I whispered, "I have to lie down. Oh Jesus. They were … tell me that wasn't real."

"Who the hell are you?" Demanded a booming voice belonging to one of the dark blue windbreakers with the bright yellow letters.

"I'm the one who's gonna throw up on your shiny new boots." I swallowed and exhaled, adding "Sir" to my warning.

Voices multiplied as more law enforcement joined the fray. City, county, federal. I looked toward the gate and my escape route. Two meat wagons, several marked and unmarked police cars filled the parking lot, obvious in their cheap camouflage.

The fire truck had gone. I calculated the odds of getting to my truck without getting shot at less than zero.

The man whose boots I'd threatened to throw up on cranked up his volume. "How about you and your mouth sit in Jacksonville for a few days until you remember who you're talking to, missy."

Bear growled at me to shut up and addressed the agent politely. "You did not declare yourself. You barged in yelling at our local heroes and didn't bother to notice that a lady is present, and at present needs to lie down in a quiet room for an hour. And the lady is going to do just that."

Moreno chimed in. "I gave her clearance to enter. She's an employee. I know who she is and where she lives. If she's needed for questioning, I'll fetch her myself. Until then, we let the lady go home."

My newly declared friend asked if I were okay to drive. I nodded and mouthed thank you. Bear took a few steps with me. I hugged him tight and whispered, "Call me."

Jelly legs carried me to my truck. I jammed the key in the ignition and remembered those eyebrows, fat furry black caterpillars wrestling on a moon pie. Moreno. We'd met months before in a maintenance shed at the eastern most edge of my island. He'd been with the emergency response team known as SWAT, responding to an event to which I was attached. He recognized me today even though I wasn't covered in blood and globs of brain matter which had belonged to a Chicago gangster, nor did I sport facial lacerations, contusions, or dangling strips of duct tape.

That day I had thrown up on someone's boots, but not his, thank goodness. He was one the good guys. And was again today.

Internal autopilot delivered me back over the bridge, to the sanctity and sanity of my aunt's island home. Built from old-growth cypress, her shotgun shack expanded over the years, was insulated, updated, reinforced, and protected with deadly force from shifty zoning boards, corrupt locals and dishonest feds. Developers mysteriously self-injured when they annoyed my aunt with their offers and threats. By sheer force of will, Aunt Hannah's little slice of paradise had been spared all attempts at destruction save hurricanes. Even the wrath of nature seemed protective of her home. Hannah Thompson was a respected member of the community, sat on several boards, attached her name to various charities. Never gratuitously, Hannah was a true believer in the principal of the American Work Ethic.

Rumor had it she had dented a mobster's skull with a cast iron skillet.

On the way home I stopped only twice to dry heave.

02 RING AROUND THE ROSIE

I stripped naked, stuffed everything in the washer, poured in too much soap, and turned the dial to hot. Although I was accustomed to sleeping through the trilling noise of my flip phone, the house phone shrieked like a banshee. I unplugged the unit at the wall, crawled into bed, and passed out.

Fire rose into a starless night sky swirling around a twenty foot tall woman. Luxuriant dark hair shrouded her figure. She spread her arms inviting me into the inferno. I snapped awake breathing hard. The cat mewled next to my head. Ralphie shared my pillow. He stretched all four legs touching my face with his forepaws and yawned. The cat closed his eyes and resumed his nap. At least I hadn't screamed. I put a hand on his tiny furry stomach and drew comfort from his warmth.

I set shaky feet on the floor, bent over, and held my head in my hands. The reek of charred human flesh, to which some long past asshole had attached the moniker of long pig set my stomach flopping. I removed the sleeping cat to Hannah's room to finish his nap in peace, stripped my bed bare, and sprayed the mattress with Lysol. Toting the bundle to the laundry room, I opened the washer. The clothes I'd worn smelled spring fresh, therefore safe for the dryer. I transferred the load and shoved the bedding in the washer. I stepped into the shower and scrubbed my own skin under a scalding spray until it felt raw. It was a race with the washer as to who could pull the most hot water.

I donned a heavy robe and sorted through the meager wardrobe, which consisted primarily of rummage sale bargains. Blue jeans, shorts, tee shirts, a funeral suit, and a couple of sweatshirts. Mother's exhortations legion, among them Waste Not Want Not, a motto shared as well with the Corps. Hence I boiled fabrics instead of discarding them. Hannah would serve my head on a platter if she discovered I threw out her good percale sheets just because they smelled like over-roasted pork.

The message light on the answering machine blinked at me, as did the missed-call light on my own phone. I ignored both. Callers could wait until I was capable of rational thought. I needed something in my stomach so it would stop eating itself. I reheated a mug of leftover coffee and dosed it with a splash of bourbon. Hannah kept fresh cream on hand at all times, and because cream had nutritional value, I topped off the Irish and poured a dollop in the cat's bowl.

The first two messages on the answering machine were for Hannah, dates and times dutifully noted in her message book. A woman identified as Nadine required a return call to discuss an upcoming fundraiser for the Opera. Mr. Stepanik called in regard to the upcoming Opera fundraising dinner and their joint attendance. Hmmm, interesting. He was a good man and a good friend to this family, such that it was with only two of us left. The third house message was Bill Thornton, island constable and personal nemesis, time stamped 1040. "You are not answering your phone. Call me." I pressed seven to erase the message. Following that, a second call, then a third call with orders issued, threatened violence barely restrained. "Call me. Now." Likewise erasing those messages leaving only data pertinent to Hannah's social life. I set the ringer to low and plugged the phone back into Ma Bell.

Beeps and tones as my cell phone connected to the mothership for message retrieval. Bill Thornton yelled over the noise of highway traffic. "I know you're home. You can't hide that truck. PPD, county, and the feds all require your attention. Before close of business unless you want a home visit." He had not closed the circuit. He was colorful in his condemnation of my continued absence. The island's top law enforcement agent was quite eloquent when provoked. I possessed the uncanny knack of provoking him whenever possible. Thornton was technically a precinct captain within the structure of the Escambia County Sheriff's Department, but we all referred to him as the sheriff, an affectation he hated.

I deleted the remaining messages from Thornton. They would be similar to the others, escalating in promised violence.

The last message featured a cultured and droning voice. "Mrs. Archer, this is Benedict Rafferty, senior financial trust officer at Martinelli Investments. We need to discuss the disbursement of your share of the sale of a property jointly owned with Pamela Martinelli. Please return this call at your earliest convenience." I pressed four to save the message. My heart sped up, breathing deepened, focus narrowed to the number on the display, prefix three one two. Chicago. I damn near died at the hands of that family. Aunt Hannah had been threatened with assault, and our island invaded by a platoon of old-school mafioso.

I deeded my culpability in that mess to Pamela's mother, vowing never to return to her city in exchange for protection from her family. Pam must have sold the software that sparked the internecine mob war because it was the only property we could jointly own. A shiny silver disk containing a half-finished encryption system upon whose ones and zeroes several dead men lay. My mother was right, I was an idiot. I should have destroyed the last copy, but I couldn't bring myself to kill the work, kill the only thing I had left of my best friend Chris, who happened to be Pam's fiancé. Instead I risked life and limb sneaking into the city for a meeting with Pam's mother, now head of the second largest crime family running the city of Chicago and surrounding suburbs. The largest crime syndicate would always be City Hall.

I closed the phone, made another Irish, but without coffee or cream, and plopped down on the sofa. Ralphie jumped into my lap. Warm, furry, guileless, another refugee from storms. Like me, Hannah had taken in the cat without asking any questions, requiring only undying loyalty. His fuzzy warmth purred under my hand. My eyes drooped. The lone figure, away from the pile nagged at me. Why was that man singled out? The sprinklers doused the fire leaving behind more meat than likely planned. Yet the single male had not been set ablaze. He had been garroted, yes, but hadn't suffered the indignity of attempted incineration.

I slept the sun past its zenith. Shadow edges were fuzzy as the skies had not cleared covering sand and sea with a dull gray light. White caps rolled in and collapsed with force on the sand. Ralphie twined in and out of my bare feet. I scooped him up. We stood at the sliding door and watched the light fade farther out of the world.

I absently scratched at my head. To my dismay, the towel had dried still turbaned on my head. It would be a fright, like a frizzy brown cotton swab. Not that I spent a great deal of time fussing at my hair. A rubber band finished my grooming regiment most days. Hair. Hair? Why hair? What about hair? For the love of Christ, the body at the bottom of the pile. Tufts of darkened hair visible, drenched by city water before it could be obliterated. The body, first in, on the bottom, last out when the medical examiners began their work. I pushed the image out of my head. Not my war, not my soldiers, not my victims. Four agencies jockeyed for control and they did not welcome amateurs. By morning, six more alphabet battalions will have joined the dance, up to and including the Coast Guard as their jurisdiction covers the sea and the water front.

I dialed Bear on whose shore this battle had washed up. He answered on the second ring and said, "I'm home. Been a long day. Going to bed."

I brushed out the dried broom that was my hair, pulled an old Cubs cap down over the top, dumped the last of the kibble into Ralphie's bowl, and set out for the 'Bama, a mile and a half west of home. It was the last American roadhouse and it occupied the DMZ separating the state of Florida from the state of Alabama. I was unaware of any ongoing animosities between the two states, but I wasn't a native.

Sunday at the Flora-Bama: church in the morning, music in the afternoon. I rarely made it to church, but I rarely missed the secular service afterward. Local musicians tuned up, and friends gathered to christen the coming week. Of late, full of tourists, life's financial blood and parasitic worms of the state. The storm had chased all but the die-hards from the beach so I held hope my sanctuary would be equally as sparse. I double timed on the high tide line in the brisk autumn air. In the spring, natives and world travelers descended on this pristine beach to heave dead fish across the state line for fame and fortune, but Sunday was home day no matter the season.

I flung open the screen door and stepped inside the shadows. A breeze carried the essence of cigarettes and stale beer, brine and sand, crowding out the aromatic horrors of this morning. The noise level was bearable. I mingled my way to the back bar. A familiar voice broke the trance. "Where's your big Bear?"

Carla, resident bartender, guidance counselor, and bouncer, pounced as if she'd been waiting for me. She pushed past a knot of thirsty revelers, and took her place behind the bar. I balanced a haunch on an empty stool and asked for a Maker's neat. One did not explain the meaning of neat to Carla.

"He's tied up at work."

"Hmm. Ain't seen the rest a yer crew nor the Sherf all weekend."

I nodded, sorted my change, and left extra singles on the bar, plotting an escape from Carla's forthcoming interrogation.

"Heard there's some trouble up Chico Bayou this morning. Figured you'd know 'bout that."

"Or be part of it?"

Carla laughed with more enthusiasm than my witty reply deserved. "Troubles up in the city instead of the island, so maybe you're not smack in the middle of it?"

Carla finally noticed a drinker waiting patiently for his turn. I took the opportunity to escape to the upper deck. I took a chair overlooking the stage, and waited for my so-called crew. At best I had a fire team. Bill Thornton, the Sherf, was not counted as crew because he had a real job, and real responsibilities, and dire consequences in the event of failure.

The City, as Carla called it, was Pensacola, Florida, good old U. S. of A. City of Five Flags, home to the Blue Angels Flying Exhibition Squadron, a haunted light house, and my Aunt Hannah, on whose doorstep I landed, homeless, damaged, and without discernible skills other than a proclivity for violence and the ability to perform mathematical feats of logic. Upon this landing, I was technically an adult, and therefore expected to make reasonably adult decisions. The jury had yet to make a ruling.

From my perch overlooking the main floor, I recognized the coppery hair of my favorite nurse. Cherryl Ellis had been on duty when I was delivered to her Emergency while sought for questioning by various law enforcement officers. She didn't like all the cheap suits and uniforms trampling through her domain disturbing patients and professionals alike. She aided my escape. We became combat friends.

Her husband Bobby, island deputy, stood next to her laughing. The pair exuded the flavor of good solid marriage and sported a squad of offspring. Children swarmed about the couple, three of whom darted about, mouths filled with laughter and all moving at the same time. One of the parental units issued an order, and five child units moved toward a sea-side door.

Children were permitted inside the roadhouse while the sun rode the sky, but vacated at twilight. Only tourists abused the rules. It had been a rare day off if Cherryl and Bobby were out on the Key with kids and kids' friends in tow. I patted pockets for cigarettes and money, and set off down the stairs for another drink and familiar company.

I didn't have to yell to grab Bobby's attention over the music as The Hermit Crabs had finished their set.

Without preamble, Bobby said, "Oh, hey, glad you're here, boy oh boy is Bill mad, you talk to him yet? Hey you got a pitcher? Come on outside, it's too nice to be indoors."

Cherryl swung out the door, following her brood. I ordered a pitcher and found the deputy perched on a picnic table while his wife chased assorted children at water's edge, yelling parental things. Her own spawn running far afield, while two non-Ellis children stayed within sight of the adult. Cherryl made shooing motions at them. Reluctantly, they moved toward the others. The clouds parted, allowing bits of sun to light up patches of the ocean, enough to brighten the beach, enough to make me glad I ventured outside to where the music and the beer lived.

I shared the pitcher into red plastic cups. Cherryl plopped on the bench next to me with a sigh, and took a long swallow. "Those kids, Lord, they are too darn skittish. That isn't the right word, but I don't know what is."

Bobby took her hand and said, "They're just different, honey, not used to being away from their folks is all."

"That's not it. Not at all. They been away from their parents before. The boy talks a mile a minute, about some kinda boarding school, about travelling with his folks, he said they even went to Paris, as in France. But that girl, I don't know what to think. She hardly talks, and when she does, it's spooky. It's not natural. God, the bedtime stories her mamma told her are criminal."

"Hey now, Cherr, they're not a problem, come on."

"Not to you, they're –"

I interrupted the marital spat. "Whose kids are they?"

Cherryl ignored me. "They aren't a problem to you, Bobby because you haven't been trapped in the house with them since Friday. That girl doesn't hardly make sense, doesn't move about much unless I make her. She's a statue in any room I'm in."

"Now darn it, they ain't doing much wrong, they're just –"

"If you say they are different one more time, I'll dump my beer on your head." She took a long drink, slammed her cup on the table and ran after the children, veering toward the tide line and into Alabama.

"Switch me sides, Bobby, you can watch Cherryl chase your kids." I stood and scooted onto his bench.

With a weary sigh he drained his beer and took my seat. He refilled our cups. "Bill is pretty tied up right now. They got all the brass pulled in to Hayne Street. City's got operational control for the time being, but the feds are getting antsy. Bill didn't hardly have words for what went on out there."

I turned to watch his kids and the extra kids and the mom who was tired while I waited for him to get around to asking me questions. I liked Bobby. He was old-school Eagle Scout. God, country, family. He could never play 'bad cop.'

"How come you show up in the middle of ..." he hesitated, searching for the right word.

I finished for him. "In the middle of some kind of barbeque? It was already out thanks to the sprinkler system."

"Aw, Jess, that's just wrong. When Bill got back to the station, he smelled rank."

"Why was he out there? It's city business."

"Because a you, because a your friend, that big guy, name of Bear. County Sheriff called in brass from all five precincts. This is big and ugly."

"And everyone is fighting for their name on the ticket?"

"That too. For sure. What were you doing out there? You tell me not to tell, I won't so long as I can."

"No secrets to keep, I swear. I owe Bear manual labor. He's done a lot of work on my nursery. I went out this morning to pay some back. Crimes were committed before either of us got to the marina."

"And you walked right in?"

"Two county sedans blocked the gate. Deputy by the name of Moreno recognized me, let me in. He used to be with SWAT?"

"I know him. He's good, wanted back on patrol unless we get blitzed. Bill may strip him good for letting you in. He's pretty mad at you. Might take it out on him."

"Tell Bill I overpowered the man."

Bobby was laughing when Cherryl returned to the table. Four of the crew tore east, back into Florida, followed by a coltish girl sulking through the wake.

Cherryl held up her cup into which the last of the tepid beer was poured. "I'm sorry I snapped at you, honey, I'm just worried. Tearing around the island helps. We gotta get out more often. I have to come more often. Cripes, you work out here."

I interrupted. "Since you ignored me before, I'll ask again, whose kids are they?"

Cherryl sighed. "Those kids are all right. Too polite, girl's shy, but heck, ours might have set that bar too high, they sure don't have trouble making themselves heard. Oh, sorry, they belong to the Reyes family. The boy's at St. Iggy's, and the girl started to the high school. Caught Bobby Junior's eye, she did. We got to know them a little since they got here, when? Maybe two months now?" Bobby nodded in agreement. "From Belize I think the Missus said. He's some kind of diplomat, Secretary to the Minister of Agriculture or whatnot. Down here doing research with UWF for a few months. Maybe your Angela would know. Isn't she over to the university?"

"As far as I know, she's got six degrees and working on a seventh."

Cherryl flapped her hand at the thought and continued. "Their mother called me at work Friday and asked if we could keep the kids so they could have a little get away, pick them up with ours. Said she'd cleared it with the schools. I was a little sore that she assumed I would."

"Their mom sure isn't shy."

"Robert Thurman Ellis"

"Aw, jeez, I didn't mean it like that. She just ain't shy about having opinions and such."

"You hush, she's just Latin is all. They're very passionate, like Italians or those crazy Greeks dancing and hugging."

I watched them watching the children, oblivious to my voyeurism. I met Deputy Bobby Ellis in lock-up here on the island. He brought me a soda and apologized for "the sherf bein so grumpy." The deputy set me free. That grumpy Sheriff had chained me to a desk in an interview room all night for no reason except spite. Deep down, I wondered if "the sherf" had forgotten I was there.

Cherryl blew a raspberry. "Her passion doesn't matter. I picked up those kids with nothing but their school books. I drove by the house thinking their folks would still be home or maybe leave something out for the kids. Car gone, lights off, no sign of anybody. Neither one of them have answered their phones all weekend, straight to voicemail."

"Hon, we got em taken care of. They're good kids. We'll get em to school tomorrow and their folks will be home and sorry, maybe bring the kids something nice."

"You're right, I'm just not feeling very charitable" Cherryl looked at me. "I'd have a half dozen, honest, but who drops their kids off without even a change of clean underpants?"

Twilight had crept in. Cherryl stood to retrieve the children, but Bobby put his hand on her arm, shook his head, and jogged to water's edge to collect the gang of children.

Cherryl sat down with a sigh. "Honestly, they're all right. I'd keep em. Just can't imagine leaving mine off anywhere. I mean who in their right mind would take them?" She was laughing as Bobby herded the children up to the picnic table to be brushed of sand, socks and shoes reapplied onto all feet.

The Ellis children chattered like magpies, all healthy, freckled, skinned knees. The eldest daughter, Theresa, shared her mother's blazing hair. Bobby Junior and Elizabeth shared their father's sun-coarsened dirty blond mop. The extra children were striking in dissimilarity to the host family yet related to each other without a doubt. Dark shiny hair, fine porcelain skin glowing, the color of Aztec gold plundered by the conquistadors. The new girl crouched down and tied her own shoes, then motioned her brother to come to her. She finished his shoes, stood, and stared up at me without blinking for several seconds. Less than four inches separated our height.

I returned her gaze, and held my hand out to her. "Hello, nice to meet you."

The girl, cheeks rosy from running in the cool air put her hand in mine and replied in kind. "ello. My name is Lilia Vasquez Monterroso." She looked away then added, "Reyes."

I glanced at Cherryl, but she was paying no attention to the exchange. I phonetically spelled the child's first name in my head. Leel-ya. I would not remember the rest.

"I'm Jess Archer. You have a prettier name than mine."

"My name means lily, for the water lily jaguar in the Maya. My mother says we are from the line of kings. She is the blood maiden of Xibalba and will return the jaguar king to his power."

Deep dark eyes, darker than brown, almost black in the failing light, held mine, as if in challenge.

"I am Javier." I was grateful for the interruption, a chance to break eye contact. The boy held his hand out in perfect imitation of his sister's courtly manners. I gently grasped his tiny hand in my left as his spooky sister would not release my right.

"Nice to meet you, Javier."

Lilia explained, "He is of Hunapu, and will remain so until he becomes a man."

"Well isn't that something?" What ghoulish stories had been inflected upon this child? A parent wanting to preserve their heritage, perhaps, but I remembered Maya legends to be bloodthirsty. As were Mongol, Greek, Roman, and Chinese. Hell, everybody left a bloody stain on the collective consciousness. Wars could not be won without bloodletting. As for the varying degrees of savageness, I left moral judgments to the pious. They were the most self-deluded, therefore, the most dangerous.

Bobby herded the flock toward the parking lot. "Round em up, let's go. Thanks for the beer, Jess."

Cherryl gave me a hug and took lead of the parade. Bobby paused a moment and whispered, "Kinda weird, huh? Blood maidens and serpents, a hidden kingdom in the cloud jungle. We been hearing this stuff all weekend, well, mostly Cherr, but you got lucky, you only got the introduction. Spend some time with her and you'll be rubbing your rosary and jumping at shadows. I mean, they don't scare me, it's just, who tells their kids that kind of shit?"

Who indeed? She spooked the deputy enough to utter a curse word. I watched the family tromp through the gravel lot and pile into a dusty mini-van. I wasn't superstitious by nature. I'd seen many faces of evil up close and sent them packing to their underworld with no regrets, but that girl gave me the willies. I shook off goose bumps, threw away our garbage, and double timed east through the surf, to the safety of my aunt's un-spooky home.

The cat required one last night prowl while I sipped bourbon on the back deck and watched heavy clouds build on top of the Gulf. I clicked my tongue several times to get the cat's attention. I'd heard Cherryl make that noise at her kids. Like working a horse, but it seemed to work on cats as well as children. I'd had my fill of the sand swirling in front of the oncoming storm. I checked the windows, locked the doors, and went to bed.

I dreamed of the burning woman again, but this time she was fifty feet tall. The wind blew a hole in the encircling flames. She had the face of a jungle cat, a jaguar. Her eyes glowed green fire. I ran and ran through the rock tunnels, but could not escape her laughter, mocking my fear and amusing her gods.

03 JUNKIE DAY CAMP

I pounded on Bear's door at 0700. His weathered brick ranch occupied the last lot at the end of Bishop's Row, so named for the defunct bingo hall slowly collapsing into its own parking lot. His truck in his driveway, hood of the engine cold. Unless the feds came and collected him, the man was home. I knocked on the door law enforcement style. Bam. Bam. Bam. No neighbors close enough to take umbrage at my banging. I took a step back and stood to the side. The door opened an inch, gravelly voice demanded, "You better be naked and beautiful."

"Let me in, dammit, it's cold out here."

"You ain't naked."

"Not beautiful either, but I brought coffee from the Waffle House."

"Show me."

I opened a lid and held the cup out, letting the rich smell of Columbian waft through the crack. The door swung open, I followed Bear's heavy sigh through the house, and into the kitchen.

Six foot plus of sculpted marble silhouetted by the early sun filtering in the seaside window. Pants, no shirt, no shoes. He held a hand out for coffee, lifted a lid, sniffed deeply, and smiled. He shared his cardboard cup into mugs and handed me one. "What gives?"

"I wasn't sure you'd let me in. Didn't want to wake your neighbors."

"They're all in their coffins. Sun's been up nearly an hour. I harbor no illusion this street will be gentrified any time soon."

"You got a good price."

Bear took a sip and nodded. "That I did, but the boy at the bank called me a ghoul. Hurt my feelings."

25

"That was the broker for the marina, and I believe he called you a goddam Yankee carpetbagger along with some unpleasant smears on your parental lineage. You hurt his bottom line."

"And hard." He leaned a haunch on the counter and sighed. "Long day."

I wrapped my hands around the mug, the only warm thing in the morning chill. Bear never wasted money on things like heat. It was Florida, but it was seven in the morning, early November. Hurricane season was drawing to a close, and the temperature had not yet breached fifty.

"Why'd the police keep you so long?"

"Punishment. Feds got mad, gave me a load of horseshit about national security. I was not impressed. And they were not amused that I was not impressed. Took me to city lockup and gave me a windowless room. But not before the coroner's crew got in to take that stack apart. The stench was ..." Bear trailed off. He drained his coffee and refilled both mugs from the second cardboard cup. "So I sat in that nice little box for a couple of hours when county comes in asking questions. Then they get run out by FBI. I ask for my lawyer. Blah blah blah, you don't have the right to an attorney because you're not arrested. I stared at the wall. They left me alone a couple more hours. Nice little gal in a fine fitting uniform brought me a sandwich and a soda."

"At least you got a date out of your time in Folsom Prison."

"By happy hour, I got homeland security dicks saying they can make me disappear if I don't tell them all I know. So I told them I was the new crime lord over all the Mexicali cartels and I'm switching up the trade routes. They were not amused. When I was looking into buying that rat hole, I ran the title search back to when the marina was built, we're talking three decades, damn near four. The previous owner had an import/export business in and outta Guatemala. Coffee, tamarind, textiles, legitimate shit. And they went broke, probably because they weren't running black market, hard to make a profit. Oh, you'll love this. Know why DHS come in so fast? Because the Coast Guard made a good case for asserting jurisdiction of the investigation."

"The Coast Guard has ultimate jurisdiction over all things water."

Bear laughed. "Yes they do, but I suspect they're bored. Nobody dropping briefcases full of white lady or bales of weed off the key anymore."

"You look pretty good for being on the rack most of the day."

"I slept between clown shows. Dreamed of my fine uniformed friend with the sandwiches." His eyebrows went up and down and a grin slid across his face. "Only folks I didn't talk to were ATF and DEA. But that'll come. City took swabs of my hands and stole my jacket and my shoes looking for trace residue. I suggested I might have changed clothes, chucking the tainted evidence over the dock. I'm lucky they let me keep my pants. I am damned lucky they ain't here tearing my house to shreds."

"Jesus, Homeland Security? I think they can lock you up forever without a warrant or a writ or even a clue."

"My little friend thinks it's something to do with the DEA. Says the men-folk were hollering about a report on a missing agent. Mostly arguing over who's in charge."

"Your little friend, a duly sworn officer of the law, just happens to sit in on a jurisdictional squabble? She must be pretty high up in the food chain."

Bear shrugged. His eyes revealed nothing, but the amusement was obvious in the crinkles around those dark eyes.

The storms of yesterday had run away leaving behind rising sunshine. We listened to the day gear up as the tide moved out and the birds moved in. Bear broke the silence. "You notice anything interesting out of place yesterday?"

I frowned and shook my head. "Same things you saw. Three in a stack and one all by its lonesome, throat slit."

He shrugged and finished his coffee. "Port Bryant is officially a crime scene under whose jurisdiction is anyone's guess. I have the day off, I may have the week off, and I plan to use the time wisely. Now go away. Thanks for the coffee."

"Since you're up and half dressed, the water pump is fubar again."

"Christ, Archer, fix it yourself."

"I'll do without if I have to traipse back into the bayou."

"You're a Marine. Nothing we afraid of."

"Nothing human. Nowhere in the Code of Conduct does it say anything about water moccasins, alligators, or giant goddamn spiders."

Bear pulled a t-shirt over his head, bent over and slipped on his boots, muttering about moochers. I ignored him. He was ready to go, but put up a good fight. I couldn't compete with a pretty cop in a fine fitting uniform, but maybe she was on duty, which meant he had nothing better to do until she was off duty, at least while his marina was a crime scene.

I followed Bear to my nursery, Gardens Of Sorrento, which butted up to Tarklin Bayou, a state preserved forested swamp. All things terrifying emanated from that stagnant black water, and my busted pump squatted in a finger creek running behind the shop. I watered my stock, most of which happened to be bonsai – little trees in pots – with water pulled through a series of filters via that pump. City water damaged the bonsai, but it was poison to the orchids with which I had been saddled. It also gummed up the aerators.

Bear pulled on thigh high rubber waders and stomped down the hill into the sluggish water. As I was less likely to encounter wildlife on this side of the parking lot, I disassembled the compressor. Something had jammed the intake down at the creek and burned out the motor. My brand new emergency shut-off valve did not perform as advertised.

Mondays were for maintenance which was handy as customers rarely graced my doorstep on Monday mornings. Cleaning, fixing, dumping, repotting were my Mondays. Bear finished his salvage work, and then spent the next half hour lecturing me on the dangers of improper shielding when using a submersible pump.

"I am not supposed to have a pump out there period. Some kind of environmental bullshit. I might kill a tree frog or something equally as important to the fate of the planet. I installed a rain cistern in accordance with paragraph seventy three, subsection nine, but I'll be damned if the city didn't give me trouble on that, too." I finished scrubbing unidentifiable biological gunk from my arms, and was toweling off when Angela arrived with lunch.

Bear went inside for cold beer, while Angela, office manager and perpetual grad student, pulled delicacies from a bag festooned with a cartoon pig and laid them out on the picnic table in the lot outside the sales room. She sighed watching Bear, "How come my friends don't look like Carpathian gods?"

I had no answer for her, too busy shoveling food into my mouth. Dill pickle, raw sweet onion, pinch of salt, briefest squirt of barbeque sauce. I squished the bun into the meat, and bit into the sandwich hugely. Propriety be damned, I was hungry.

The afternoon had warmed and the air thickened. The beer was necessary. Bear doled them out and grabbed a sandwich. "Wasn't no crocodile blocking that intake. About ten pounds of slime, some flora, and two small fauna."

"Assholes with Kalashnikovs I can handle. Creatures in the big dark empty of the bayou, not so much."

Angela and Bear flirted while I ate. I tuned them out. The pork was smoked to perfection, bark crisp and peppery, quieting the monster in my stomach. Pretty sure I hadn't eaten yesterday. Unbidden, an image of the carnage rose like swamp gas. I laid my sandwich down and took a deep pull of beer to choke down the bite in my mouth.

Oh Lord. Hair. Tufts of charred hair, yet a tress had remained intact, attached to the person on the bottom, the body on the bottom of the pyre. Shielded from the worst of the flames by the other two victims.

"Archer, you okay? You look green," Bear asked.

I shook my head. Bear stored standard fuel to fill boats and the occasional float plane that wandered inside the channel. That was the accelerant. The sprinkler system doused the flames. It had been a hot fire, but not hot enough to cremate the victims. That required a furnace. The arsonist did not understand basic laws of a material fire or maybe he didn't care.

I exhaled shakily. "It was a woman, her hair, it didn't all burn, she had long hair, and it wasn't completely gone. She was under the others." My voice barely above a whisper.

"No," Angela gasped. "I heard about a fire on Myrick, on the radio, driving in this morning."

"It was my place. Somebody killed four people Saturday night or Sunday morning, then started a fire," Bear told her.

Angela put her sandwich down. "My God, who were they?"

"Don't know the victims, don't know why they were at my marina. Lock on the door isn't hard to pop, neither is the gate. Mistaken identity or previous owner's business. Either way, I got no information."

I pushed my sandwich away as my stomach would tolerate no more. My beer was empty. I reached for Angela's, but she snatched it away and held it over the gravel, threatening to pour it out. "You want to keep secrets? Fine, but we have to get the orchid room ready. If you make a face, I'll pour it out."

"What secrets? I am not keeping secrets. I didn't see you yesterday. And I didn't have anything to tell." I diverted the conversation by launching into a tirade listing cost overruns and maintenance and tourists and my deep abiding hatred of orchids. Angela had unilaterally contracted a damn gross of clones, pods, bulbs, essentially starts of terrestrial and epiphytic orchids. My terror at executing a thousand dollars' worth of innocent plants was an understood if not fully articulated concern.

Angela packed up the garbage and gave Bear a sympathy hug, told me we had work to do, and disappeared into the gloom of my fiduciary purgatory.

I followed Bear to his truck and asked if his cameras were operational.

He nodded. "Why I came with when you barged in this morning. I started watching the playback. And you're right, it was a woman on the bottom of that fire. I'd rather fix your pump than watch snuff porn. I'll get it to Bill. I ain't taking it to the feds. You think he'll protect the source?"

"He hates the feds more than you do."

Bear nodded. "True. You be home soon? We'll pull the files down local, run them through your transmogrifier, maybe get some idea what we're dealing with. We can decide what to give the law. Honest to God, this doesn't feel like it's coming at me personally, but until I know for sure, we hold off doling out information. Idiots didn't ask about the cameras while they kept me in lock-up. All those suits and nobody noticed my cameras. Hell, I didn't even think of them in all the excitement."

I stood in the parking lot and watched Bear turn out onto Sorrento. He'll bring the data to my system, which consisted of a modified laptop, and an overstuffed desktop containing multiple processors that tended to heat up too quickly. I also had a masked router, a laser printer, an oversized monitor, and most importantly, a box of mice to fit any and all computers, none of that cordless crap either.

Angela's voice interrupted my thoughts. She was issuing orders concerning bulbs and rhizomes and lighting and bark and humidity and water pH, etcetera ad nauseam. Calculating distance variations within the theoretical laws of quantum mechanics made more sense than orchid care.

I kicked Angela out of the shop as Happy Hour drew near, and grabbed myself a cold beer from the mini fridge in the office. I spent an hour replacing grow bulbs, wiping bugs from the windows, and spraying everything for spiders. I dug through the junk drawer and found a pair of tongs to pull a bird out of a fan casing. I tossed the poor thing into the brush hoping St. Francis would work his charms. I hadn't known the bird personally and had not witnessed his passing. I locked the back and side doors, plopped down at my desk and checked my phone for messages. Nothing important, thank goodness. I'd forgotten to call the financial guy in Chicago about the alleged disbursement. I should have changed my name, moved to Ukraine, and stolen a new phone when that man uttered the name Martinelli. Instead, I tacked a sticky note to my desk with the investment adviser's name and number.

The cowbell over the front door clanked. Besides forgetting the phone call, I had also forgotten to flip the closed sign forward, and lock the damn front door. At this rate of forgetfulness, my desk would be covered with sticky notes. I stepped into the sales room and watched a large male walk toward me, six foot plus a couple inches, long gray hair woven into a single braid laying over his left shoulder. Creaky leathers, vest with identification patches, age past forty. No visible tattoos, but not much skin showed except head and hands. He was dressed for cold riding. The man was stoic sized, but not fat. No weekend warrior this. He nodded when I caught his eye and wandered to my left. I called out, "Yell out if I can help you with anything."

I took position at the potting desk searching for a weapon. My choice was a seven inch curved propagation knife or my scathing wit, equally dangerous.

His boots scuffled on the concrete floor allowing me to track his location. I scanned the orchid list, cursing the ancillary costs piling up under the right hand column, and watched the customer peripherally as he crossed the aisle.

He stopped in the second row and held up a small plastic training pot, a leafy eight inch tall tree sticking out of the middle. "What is this? Looks like little tomatoes." His voice a low grumble.

"That's Jerusalem Cherry. The plant is toxic but it tolerates abuse. It prefers partial shade."

"It smells funny."

I nodded. The plant did smell funny.

The man meandered through the sales room, touching leaves and reading labels. Perhaps he wanted a lovely bonsai with which to decorate his club house. My knowledge of the genus Bikerus Americanus Utlagatus, also known as Outlaw Biker, was limited to folklore, bad movies, and the occasional overblown news report.

He approached my bench empty handed and asked, "You know Red Max?"

I turned slightly toward him, an eyebrow raised in query. "I know a man named Max." The sterile and wickedly sharp propagation knife within reach.

"You work with him at St. John's."

The nameplate read Martin, another patch identified him as Sergeant at Arms. Various patches alerted the world to his specialties. No fleur-de-lis or troop number. He wasn't selling me popcorn. I carefully came to attention and waited.

"Max said you don't waste alotta words." He paused, choosing his own words. "But he said you're okay. That you got his girl home safe."

"Your friend is a goddam gossip." I looked the man up and down. I was toast if he wanted a fight, but I was angry. "How do I know you aren't a cop?"

"Do I look like a cop?"

"You could be undercover. Gang task force maybe."

"Maybe you're the cop."

I laughed out loud. "For God's sake, I sell trees."

Up close he wasn't unattractive. Hazel eyes, a corona of gold surrounding the pupils, but his face was off kilter, as if Picasso cubed him. Not obvious at first glance, but he took a spill some time back, and all the kings horses worked hard putting him back together with the up and down arrows mostly in alignment.

The silence of my appraisal hadn't made him nervous. He smiled and held out his hand. "The name's Steady. I got a problem and Max said you might be able to help."

I returned his handshake. It was firm, his hand warm, and he didn't try to crush my knuckles. Point in this man's favor, but brother or no brother, I would beat the shit out of Max. I'd sneak up behind him and whack him in the head with a spaghetti pot. Do one favor, next I got a line of idiots out the door. Only one idiot thus far, but there would be more idiots, of that I was sure.

Mr. Steady Martin stepped away from the bench and pulled a bougainvillea from the shelf. Crimson, twelve inch canopy in full bloom, one inch trunk, copper glazed pot. She was a beauty and she wasn't cheap. He brought it to the bench and set it down in front of me.

"What is this?"

"Bougainvillea, also known as Paper Flower. Difficult to kill. Responds to a hard trim by blooming more. It's hardy and likes the sun. Doesn't like to dry out, though, which it will in a bonsai pot."

"Hm. Usually see them in a fence row. Pretty, but full a thorns." He stared at the plant for a long moment and sighed. "Our lives, it's hard on the kids, you know?"

I poked at the dirt in the pot and nodded. I understood his dilemma in a roundabout way. My parents hadn't been outlaws, but the lifestyle was not absolutely dissimilar. Any given day a chaplain could come to the door and tell a child that one or both of his parents were gone with no explanation other than service to country. The consolation prize was a lovely folded flag suitable for framing.

Steady's eyes were shiny not with narcotics, but sorrow, tears that would not fall. It was time for me to play counselor.

"Come on back to the office, I got coffee." I pulled keys out of my pocket, locked the front door, turned off the lights in the sales room, and led him through.

I set the plant on my desk and started the coffee. We didn't speak while it dripped. He stared inside himself and I stared at the dark brew streaming down into the pot. I placed a mug in front of him. "I might have some chunky milk. The sugar hasn't gone over."

He shook his head, leaned back in the chair, and choked out a sordid tale of drugs, self-indulgence, and daddy issues. His little princess had run off before, but this latest guy was super bad, not even home grown.

"She run off again last week. Her parole officer called the house and said she missed her appointment, which means she missed her test, which means he's gonna violate her. I ran down all the places I know she knows. Girl won't answer her phone, but I got a lead where she was, using that GPS shit. Then the signal went dark. Battery musta died."

He pushed a creased four by six photograph across the desk. A smiling blond, sweet little sixteen, straight teeth, eyes white and healthy, skin untainted by teenage acne.

"You referred to her parole officer. Is this photo recent?"

He shook his head, reached inside his jacket, and removed a folded sheet. "She's twenty now."

I unfolded the paper carefully. A crease ran through her forehead and another across her neck. mugshot colors muted on the cheap copy paper. Four years looked more like four decades. Looking into the eyes of the woman in the photograph, I wondered if she was still alive.

"I can show you where I think she might be, where I've seen that barrio rat she run off with. I ain't got a picture of him, just seen him. No name yet. I'm working on it."

I put my head in my hands and rubbed my eyes. Fucking junkies. Blame everybody and everything, but never the sweet little angels. I tamped down my anger, at the intrusion, at the assumption that I would risk my liberty and my life to drag a scag back from the brink, if she was still alive. That picture was brutal. She went from sixteen to sixty in four short years. Chances were good she was done. No. No. No. I will not get involved – not again. Goddam Max. Couldn't keep his mouth shut.

I looked up from the picture. "She'll see you and run. Give me the coordinates of your guesses and a rundown of what I might be walking into."

He gave me two addresses. I plugged the numbers into a mapping program. I opened the image to street level and turned the monitor around. He nodded. I wrote the physical addresses on the back of the mugshot while he briefed me on the local wildlife and situational concerns.

I looked him straight in the eyes for several seconds before delivering my speech. "I will see what I can do. She will likely return to the life she's chosen. You know that. This isn't your first try, but it will be my only try."

He finished his coffee and clapped the mug on the desk. "How much?"

"Nothing. Or your life savings. Either way, I'll assess the situation. If I decide to move forward on the extraction, and she's alive, I bring her out. If she's dead, I contact the city and let them handle it. But my do-gooding stops here. I signed up to serve breakfast, as in community service without a court order, not bail out biker babies. You get that through to Max."

His eyes narrowed quickly. Then he sighed and softened. "Max said you done good, saved his girl. She got herself in trouble. Like mine."

"I could point out the obvious pattern, but that would be superfluous."

"He said you got a smart mouth, too."

I stood, signaling the end of the meeting. "And yet, here you are. I'll call you when I've finished recon. I'll have a list of things I'll need. Be ready to roll. She'll need to be taken somewhere and locked up for a while, probably a long while. She'll need serious medical attention. It would be best for her to be far away. No family, no friends, get her out west if you can, somewhere lonely and quiet."

"Max's little girl is –"

I finished his sentence. "Not my problem anymore."

"You think this is easy? Asking a goddam civilian for help? My brothers, we should be doing this. Busting this shit up."

"Yet your lifestyle has certain profile disadvantages."

"That's about right." He stood, signaling he was taking his own sweet time to leave my office. "Why you doing this? You sure as hell don't approve, but you're willing to help. Why?"

"Latent case of Samaritanism."

"Bullshit. Lady Marine and all? Max thinks you miss the action."

"You two are gossipy old women." I pointed to the bougainvillea on my desk and asked, "Do you want that?"

"Gift for my wife. Can I come back and get it? Can't carry it right now."

I told him the price, rounding to the closest dollar for the tax man. He counted out tens and ones and tossed the pile on the desk

I followed him out of my office and unlocked the front door. He hesitated at the door, looked down at me, and said, "Heard a rumor you did for Joey Steps."

I forced a laugh. "Now I know you all are gossips. Joey's mouth got the best of him. He tried to move on somebody else's territory and it ended badly for him. It was in the papers."

Steady held his hands up in mock surrender. "Sounds about right. He wasn't real bright. Fuck him. You know it's funny, though. I hate drugs, I'm okay with a little grass, little blow now and then, hell, it's safer than beer. We got the hard stuff out of our system a decade or more back, got all grown up, don't even run it no more, and now our goddam kids are dying from it."

He walked away and mounted his iron horse. The patch on the back of his leather displayed a life sized red skull floating over crossed M1s with bayonets fixed. Over the top of the skull, red lettering on black, a curved patch read Twelfth Knight.

No, it wasn't funny what their kids were doing. It was the madness of fools who in turn raised their offspring in folly. I listened to his engine fade into the evening on lonely Sorrento Road after cocktail hour had passed. There's no time like the present for a little bourbon. I poured two fingers and studied the dull portrait of my target, Taylor Martin. Even if she were alive, she was not so sweet now as she was four years ago. She never would be again.

After this, my books were closed. No more errands of mercy, no more do-gooding. Max had gotten my attention because I worked with him in the kitchen, and he had served with distinction. Technically a brother, but this Steady Martin was not my brother. I owed him nothing.

04 NIGHT VISION

Bear's truck squatted in my driveway like a fat dry toad. I climbed the stairs to find the inner door standing wide open. No security whatsoever. I yanked open the screen door and stomped into the house. Before I could yell, Bear announced, "I don't wanna watch this alone." He pointed to the counter where fresh coffee awaited.

"You helped me install that steel security door. It doesn't work if you don't lock it."

"Yeah yeah yeah, user error. Bring the pot." My laptop was on the table, powered up, and apparently loaded with poisonous data.

I poured mugs and scooted a chair next to him. We waited silently as the screen filled with video icons. The system recorded still images at three second intervals, twelve hours at a time, then uploaded a compressed loop to a private offsite server. I would have preferred a live video feed as the jerkiness of the stills unrolled ongoing events in bursts of black and white, like kids' doodles in a notebook, flicked to create cartoon motion. Except these weren't stick people.

Bear double clicked on a file labelled 05110000x12ETM, indicating day, month, start time of data collection, span of collection, and location – Exterior Terminal Main gate. That particular camera was statically mounted and oriented to the western front of the building. I argued for a sweeping camera at that gate, and another camera mounted on the building facing the gate so we could read the faces of who was coming in and going out. Bear overruled my suggestions as overly paranoid, bordering on nuts. I decided against pointing out the irony and sipped my coffee.

Bear poised the mouse over the image control slider and clicked Play. "Sunday, midnight, we'll be able to see when the fun started." A gigantic moth, magnified by the camera, trapped in crisp black and white, terrorized the night, movement strobed by the virtue of still photography. Four sets of glowing eyes darted across the gravel lot unmolested as the stills sped by.

Seventy six minutes into playback, a large van, windowless, light in color, moved into view. Bear switched playback to manual and clicked through the arrival. He tapped on the screen and said, "Ford Econoline. Maybe ten years old." The image quality enough for him to read the shape of the vehicle and make a guess at the model, but the focus area was too large to obtain important details, like a damned license number. The van ran dark, no headlights. It veered right and stopped near the service door. One person moved out of the passenger side door, jerk walking his way toward the back of the van. The driver magically joined him, and the pair assisted three hooded figures down and out of the cargo doors. The smaller man led a processional toward the door, single file. He appeared at the door with a pry bar. In the space of six seconds, two images, he had the door open. Bear growled.

"Stop. Are those people roped together?" I whispered, tapping on the screen.

Bear reversed through several images. The low light infrared picked up the lighter color of rope linking the prisoners. "Looks like it. Two guys, three prisoners. Easier to control when they're roped together." He whispered as well, although we were alone except for Ralphie. The cat kept our secrets. Bear paused playback and switched to another file. The date stamp was the same, but the location read ISW for Interior South West. He clicked forward to synchronize the file with the newcomers breaking and entering.

Although not in color, the detail of the interior camera image was sharp enough to capture faces. The taller of the men removed the hood from what was obviously a woman. In one image she was hooded, in the next, long hair had fallen over her shoulders. He cut her loose from the prisoner tether, but her hands were bound. Through dozens of frames the men spoke at her, but the

40

expression of contempt never wavered and her lips never moved. The smaller man stepped around her, his left arm appeared under her jaw. In the next still, her head was pulled back, a knife at the right corner of her neck, her chest a bib of darkness. Oh sweet bleeding Jesus. Bear stopped the playback and stared at me, unable to believe his own eyes. I grabbed his hand and gripped it tight.

Bear resumed playback. The hood was removed from the second man, still tethered to the third prisoner. The taller assassin spoke at this prisoner through several frames. The smaller man slit the throat of this second prisoner after gaining nothing from him. The third man's hood was removed. In the next frame, he was on his knees next to the woman, his mouth opened and closed at her unmoving body. The smaller man, tired of listening, pulled the prisoner's head back and slit his throat as well.

The assassins, moving as marionettes, stacked the men on top of the woman.

Bear asked, "Do you want me to stop?"

I shook my head. "They did not beg for their lives, they accepted their fate with honor. We need to bear witness."

The taller man left the frame. "I know where he's going." Bear forwarded until the man returned carrying gas cans. He handed one to his partner. Each emptied a can over the pile. The imagery caught a match in mid-strike, then a bloom of white obliterated the image. The camera's light sensor adjusted to the increase in light and we were able to watch the pyre grow frame by frame. The assassins were lost in the dark background. The fire burned through eighty seven images before the sprinklers engaged, smearing the lens.

Bear opened the exterior gate file and synched to the last time stamp on the interior loop. A man silhouetted at the service door, backlit by fire, robot walking to the big van, a side view as he cleared the front of the van and climbed in the driver's side. It took twenty one seconds, seven still images for him to back the van around and drive out of the frame. It was the taller assassin.

Without a word, I retrieved the whiskey from the liquor cabinet, poured two generous helpings, and set one in front of my friend.

"Jesus H. Christ. That was a ceremony. The tall guy in charge. He killed his blade man, but didn't put him in the fire."

Bear swallowed, then blew out a pent up breath. "I don't recognize any of those people."

"I know you cleared the title to the marina, but this makes me wonder what the bankruptcy management team was running in and out of there. Maybe we need to look into just how angry that twerp from SunTrust was. Unless you have objections, I'll run these through the transmogrifier, clean them up, and poke around for some identification."

"No objections. I don't wanna have to see them again. I downloaded everything to your server. I'm going to wipe mine."

"Let me work on the images. I'll strip everything out, meta data, background, any digital footprints, then deliver usable images to Bill."

"How is he going to keep me out of trouble? Your constable don't owe me shit."

"He likes you more than he likes me. We'll start there."

"And he's going to want to know why the hell I didn't turn this all over yesterday and I don't have a good answer." Bear tapped a finger on his phone screen. "Program on here provides access to the surveillance storage. Give me the word. I wipe the whole thing clean and delete the account." He stood and finished his glass. "It's getting late. I need my beauty sleep." He gave me one of his patented giant hugs which seemed to go on forever yet stopped too soon. My brother in arms, for better or worse.

After he'd gone, I re-scanned the video files and captured an image of each of the actors. I fed the data into the editor, stripped all the identification, cropped each image to just the face, and enlarged by degrees until the pixels grew too large, losing definition. I sharpened the first image. The crisp black and white transformed the woman into a glamorous movie star the likes of which the world has not seen since the Fifties. High cheekbones, strong forehead, wideset eyes with the slightest upward tilt. I sent her to the printer and began work on the male prisoners.

The second victim looked as though he belonged with the woman. High cheekbones as well, aristocratic nose, not born of peasant or working class. The third prisoner, the man who mourned the woman, wore a fat pug nose, but I couldn't tell if he'd been hit or that was just his snozz. His hair longish, dark in the image, again, possibly attributed to the limited degrees of gray in the image spectrum. I sent the men to the printer and examined the image of the dead assassin. Shorter than his partner, squat in build, but in death he had looked thinner. Not starved, but certainly not a fan of processed foods, nor did he look as though he were part of any ruling class. I cropped and cleaned the image, sent him off to the printer, and started on the live assassin. Taller, leaner, his facial features could have fit any number of indigenous stereotypes, but his height said his ancestors mixed with the conquerors. Identification based on perceived ethnicity was an exercise in futility, but it kept my mind from revisiting the horrors we had witnessed. Fortunately, the cat didn't care if I profiled these people based on fact or fiction. I dubbed the living assassin Angel and sent him to the printer deck to keep the others company.

I shut down the equipment, stowed the images in a manila folder, locked the folder in the gun safe, and retrieved a different picture by which I would locate and profile someone hopefully still alive. I jammed a grungy Cubs cap over my hair, filled a water bottle, stowed my little .38 in its holster, and cruised through a ghost town after midnight. My destination was the first address on Mr. Martin's list.

As I couldn't watch the entire building, I made a circuit and discovered the southern end of the building had suffered minor fire damage, and the outer stairwell dangled drunkenly. I backed into a hidey spot on Hernandez midway down the block. Few vehicles shared the street with me, two of them without wheels. My truck, not new and not without blooms of rust, blended into the landscape. I settled in for watch.

The building resembled a soviet prison, designed in stark block when it was newly built by some politically clouted grifter thirty years past. Creatures whose parents had attempted learning in this citadel now haunted its empty corridors. Two stories tall, the abandoned education factory occupied two long blocks of a dying street in a dangerous neighborhood, held hostage by greedy councilmen and racial hucksters. The property was surrounded by chain link topped with razor wire, as if there were anything left to protect.

Figures in the dark, moving by ones and twos, oozed past my hiding spot. In turn they would pull back a piece of fencing, stepd into the lot, and move toward the north stairwell. The door did not appear to be locked, and the window was intact. Movement of the squatters was not furtive. They were of no interest to anyone. No one glanced my way. Steady had provided me with the sparse data he and his brothers gathered via their own surveillance. Trust but verify the maxim for continued existence. I planned a watch for two to three nights, and create a plan, maybe two plans.

From the south, crossing beneath the sickly yellow light of a functioning street lamp were possible targets: Thin female, blond, underdressed in the November night, exposed skin so damned white, if she weren't sickly, her skin would have glowed in the dark. She was accompanied by a male, also underdressed. His skin was darker by several shades. Maybe his work took him out into the sun more often.

The female scurried to keep pace with the male. He walked with assurance, a swagger, head up. It was too dark to see if his eyes were as watchful as his gait suggested. The female stopped to fix a shoe, balancing on one foot like a drunken flamingo. Without turning he waited until she was next to him. As they neared, I confirmed the female was my quarry, Taylor Martin, biker baby. The male approximated the description Steady had given. Mid to late twenties, five foot eight, Latin origin, whatever the hell that meant. The man's coloring ruled out Nordic princess or Algerian sheepherder, but the man could have been any one of a thousand men in the city, ancestors from a fifty different countries.

The male pulled back the chain link flap and scanned the street up and down waiting for the woman to stumble through. If these two scored a night's worth of poison, he had not yet imbibed, his movements too precise, too sober. Taylor, however, was stoned and moving in slow motion, unsure of her steps.

I watched them disappear around the north end of the building Another hour passed with no more chickens limping home to roost. I added that item to my mental notes on the tenants. One night does not a database make, but it was a start. I needed sleep and I needed to be home before daylight. I turned north on Davis then crossed over to MLK, unsettled by the sight of the target's boyfriend. He seemed too healthy, too alert, his movements unhindered by drugs or alcohol. Maybe he preferred to get bent in the privacy of his squalid home. I was not happy with this development.

Thank goodness my truck knew the way home. I dropped clothes on the floor and crawled into bed. My skin crawled even though I hadn't entered the flop house. The cat curled up next to my head, providing warmth, his motor blending into the hypnotic roll of the night tide.

Those gossipy old bikers were wrong. I wasn't bored. The shop kept me busy and broke. I had friends, I volunteered, I spent time with Hannah doing cultural things like taping myself into a borrowed gown and not snoring through her beloved opera season. Maybe a sluggish thyroid filled me with ennui.

"Looking for a mud puddle," drifted the soft voice of my late mother. She would bath and dress me for church or the theater, a museum, or dinner. Within minutes, I would be knee high in a mud puddle. I was not a graceful child. I fell over a lot. Skinned knees, raw elbows, bruises, abrasions, scrapes, all the hallmarks of childhood. She loved me, but despaired of me. It was now Aunt Hannah's turn to despair of my ever becoming domesticated.

I dropped into sleep without noticing until I stood on the ledge of a chasm, gaping at a blackened serpent rising from the steaming depths. It loomed over me and opened its mouth. Imprisoned behind poisonous fangs stood Lilia, the Ellis's spooky teenaged house guest, crying soundlessly for her mother.

05 WAFFLE HOUSE BLUES

Trilling bells broke into my sleep. I pried up an eyelid. Number displayed as Thornton's. Groaning, I set my feet on the floor, stood and stretched, hoping he would give up before I'd finished yawning. No such luck.

I pushed the green button to answer. "Hey, Sheriff, what's up?"

"We need to talk."

"I haven't eaten breakfast."

"I'm on the stairs."

I closed the phone to cut off his rant but oddly his voice was still audible. He'd waited thirty six hours. He was unhappy and standing on my porch. Christ Almighty, it was seven in the morning and the sun was just peeking over the horizon.

I brushed teeth, donned yesterday's outfit, pulled on boots, and poured cream into Ralphie's dish. The cat stared up at me, eyes squinty, asking where the rest of his breakfast was. I opened cabinets until I found a half loaf of oatmeal bread that hadn't turned fuzzy. I pulled out a slice and laid it in the bowl to soak up the cream. Wasn't he supposed to catch mice? He swiped a paw at my hand.

I locked the door and clomped down the stairs, sliding into the passenger side of the county issued cruiser. Thornton raised an eyebrow at the state of my attire. I shook my head and sighed. He gunned the engine, fishtailing down the crushed shell drive. He left a little rubber on the pavement pulling out west bound. Thirty seconds later, he turned into the Waffle House. I should have walked, saved the taxpayer's some money replacing tires.

Silence reigned until we'd been seated. The waitress, well known to our island hero, asked after another of the deputies whose name I was unfamiliar with. They bantered. He asked about her twins. He turned that smile on and off at will. His dark hair, unruly at the best of times, was a little longer than regulation, but it suited him. His skin was grainy, his eyes sported bags large enough for a weekend getaway. Two plus decades on the job, yet he retained a boyish charm belying the steel rod that ran stem to stern. He had never been bent, bought, or frightened. He could be angered, a skill I had perfected when I came to live on the island long ago as a feral child who had roamed too far from home.

"Hey now, whatchoo all want? Billy will have me talking here all morning if you don't order."

Coffee, milk, scrambled, extra bacon, and extra grease on the hash browns. The milk was ice cold and spiked my forehead. I reminded myself to get some kind of food for the cat before it starved to death. We plowed through our plates in silence. Bill sighed and leaned back in the booth. "You've been scarce."

I nodded, pushing my plate away, crossing the knife and fork, indicating I was finished. Mother had beaten a few manners into me in the short time she'd had the opportunity.

"That scene at the marina, that was about the worst I've seen outside of service."

I nodded again. A lot of his job consisted of scraping drunk drivers off the 292, but the man deserved credit for ending a drug war on his island. A war costing the lives of a dozen narco-soldiers, and regretfully the lives of two deputies, followed by the arrest of a score more scumbags local and imported. That incursion was large enough to warrant coverage on a Voice of America broadcast when I was scratching fleas in boot camp. Thornton's success ultimately led to a permanent precinct on the island. Bumbling local yokel, he was not.

"You pulling this silent shit?" His voice harsh, barely above a whisper.

"What do you want me to say?"

"What happened out there? I got to the party late."

"It was done and cooled by the time I arrived. You know Moreno let me in."

"Yeah, he told me. Said he got you back out when you turned green."

"He's a good guy. Did he tell you I threatened to throw up on some agent's boots?"

A smile flitted across his face. "Yup, you done that before. At least they're not mine. I don't know how you survived the Corps."

"It's a wonder." I said. I slowly pulled the manila envelope out of my jacket and slid it across the table. Bill raised an eyebrow, and pulled the envelope into his lap. He slid a print partway out. His face tightened briefly then relaxed into his patented cop scowl. He stared at the image for five slow seconds and slid it back in.

"Tell me."

I glanced around looking for ears too close to the table. "From the available data, the situation began with two assassins, three victims. The image marked Angel is the only person to emerge from the building alive. His picture isn't as clear as the others. I can only pull so many pixels out of thin air. He may have known about the cameras, but expressed no concern, no furtive flittering, no masks.

"Aw, Jesus. Bryant has cameras. Nobody thought of that."

"Three static mount cameras on utility poles outside of the warehouse. They face the building. Four inside, aimed at a center point and mounted against the dispatch tower, which you can guess limits the amount of coverage. No video. Every three seconds a still image is recorded." Bill opened his mouth to interrupt. I held up my hand. "Let me finish, please. Bear is not involved in this beyond someone unknown choosing his property to send an ugly message to someone else unknown, to either of us anyway."

"I know that, hell, we all know Bryant's not part of this. Feds got nothing on the victims so they're trying to press Bear. Spinning in circles more like, but they gotta fill in their reports, make it seem like they're doing something. They're pissed they can't find anything on him, can't get to his service records."

"We are all redacted to some degree, even you."

"It wasn't my warehouse. Problem at this moment is you've got surveillance footage and you're sitting on it. That doesn't look good."

"It doesn't look anything. Bear was in custody until yesterday morning. No one asked about the cameras. He pulled the data and stepped through the first few frames. He lost his appetite quickly if that gives you an idea of how bad it is. I showed up in the morning and dragged him out of the house for some electrical work. He came too willingly. He didn't tell me about the surveillance until last night. It didn't dawn on anyone to check the damned cameras. We assumed the big boys would get identities using their fancy space age computer systems."

Bill shook his head. "Finger prints too badly damaged. They pulled what they could, but so far it's a no-go for any federal database. According to the coroner, the dental work on the odd man out is nonexistent. Missing a couple molars, a lot of wear and tear, no professional attention."

"He was one of the two assassins."

Our waitress brought more coffee and poured without a word. When she walked away, Bill asked, "How am I supposed to present this?"

"The images are isolated. I cleared the background, then painted it black. Nothing to identify the location."

"Somehow, I am gifted with professionally printed portraits of the dead at Bryant's marina, kind of a coincidence."

"Make something up, anonymous source. Pretend you had a private eye surveilling the marina. Nobody's prints are on those pictures but yours."

He wiped his mouth, looked around for witnesses, and then zeroed a hard look at me. "Do the rules mean anything to you people?"

"That depends on whose rules. When you need the footage, you will have it, raw, unedited, but you will have the decency to give Bear a head's up, let him get an attorney."

Bill took a deep breath, held it, and then blew it out. He knew I wouldn't budge, not when it came to "my" people.

"Fuck it. It's a helluva lot more than anybody has now. Feds sitting around making PPD fetch their damned coffee. I'll get one of the city guys to cover the source, maybe get them some credit."

He scooted out of the booth and stood, stretching his tired back one way then the other. "I'm not gonna say thanks. This shoulda been turned over Sunday, but I guess everybody overlooked it."

"Nobody asked. I wasn't thinking of it and neither was Bear. When he did remember, after you all let him go home, he pulled the data. It's terrible, even in black and white stills. You didn't have to spend ten hours parsing the data to pull out something useful. I did. And it was …" I paused, looking for the right word. "It was barbaric. The assassin was making a statement to someone, but not you, not me, not Bear. I don't think the message is for us at all. It was professional kill, but it was personal. To someone."

"So when I need the rest?"

"My people skirt the rules, Sheriff, we don't flaunt them. The data will be made available, when you need it, when Bear is protected."

He dead-eyed me for a long count, interrupted by our chatty server, "See ya, Billy." His smile at the ready for her. He stomped out the door, shaking his head and muttering. The cruiser left rubber on the tarmac. More waste of taxpayer dollars.

Speaking of dollars, Bill skipped without paying. I tipped the mother of the twins an amount large enough to ensure her silence concerning the clandestine rendezvous, but not so large as to arouse suspicions of an assignation with the island Sheriff.

No safer place in the world than the Waffle House.

06 GARDEN CLUB

I walked home, retrieved my truck, and drove to the nursery. Angela's aged and hard-used Beemer perched in the parking lot. No sign of her in the salesroom. The aroma of fresh coffee lured me toward the office. It could be a trap. Angela occupied a high position on the short list of things for which I harbored irrational fear. She was third behind giant spiders and alligators. I still hadn't figured out why she gave up a promising career as a civil servant to join me in a venture that so far had generated not much more than aphids and headaches. Maybe I was her community service, and she was sentenced to work here to atone for crimes and misdemeanors.

A clang of metal rang from the classroom. Shelf brackets lay scattered among galvanized screws, the cordless drill, and the ladder. Oh shit. I promised to install shelving for her stupid orchids. Our stupid orchids, since it was my name on the contract.

Last fall, Angela had talked me into a sizeable purchase. She moved those orchids rapidly for a surprising net gain. But those plants were established and healthy and had leaves and blooms. Not this time, oh no. This time, we filled three dozen clay pots with expensive potting mix, and buried hairy tubers and rhizomes beneath the surface. I possessed a basic understanding of orchid culture, but these seemingly empty pots represented a significant investment in a medium of which I had limited knowledge and little interest. She claimed to have gotten some interesting species including vanilla pods and various fragrant varieties. She promised we'd be significantly blooming within a year. Hell, I could be dead in a year, from any number of things including her.

I pulled wood planks out of the store room and stacked them on the work table. We'd already discussed the pros and cons of permanent wall shelving versus stacked risers. My abiding hatred of orchids counter-acted any weight my opinion carried so shelves attached to the wall it would be. She wanted the shelves high to catch the convection of rising heat, but mostly to ensure no one could molest the sprouts – if they sprouted. We'd had incidents of unwarranted touching committed by customers on plants that weren't ready to be handled. I was brought around to the idea of high shelving when Angela threatened to break the fingers of a nine year old whose mother was less than attentive to her ill-mannered offspring.

Angela's assessment of the situation that day was valid so I was loath to intervene. Then the stupid cow took a swipe at my friend. I closed the distance, grabbed the woman's arm, swung her around, jammed her wrist between her shoulder blades, and goose-stepped her to the parking lot. Idiot child screeching in our wake. I informed the woman that we had security cameras and her behavior would result in arrest. At week's end, Angela posted an ornate tin sign prominently in the front window: No children. No pets. A bill for the sign had never rolled through accounts payable.

The whirr of the drill and the scraping of the ladder being moved about filled the afternoon. Conversation was not committed. Angela silently handed up water trays, then bricks, then her mystery pots.

The previous tenant of my nursery left behind a palette half stacked with red clay bricks. After scrubbing and disinfection, those bricks save me at least a hundred dollars. In my small world that was significant cash. The pots of sprouts would on top of a brick sitting in an inch of water, thus keeping their little orchid feet dry. Orchids responded poorly to damp roots, but humidity was their best friend.

Nearing the end of our task, Angela broke the silence. "Any word from Hannah?"

"No one from the embassy has called. I can only assume she hasn't caused any serious trouble." I stopped the drill long enough to cuss and yank a harpoon of old cypress out of my thumb.

"Your behavior towards the orchids is petulant and unwarranted. We sold out the first batch within weeks," she reminded me.

I stopped sucking on the wound. "Out of fear. We got them on consignment from gangsters."

"From your aunt's gardening club."

"Same difference. Those were whole plants, with stalks and blooms. They practically sold themselves."

"No. I sold them."

She was right, but I tuned her out. Something was on her mind and she would get around to it when she was ready. I was too damned tired to balance on the ladder, safely use a power drill, and argue at the same time.

She asked, "Have you talked to Bear? Any word on the fire?"

I tightened the bracket. She handed up a shelf and I slid it into place. She handed up a brick which I considered dropping on her head. Instead, I held out my hand for a pot and said, "Maybe we could get a couple of indoor trees, like a ficus or an olive? Would that work? See if we could mount an orchid on the trunk, like at Selby Gardens. How cool would that be? We'd need more ventilation, a couple more windows..." I placed the last pot and backed down the ladder.

She stared at me as if I'd grown a third eyeball. "I asked you about Bear and you start talking about air circulation."

"Aw jeez. I don't know any more than you do at this point. The marina is closed for the time being. He was over here yesterday working on the pump. Remember? You brought lunch."

"What's he going to do?"

"Do? Wait, I guess, until the scene is cleared, then clean it up and go back to work, providing the cops haven't impounded everything for evidence."

"My God. Someone murdered three people and set them on fire at his marina. He's your friend. I think you'd be a little more concerned."

"I am concerned. But there's nothing I can do. The only cop I know to ask is Bill and he doesn't like me so he's not going to tell me anything. I can worry or I can work. I can't do both."

I stowed the ladder, put the tools away, and swept up the errant screws, all the while enduring her silent treatment. I cared very much about my friend, but there wasn't one damn thing I could do for the time being, and I didn't know how to politely make Angela understand that there was nothing to do except wait and watch. She was a civilian and I didn't have much experience with them, but she had become a friend. My last civilian friend was murdered for a shiny silver disk. I didn't want to lose another one, and I didn't know what to say so I said nothing.

I grabbed two beers and tracked her to the sales room. Angela had my gardenia on the potting bench. My gardenia. Last remnant of a previous life and loss. The poor thing had bloomed since moving to the nursery. Propagation was occasionally discussed, but I never had the nerve. Now she held it hostage. I set her beer on the table and raised an eyebrow at her.

"It's time to try and make little gardenias." She dorked around with my plant, misting it, gently wiping the dust from the leaves. She gave it a final inspection and placed the plant back on the shelf. "You and Bear excluded me from whatever conversation was going on."

"You're right, we shut it down. One of the dead was a woman. It was savage. Nobody wanted to dump that image on you."

She nodded. "I guess I can accept that. I'm sorry I was such a bitch today. I don't like being shut out. I actually care about you. Bear, too. If there's anything I can do, name it."

A thought popped into my head. The voice of reason, so like my mother's, tried to override the thought, screaming: Shut up Shut up Shut up.

"Do you still have those goofy coveralls from the department of Agriculture?" I asked.

She nodded.

"Can I borrow them?"

"They'll be too long. Too tight. Why?"

"A job, a favor, unrelated to the marina."

"Hmmm." She agreed to loan me the uniform, but said she would wear it and find something suitable for me. I tried to scare her off with an abridged version of collecting a friend's daughter from an unsuitable relationship.

"In this day and age, really. Women making unsuitable decisions. And you need a costume to facilitate this, what do you people call it? An extraction?"

I locked up the shop and followed Angela's sarcasm to her apartment. Snaking through the city after her was like trying to catch quicksilver. I already regretted my decision to involve her. On one hand, any job carried the potential for danger. On the other hand, I needed the damned uniform. With it, I would blend into the landscape as a non-law enforcement governmental agent. If I encountered any ghouls, they'd see the coveralls, forget the face, and give me a wide berth.

She'd left the door open. Operational security was not her strong suit. She rented, leased, or owned an abandoned print shop off Baylen. She'd converted the upstairs into a living space. The building would have rented for a quarter mil a month in Chicago, but not in this city. Even on the meager wages she received from her work at the nursery, she would have beer money left over. Her only extravagance was a fancy coffee maker complete with milk steamer and bean grinder.

I found her rummaging through a closet in the bedroom. She tossed a denim shirt at me. "You may have to wear your own jeans. Wait. Wait. Here." She stood and held out a wrinkled beige-ish pair of what may have been pants in a previous life. "They don't look too good, but they are legitimate government issued crappy khakis."

While I changed into the dirty clothes, she donned her old uniform. The banana colored coverall glowed with good vibrations, but the smiling orange FLUSDA logo creeped me out. The khakis were too long, and the denim shirt had belonged to a large man named Bruce. I tied the excess shirt in the back, and let the front drop over the top of the khakis. I'm glad Bruce left his pants. Too big was easier to camouflage than too small.

Angela insisted upon driving while I navigated through the city. Gentrification was hit or miss. Our target destination spitting distance from her apartment, but a million miles between lifestyles. I refused to be drawn into the intellectual equivalent of tiddlywinks by taking any side in a discussion of outcome equity, personal choices, and privilege in a country that could afford bakeries devoted exclusively to dogs. I don't have anything against dogs, but I'd seen how the rest of the world was ruled. I preferred my little corner, warts and all. I preferred to feed the dogs than eat them. I also lacked sufficient sympathies regarding stupid choices.

Angela remained silent through the drive, offering the occasional non-committal "hmmm" as I barked directions. We parked in my hide of last night. We listened to the ticks of the cooling engine. It was full dark, but too early for the vampires to emerge.

"This favor, you don't have to name names, but what's the mission-accomplished part?"

Allowing her to accompany me was not only harebrained, but dangerous. She was armed, but I was more worried about her running out of bullets in the event of a siege. She wouldn't run.

That much I knew. Her debutante persona camouflaged a streak of fearlessness.

I blew out a heavy sigh. "The favor is for a friend of an acquaintance. His daughter is mixed up with a dealer and is living in that flop house. She's pretty far down the rabbit hole. Guy she's with looks dangerous, like he's keeping her supplied but doesn't partake as a habit."

"Hmmm."

"Hmmm what? You asked, I answered." I spotted our quarry leaving the roost and pointed. "There. That girl. With the swaggering fireplug."

City light allowed Angela to pick out my target. "Won't be a fair fight."

"It's not her I'm worried about."

"Do we follow them?"

"We do not. Reconnaissance only. This is where they roost after tanking up. Best shot for extraction is here unless I can catch her alone, outside, which turns our field trip into kidnapping."

The residents emerged in singles and pairs in no specific pattern or time frame. If they had cars, they wouldn't be living here. This was the bottom of the proverbial barrel. These folks were the walkers, and that gave me two places within a mile that I knew of, where they would most likely go for whatever they needed. The number of tenants had not altered from last night. An hour passed with no more lice crawling out of the woodwork. Time for a walk through. Alone.

I pulled the ball cap low on my forehead, and checked my penlight. "If I am not out in fifteen minutes, drive to Hayne Street. You do not call 911 until you are in the PPD parking lot, locked behind the gates." I forestalled any argument by climbing out of the car and pushing the door shut gently.

I walked to the corner, comforted by the click of the door locks engaging, loud in the still air. Traffic was non-existent. I crossed the street, pulled the chain link back, and checked both ways for people.

"You forgot your clipboard." Angela whispered.

The damned woman was a wraith. I hadn't heard her following me. Maybe I was getting too old for these adventures. I should accept my fate, sell trees to tourists, and walk the beach collecting shells. But first, I kill Angela. I bit my tongue when she scared me. Didn't matter, I had nothing to say. She snuck up on me fair and square. Operational security failure.

I nodded and held the fencing back. She climbed through and waited for me to join her. I pointed to the north stairwell, then pointed upward. Twice I had seen the target use this portal. We climbed the two half-flights on tiptoe. Underneath the intact mesh window, the door sported a hole where a lock had been bored out. A brick propped the door open, and a stench floated on the stale air leaching out of the building. Rot, corruption, human waste. Not for the first time I wished I'd spent more time with Jane Austin than Edgar Allen.

Angela grabbed my shoulder and tugged. I turned and jerked my head back toward the stairs. She shook her head and gestured for me to move forward. I pulled the door open. It moved silently. Someone had taken care to oil the hinges. It was surprising, like a flower growing from a crack in the sidewalk.

I stepped into that foul world wishing I hadn't taken petty pleasure in seeing the fear in my friend's eyes, wishing I hadn't brought her on my field trip. It was wrong and it was stupid and it was the mark of an amateur. Echoing in my head, the voice of my mother telling me to grow up, get a grip, and deal with the situation at hand because only the living received the gift of hindsight.

The door swung shut silently except for a metallic click as it rested against the doorstop. I closed my eyes, snapped on the flashlight, counted to five and opened my eyes again. They would more easily adjust to the introduction of light in the blackness.

I swept the light counter-clockwise, up from seven, around to five and back again, looking for stragglers, clues, giant spiders. Nothing scuttled out from under the thread of light in this purgatory. Cockroaches had higher standards. Angela kept pace behind, hand on my right shoulder for guidance, no doubt her other hand on her weapon. Mentally mapping the layout, one long wide corridor, two sets of doors per classroom, six large rooms on either side. The perfect model of prison architecture. The only sound was Angela trying to breathe through her teeth.

Mattresses, blankets, latrine buckets, boxes, fast food detritus, I did not see any needles nor syringes shine back at the light. Interesting. Their drug gear on them or carefully stowed, tidy in their accommodations, meager as they were. Curious, but I didn't fancy checking the buckets to see if they emptied their shit. We swept back down the corridor. On return inspection, the open rooms had a feeling of order, of being reclaimed each return. This was instinct, not logic, but it made sense. This was a commune, of death, yes, but even this far down the hole, these folks retained some humanity.

My girl would be in one of these rooms. Her buddy didn't look like the kind of guy who shared his manger with other dogs. He would mark a space for himself and his property. I led Angela to the exit and put my hand up for her to wait while I checked the landing. Clear. We tiptoed back down the metal stairs. I held her shoulder while we crossed the dead lawn to the fence. The light was bright enough for me to recognize that she was about to bolt. The eyes had taken on a panic sheen, nostrils flared. We crossed the street to the car, locks disengaging loudly. She tossed me the keys without a word and flung open the passenger door.

I whispered, "Don't slam it. We're supposed to be incognito."

"I don't plan on coming back here. This will be the only time someone sees this car."

"If someone sees the car, they see me. Actual human people live in this neighborhood. Some of those folks work and pay bills and want this shithole bulldozed. Those people especially can't see me, or you."

She did as asked, pulling her door shut carefully. I turned left onto Davis, lights off. I slowed for the stop sign, checked for traffic and cruised through the four-way without stopping. As we passed the north end of the property, Angela blew out a heavy breath and said, "I am not some sheltered child, for God's sake. But people live like that. I mean, you see it on the news, but you don't believe it."

My turn to murmur "hmmm."

"Do you know where they go when they leave that place?"

"To feed, to fix, to make money. The target's father gave me a rundown of what data he'd collected, but it's sparse. Neither he nor his buddies can surveil without being spotted."

"Have you seen anyone get into cars?

I shook my head.

"Then they'll probably up head to Parker Field. The police have shut down most of the open air trading up and down MLK, shut down the business fronts, got the city to bulldoze a couple of the burnt out lots. We had the usual squad of clowns demanding an end to the, and I quote, destruction of our historic neighborhoods, end quote. But work is getting done. Sixth Street has a lot of calls for service, but it's predominantly residential."

She was a native. She'd know this shit so I kept my curiosity to myself and took Sixth north. I pulled my hat lower and scrunched down in the seat, pulling my chin into my neck, changing my profile. Angela laughed at me then followed suit. I came to a full stop then slowly crossed over Davis heading west. The park had two ball fields, but tonight the kids were at home, mostly. Noise of music, cars rumbling with the loud insipient bass of the tuneless. No one noticed us. I turned left at the far side of the field. A thin weedy field separated our street from traffic on the 110, light at this time of night.

"Circle back around, maybe we can spot your quarry."

"No. We got what I needed for tonight. No reason to risk exposure."

"Because I'm here."

I sighed. "This car, even with the dents and the dust is recognizable. Someone will notice. Do you have a reason to be in this area? Some folks won't ask nicely."

"Okay, it's not me. Sorry."

"Angela, I need a lot more information to make a safe extraction. Her father told me the boyfriend was a squirrel, a user, but that squirrel is too damned healthy. Maybe he doesn't use as much or maybe he was stronger to begin with. I don't know, and I don't know shit about junkies except I don't like them."

"The quality of your mercy is severely strained."

"To show an unfelt sorrow is an office which the false man does easy." The benefits of a semi-classical education allowed me to respond to insult with insult. Yes, my mercy was strained, but I suspected hers was a bit false. Of course, that could be my vanity talking.

We wound south through the city stewing in our own silence. There wasn't much to say. I pulled into the lot behind her building, parked next to my truck, and turned off the car. I asked, "Do you want a lecture or do you want to get some sleep?"

"No lecture, not tonight. I am aware that there is no fix for stupid. But it's heartbreaking to witness. My mom counsels first responders who have to go into places like that. It takes a toll on them."

She pulled the keys out of the ignition, slung an arm around my neck, and pulled me in for a hug. "I gave up a date to come with you."

"You're an idiot. I'd sell my soul for a date."

"That's why you are eternally alone. You don't have a soul."

I climbed into my truck and kept watch until the outer door clicked shut. Seconds later, an upstairs light cast shadows on a person shape through the curtain.

Angela was wrong. I had a soul. It was dusty and abused, but painfully self-aware.

I navigated by instinct until my headlights shone upon the stairs to Aunt Hannah's house. I slept the sleep of the wicked, untouched by dreamscapes, whilst the rest of the world slept easy.

07 SHOULDA TURNED LEFT

I woke with the cat sitting on my head biting my ear. I hadn't gotten him kibble and he was making me aware of the oversight. I dug around the cupboards as coffee brewed and found a stash of canned tuna. Wise to the whirr of the can opener, Ralphie, leapt at my leg and deployed all eighty claws climbing his way to the counter. I grabbed him by his scruff, dropping him and the can at the food bowl. I warily filled his water while he growled through the fish.

I stumbled through a cursory shower, then played phone messages while the cat cleaned himself on my wadded sheets. I shoved him off and made the bed listening to Angela stumble through an apology. For God's sake, she didn't make me take her, that stupid was all mine, yet here she was taking responsibility. I was too tired for introspection or philosophy or wondering why the woman felt she owed me an apology. I was a terrible friend.

No word from Hannah, and no yelling from Captain Thornton. I scrolled back through the list of incoming calls. The call from area code three one two had yet to be addressed. I pushed send and waited through the rings, trying to remember what time zone Chicago occupied. A cultured voice answered, "Martinelli Investments, how may I direct your call?"

Reaching back through the cobwebs of memory, I said, "Rafferty, Ben Rafferty."

The slightest hesitation before her terribly cultured faux Brit accent returned. "Mr. Rafferty is not available. Would you care to leave a message?"

"Yes, if he has something for me, he can mail it to …"

Jesus, they knew where I was. They brought a fucking war to my island.

"He can mail it to my home address."

"And this is in regard to?"

"Barring your misplaced preposition, Ben is keenly aware of the matter about which I am calling. The name is Archer." I hung up, pleased at my petty behavior, my style of late. Not enough sleep, too much time alone. Time with the cat didn't count because he didn't like me either.

I dressed in clothing from the hamper, and popped into Wal-Mart on my way to the nursery for a new roll of duct tape and a bag of extra-long zip ties. My kidnapping supplies had run low and I planned to collect the errant princess tonight, guard dog or no. My odds of prevailing mostly unscathed were decent because I never fought fair, not if I could avoid it. My conscience would be clear if the boyfriend made himself collateral damage.

Angela had not yet arrived, which left me with the morning housekeeping. I made coffee and sifted through the mail, turned on the misters, and discovered a half used tube of brown greasepaint in a desk drawer. It smelled vaguely of mouse shit, but it coated my fingertips easily. I crammed it in my back pocket to complete my kidnapping disguise.

My gardenia survived the long ride down from the frozen North Country, and now flourished under proper care. Angela was right, though, it was time for the plant to propagate. I cleaned and honed the shears, dipped the cuttings in powdered hormone and stabbed them into a tray of damp peat moss. I snipped as many stems as I thought the mother plant could handle having removed. I placed both mother and her tray of babies on the shelf and added water to the humidity tray. I tacked a bright red sticky note on the shelf, reminding the reader to check the future sprouts every damned morning and evening and at lunchtime.

I chalked an outline where talk of an indoor pond had been discussed during prior drinking sessions, then sat on the floor with my notebook, sketching a rock climb, maybe six foot tall, water moving down the front. To splash or not to splash, probably not, too much evaporation. There was enough room, if I reinforced the pillar, waterproofed it, but thick black plastic was expensive. A cursory search of the internet netted me no savings for a necessary pond liner. Maybe a deal could be struck with Frank the grumpy landscaper a half mile up the road.

The bell over the front door tinkled. A large male standing in the doorway blocked the late morning sun. I stood and brushed dust from my pants. It was Mr. Steady, or was it Mr. Martin? Now was not the time for flippancy. His crooked face bore a murderous look. I motioned him to come through to the office. He shook his head. "You doing this or what? Been long enough."

I told him to wait, retrieved his plant from the classroom, and stuffed a letter opener in my back pocket. I carefully placed the bougainvillea in a paper shopping bag and taped the top closed. I tried to hand it to him. He stood immobile. I placed the bag on the floor between us. He stared down at me from his great height and growled, "So?"

I met his gaze. "It has been forty eight hours. You specified no time frame nor did I offer one."

"What the hell have you been doing?"

Cruising the wastelands for the last two nights, you overgrown misshapen goon. I took a long breath to calm the rage. "I've been tracking her movements since Monday night. I also did a run through of the flop house. I have two plans for extraction and the situation will determine whether I use either."

His fists were clenched at his sides, his stare hard, and his countenance terrifying. Little did he know that I have faced terrifying faces belonging to terrifying men so I knew how to wait. It took him a long count of thirty to speak. "I seen her last night. She looks worse."

I wanted to rail at him about spooking my prey, but it was his daughter. I placed a hand on his hairy arm. "She's alive and she's eating. That buys me enough time to get her out in one piece."

"When?" he pleaded.

Leaving out the bits about how his daughter most likely earned her fix, I told him, "In the next few days. Her friend is healthier than you led me to believe. He doesn't give her much alone time. I will call you. Be ready."

Again with the hard man stare, he frowned, his eyes grew moist. He bent down to retrieve his plant, straightened to his full height, nodded at me and left my building. I blew out the pent up anger. How dare he question me. How dare he bleed for his misplaced daughter. How dare he feel helpless in the face of utter madness.

I was familiar with the area in which my target entertained her work and pointed my truck in that direction when the sun had dropped below the horizon. Some of the best smoked pig in the city was found at Parker Street Grocer and Meats. An aged grocery, a rundown tavern, and cinder block garage took up half the eastern block. The joyous noise of football at Parker Field directly across the street filled the night air, occasionally drowning out the heavy bass thump from the open bay doors of the garage. Nice night to be outside, no breeze, mid-60's. Drone of the highway a hundred yards away provided a steady hum underneath the talking and music and laughter and the cars on the street.

The term "organized crime" was a misnomer. Crime was organized by whoever was on top, a position earned by knocking off the previous management. The current management had shut down the shootings and open drug trafficking on the block, which made the city less likely to come in with writs and bulldozers. This park was smack in the middle of a real live neighborhood peopled with real live humans who lived and worked and played here, and were little part of illicit activities. No bullets whizzed across the field of picnickers in this part of town, fall grasses filled berms uncluttered with spent brass. Folks dropped their kids at the field, grabbed a bite, a beer, a coke, and wandered back afield to watch their children hurtle pigskin or crack a leather ball.

North on Hayne, ducking under the highway, and coming back down MLK, I approached the target zone from the west. I backed into an overgrown alley behind an urban forest of scrub brush obscuring the remains of an old shotgun shack leaning heavily toward its neighbor. Quick inspection assured me no squatters had taken residence. I climbed back in the truck and sat there drumming my fingers on the steering wheel, listening for approaching hostiles, plotting a scouting perch. Futility and folly. There was nowhere to hide and observe. Not without a lot more equipment. A pajama clad ninja toting a night scope and smeared with camouflage grease, no, that wouldn't raise any alarms. There were families sitting on the bleachers watching the football game, people standing outside the fence talking. This wasn't a shooting gallery, this was a neighborhood hangout regardless of some bad business. I, however, was not part of the neighborhood, and I hadn't thought to bring one of the Ellis kids as part of my clever disguise.

I pulled my hat low, zipped my stained sweatshirt, and shuffled up the pitted sidewalk to the corner. No driver's license, sixty eight dollars in cash, tiny smudges of smelly camo rubbed into my skin at strategic points mimicking a lack of hygiene. I'd planned to slink into the tavern, play at being a barfly looking for a new perch. Waiting to cross, I heard the sound of a throat being cleared.

An old man sitting on his porch, dimly lit by the yellowed streetlight across the road. I stepped forward, spying on him from behind a row of shrubs. He stared at me and cleared his throat again.

I stepped to the porch steps and let him look me over. He nodded and waved me up.

I stepped up to the deck, not hurrying, hands in my pockets. He gestured toward an old vinyl chair. "You looking for something?" His voice low, but not unfriendly.

I crossed in front of him and took the empty chair. No use lying. "Yes, sir. A girl. Her father wants her home."

He twitched his head toward the grocery. "New man own the block now, he own the girls, too."

Neatly trimmed viburnum provided a natural screen from the casual observer and glossed over the scent of spent hydrocarbons. It was a peaceful place from which to watch the nightly show. I spotted a young boy, pre-puberty, lanky, running north, chasing after a sedan which had rolled through the stop sign, turned right and pulled into the grocery parking lot. The boy caught the car and leaned inside the passenger window for a five second parlay. He sauntered back toward the corner and handed his package to another child who in turn threaded his way south through the loiterers, past picnic tables filled with an eclectic mix of diners, not all involved in the dark trades. Children as runners. Police snatch them up, they did no time, and fear kept their little mouths shut. Business conducted in the open, but not obnoxiously.

My target's owner emerged from an open bay of the garage. Laughing at something, he raised a hand without turning around. The garage door rumbled down, lessoning the steady bass thump. The boy who collected the package from the runner sped toward him, stopped and jabbered up at him. The man entertained fifteen seconds of chatter then raised a hand as if to cuff the child. The packet fell to the ground, the child scooped it up. He gave it to the man, then ran north and took a position outside the tavern, disappearing into the shadows.

"That's himself, king a the block. They call him ha-say-vi-yoo-dos, the Widow Maker. He done made a few widows round here, a coupla more folk droppin off the radar than usual."

"Like who?"

He ignored my question. "He come up in here six month back. Run off the crew who run off the bikers. Nobody shootin no more. Day business picked up nice, weekends the kids play pretty safe."

He had shared too much. I sensed the end of cooperation. "All I want is to get the girl home. Nothing else."

This wasn't Philly or Chicago, this was a purchase only drive through. No bodies propped against buildings or sprawled on the ground. No tents, no dirty mattresses, no homeless pushing shopping carts and muttering to their gods. It looked and sounded like any crisp November evening. Too late for the school crowd, but I figured the king's runners weren't likely to be called in as truant.

I scanned the clusters of people and spotted Taylor parked at one of the street side picnic tables populating the gravel parking area between the grocery and the tavern. The people seemed to be segregated by business interests, and further sorted by gender. Two tables of non-coms, veteran drinkers enjoying the temperate night, separated the tables of working folk.

Taylor's owner swaggered toward her table, reached around her, and grabbed up her sandwich. He tore off a bite and tossed it back on her plate. I couldn't hear their verbal exchange. He hadn't touched her, but she didn't like what he was saying. She jumped up from the table and waggled her finger at him. He smiled and shook his head, teeth white and shiny in the light of the parking lot. The girl's shoulders slumped. The king walked toward the shadows, and she followed him like a beaten dog.

"That yer girl?"

"Yeah," came out in a breath.

"You ain't no cop."

"No, sir."

You act like you got practice, watchin and waitin.

"Yes sir. Marine."

He chuckled softly. "Don't that beat all. You dint push no papers?"

"No sir."

"Did my stint getting shot at running around that goddam jungle, rotting my boots, rotting my skin. Lotta fellas looked like me, but by the time I got home, all them bastards had to call me sir." He chuckled lightly.

"Coffee's good across the street, can I bring you something?"

"Grocery ain't got no pot on this late. I got a Silex on the stove. You get yourself a cup here. Just because a lady walk over after dark don't mean they be good to you." He tossed the dregs of his own coffee over the porch rail and handed the mug to me.

He reached a bony arm across the screen door and pulled it open for me. The kitchen was lit by a yellow light over an old cast iron sink, chipped and stained, but clean. The kitchen smelled of coffee and pine and old linoleum. I filled his cup and pulled a clean mug from a rack over the stove.

He held the door again, taking care not to let it slam. I took my seat. He held up a bottle of Early Times. "Night's comin on a chill."

I accepted a pour. Seemed rude not to.

He poured a tipple in his own coffee and set the bottle down. "Less you local or a workin gal, you ain't gonna get served."

"I've been over in the daylight. That pork's the best in the city."

"Night time different. Business different. Only way you get your girl is if you drive up and ask," he pointed toward table to which our girl had returned. "You ask that heifer in the loud green dress for a date. She feeds and runs the girls for the new king. Then you gotta figure out how to get your girl specific. You seein the problem yet?"

Oh yes, I saw the problem. Wasn't just a skin color thing as there were lots of different crayons across the street. No, I was implausible as a buyer of the various products for sale. He invited me to his porch because he spotted me as a civilian in this urban war. Dammit. I'd been bumbling this job from the beginning.

He interrupted my self-flagellation. "Look at this. You see how this works."

An expensive dark sedan stopped in front of the "girls" table, and the fat woman, draped in yards of poisonous green polyester, waddled over and leaned in the passenger window. Within seconds she stood upright and flicked her hand. The car moved forward, slowing through the right turn, stopped, and idled at the curb. This time no young boy ran after. Taylor navigated the gravel to the waiting car. She slammed the passenger door. Alone, she was alone. The asshole who bought her time would pose no threat.

I thanked the old man and ran off the porch, his soft laughter followed me around the corner. I ducked behind the screen of shrubs and dug in my pocket for the truck key. I yanked the door open, a scream caught in my throat.

Lilia sat in the passenger seat dressed as a street urchin straight out of Dickens, eyes wide in surprise, a small "oh" escaped her mouth.

Fuming, I climbed in the truck. This was my chance to catch the target away from her owner. I closed my eyes and engaged the door locks. I took a deep breath, held it for ten seconds, then let it out.

"Lilia."

"You have eyes like my father when he is mad."

"Does he beat you?"

"He would not ever. He would take my toys and have anger at mi Madre. Accuse her of raising a nahual, practica u meyah xwaay, the sorcery. He says I move like the jaguar."

"I may beat you. And break all your damned toys." My prey was long gone in the thirty seconds it took to stop having a heart attack at the sight of this child hiding in my truck.

I backed down the alley, emerging onto an empty Sixth street. I ran through all possible scenarios of retrieving my prize and keeping this stupid girl safe. None. Nada. Zippo. Zero. The child's voice burned through my musings until I slammed on the brakes and skidded into the parking lot of a church currently not in service.

"What the hell are you doing here?"

"I followed you."

"From where?"

"La escuela, the school. It is empty. Only los fantasmas live there now. You know, the ghosts."

I was woefully inadequate to the job if a fourteen year old pampered princess from a moneyed family, who spoke English as a second language, could find me so easily. I'd been mucking along like an amateur since I agreed to grab Taylor. My heart wasn't in it. And just who the hell was this kid? Cherryl said the family was from Belize, some diplomatic thing. Her profile in the low light was familiar ... Oh Jesus. They can't be ... no ... oh Jesus. I stomped out those big ugly thoughts. Oh Jesus, I was on the far side of midnight with a spooky runaway in my truck. I checked both ways and eased back onto the road.

"Ah Puch split the earth and shows me his fire. He opens his mouth, Buluc Chabtan rises on his breath and comes for me. He will take me to the shadows. I do not know what I am to do."

Half the words she spit out were Spanglish and the other half were clicks and throat noises the cat made yarking up a hairball. The words I understood unnerved me. The words I hadn't understood scared the hell out of me. I managed to keep the truck between the yellow lines by sheer force of will.

"Lilia, how the hell did you find me?"

She shook her head as if to clear it. She said nothing for several long blocks. I took care to drive as invisibly as I could. I left the house this evening with plans to kidnap a junkie. All I found was a teenaged kid who may be an orphan.

"Me abuelita, she comes to my school and she takes me away, to a big house far away behind the gates. The house is filled with gold and marble. She tells me to stay silent. He is

74

importante, that he will make me his family. He will make us wealthy. She held my arms that I could not run. There were many men with guns. She makes me stand silent in front of this man who is the owner. He is older than my father. He nods. She smiles, like the cocodrilo – with big eyes and much teeth. She tells me to sit outside while she speaks to this man. Then she takes me back to my school and tells me I will be eaten by wayob if I speak of this."

Tears shined on the child's face. She took a deep shuddering breath. "Mi madre, she knew what had occurred. She was angry. She says that we must leave, before her mother sells me to this man. I do not know what she means. I beg her to tell me. She cries so hard. She tells me she was sold to la familia de mi padre because of her beauty. She says she will not permit my more sacrifice. I do not know what she means. I miss her so much. She tells me stories of the water and the sun, and of the jaguar god who will come to protect us. Now she is silent."

The child stopped talking as abruptly as she started and remained silent until my headlights splashed the row of wax myrtle along the fence surrounding the House of Ellis. I turned the corner and pulled in the driveway, killed the lights, but left the engine running. Drop the child and run, or perp walk her to the back porch, and let her fend for herself?

Too late. Cherryl banged out the back door. I knew little of family or parents or, according to some, morality, but I knew the anger on her face, visible even in the dim yellow of the yard light.

"Lilia, keep your mouth shut. If she belts you, you take it. If she belts me, you take it. Say absolutely nothing except Yes ma'am, No ma'am. Do you understand me?"

She nodded, eyes wide, watching Mrs. Ellis stomp to the truck. Cherryl yanked open the passenger door and ordered, "House now. Bed."

The child hopped out and double timed into the house without a look back.

"You." She sputtered through several starts without raising her voice above a hard whisper. "I should be surprised. Somehow I'm not. What the hell is she doing with you?"

I stepped out of the truck with my hands at eleven and one. Cherryl was not amused. Lies failed me, rarely had an interrogation seemed so deadly.

"I …"

"I, I, I? What? I what? I just happen to be driving around with a fourteen year old girl at two o'clock in the morning?"

"I was on a stakeout. She came to me."

"And?" Cherryl demanded.

"And she was babbling nonsense about pucks and jaguars and witches and her mother."

"Oh sweet bleeding Jesus. Can't hardly get a peep out of her for days, now she can't shut up about her mother. How she was trapped in the shadow of a cave or some damned nonsense."

I shivered, but not from the chill. "That girl found me somehow, I think she is looking for her mother, talking about some kind dream where her mother is calling to her from a well. I didn't catch all of it. She tends to mix her Spanish and English."

"It's not just Spanish, it's Mayan, for the love of Christ. Her teacher called today. Couldn't get ahold of her parents. I had to leave work to get her. Mrs. Shields said Lilia jumped up in class, yelled something that sounded like buloo-socku-cutchel, and tore out of the classroom. She locked herself in the bathroom and wouldn't come out until I got to the school and cooed her out. She was pale and shaking like something scared the daylights out of her. She wouldn't speak, just followed me out to the car. Ran to her room when we got home. I swear I was ready to smack her. My God, the child is unhinged."

I hesitated. Afraid to speak, more afraid not to. "Those people, at the marina, I think it's her parents. That child looks familiar … "

Cherryl held her head in her hands and heaved a great sigh. "Of course she does, you met her three days ago. And you hear this loud and clear. We have no way of knowing who was in that fire, now do we? Jesus Christ, unless you've gone native, unless you can read the goddam tea leaves, unless you can kill a chicken and read the blood splatter, you just keep that nonsense to yourself. Do you hear me?"

Loud and clear. The woman was a devout Catholic, but this was not the time to point out the irony of her religion's peculiar ceremonies like drinking the blood and eating of the body of Christ, the man she had just cursed, so I waited, and waited some more. I waited until she could speak. She was unhinged. She knew the truth and didn't want to know.

"What am I supposed to do?" She asked.

"Keep them home, call in sick, load the guns, leave town. Something is wrong, badly wrong, Cherryl."

"Now she's talked you into her bloody fairy tale. Her parents took a dirty holiday knowing the kids would be taken care of. And they were right. They are taken care of. But Jesus, how did Lilia find you? Why you? Has she been out before? Is this an ongoing thing?" Cherryl's voice was gaining traction.

"Stop. Now. Lilia has not been with me, not ever. She scared the living daylights out of me. And I missed my target because of her. I guarantee you that child has not been on my radar or I would have returned one very sorry little girl."

Cherryl's shoulders slumped in resignation. I stepped closer to her and whispered, "Would it be so bad just to load the kids up and get them out of here for a couple of days? Off island, west maybe. Chase the sun to a different shore?"

"Sure. I'll pull a credit card out of my butt and set us up at the Ritz in Lauderdale. Yup, that's just what I'll do." Her anger knocked me back a step. Without another word, she turned and stomped back toward the house. The back door did not slam. The deadbolt loud in the morning still.

I backed out of the driveway thinking very dark thoughts, grateful for once I wasn't a parent or one of those children. One child specifically.

My déjà vu had not come from Sunday's walk on the beach. That child spooked me when I met her, with wild stories of blood lines and jaguars. The tale had mixed with the terror of Sunday morning and grew into vivid nightmares. I didn't know why until I found the child in my truck. Her profile so like the woman forever frozen in black and white.

The part of the brain that still believes in hungry tigers hiding in the bush, crocodiles in the pond, the instinct part that allowed humans to walk upright, recognize and run from predators, that part of my brain had finally recognized the horror Cherryl refused to acknowledge.

08 SITUATION FUBAR

I caught two hours of sleep parked in the back of the lot at St. John's Mission house. Wild Bill Darby, decorated Marine and three-time Asian theater volunteer, ran the kitchen, serving breakfast to scores of lost souls. Most guests were in and out before eight. Lingering over a second cup of coffee was not encouraged.

Donating time to the soup kitchen was the penance Aunt Hannah extracted for the accidental homicide of Joey Steps, aka, Joseph Stepanik, Junior, late son of Hannah's very special friend, Joseph Senior. Length of sentence: Fifty two Thursday mornings. This was not Calcutta and I would never be nominated for sainthood, but I sent up a silent prayer requesting patience or lock jaw so I could pretend a zeal for serving the downtrodden. God was not listening this morning.

Cutting through the early morning clatter of pots and pans, Darby's booming voice hurled orders at his numerous volunteers. Because I was ten minutes late, I was assigned the guest bathrooms. I donned mask, heavy rubber gloves, and filled a mop bucket with bleach.

I emptied the bucket of its brown water, scrubbed vigorously and rejoined the kitchen crew. I locked eyes with fellow volunteer and resident blabbermouth Max, and gestured to the door. He shook his head and pointed at an imaginary watch on his hairy arm. Four hours and a hundred and twenty nine meals later, silverware sterilized, floors swept, pots, pans, dishes rested in their cubbies. I grabbed the trash bags and banged my hip into the fire door. I tossed the bags into the dumpster and patted my pockets for a smoke.

"Goddamit, Archer, get in here now." Darby yelled.

I ran inside cursing Aunt Hannah and God. A tall, skeletal junkie had another tweeker strong-armed against a block wall in the dining room. One hand wrapped around the victim's throat, the other running up and down its jacket and pants, looking for product or money. One of the combatants had identified as female or the male volunteers would have handled the situation themselves.

The smell of the fighters struck me at ten feet. Breathing through my mouth, I pushed between the two screeching scarecrows. Max wrapped his giant arms around the aggressor and plucked him off the floor. Matched in height, but not in girth, Max toted him to the door. The female slapped at me. She wanted her man. She hurled words that made three retired Marines blush. I pinned her stick wrists behind her back and forced her to the door. I pushed her through and released her arms. Still spitting invective, she shoved her way past Max and ran down the sidewalk. Ugh. The stench was on me, in my clothes, hair, skin, and soul.

I scrubbed all exposed body parts with blue industrial soap, and yelled, "Are we done? Garbage is out and the fridge is locked."

"Yeah yeah yeah, get outta my kitchen. Go smoke your damn smokes." Darby flapped a hand in dismissal. He was done with me for the day and looking up recipes for tomorrow.

I caught Max waiting in the alley. He offered me a smoke, not my brand, but I gratefully accepted.

"You know he used to run a soup kitchen up north? Quit it all to hell and brought his family down here. Said it was less dangerous." He shared, snapping the lighter shut.

I laughed obligingly, drew on the cigarette, and checked the alley for creeping dangers. I was angry at Max, but I was too tired to work up any righteous rage. Next time one of these dopes asked about saving their messed up kid, I'd be in Pittsburgh.

"Steady told me you didn't say much. Issued orders. Wouldn't give him a price, like he's gonna owe you."

"I'll bill him for recon and incidentals and you guys do this yourselves."

"Naw, he's okay, worried 'bout his girl. He don't take orders real well."

"I know, I know, from a woman."

Max scuffled a boot on the concrete, "In general, but it sure would help if you were a brother."

"Your friend is not my brother." I took a last drag, ripped the filter in half, and ground the pieces into the dirt.

I left Max in the alley, and made my way to Navy. My eating habits of late were disrupted by the smell at the marina. I hoped a burger would stay with me. Sitting in the parking lot wiping grease from my hands, I called Steady and dictated a wish list only he could provide: One burner phone, two if his personal use phone was a so-called smart phone, a car nobody would miss overnight, gun unattached to criminal activity, and an anonymous ride into the city – preferably one of his men. I reminded him the list was non-negotiable. One missing piece would bring the mission to a halt. He said I didn't need to remind him. We agreed upon a rendezvous point on west Hernandez, a club property. We'd meet, exchange pleasantries, and then meet back when I had retrieved the package. It was near the hospital, just in case. I hung up, confident all products would await my arrival. Confident that if the products weren't delivered, I was off the hook.

I drove to work, but Angela shooed me out of my own nursery, telling me to be careful if I were 'working' tonight, promising she would lock up as she had on a hundred other occasions. Too tired to argue, I steered the truck home, climbed the stairs, set an alarm, kicked off my boots, and planted my face on the bed. I woke in darkness to the trilling of my phone. I flipped the lid. It was Bill. Nothing good would come of talking to him. If he wanted me, he knew where I lived. I closed it and slept another hour.

I splashed my face and tied my hair, tucking the tail down the back of my shirt. My replenished kidnapping bag was packed, and sitting by the door. I located clean underwear, dressed in disposable clothing, and pulled on my boots. The far off drone of an American made motorcycle cued me to lock up and walk down the lane. The bike slowed, made a U-turn, and stopped next to me. Without a word I secured the pack, and wrapped my arms around an unfamiliar leather clad gut, settling in for a cold night ride with a silent stranger.

He pulled into the lot on Hernandez and waited for me to dismount. He offered a salute in the near dark and rolled parade speed down the side alley. Headlights flickered briefly on the side of the building. I walked toward the vehicle and climbed into the driver's side of a neglected Toyota sedan. The car was covered in dust, oxidation ate at the wheel wells. Steady glared at me in the glow of the dashboard while I checked the brakes, locks, and windows.

"Plates are clean." He handed me a onetime use phone and held up its mate, assuring me both were purchased with cash from different stores. He pulled a bag from under the passenger seat, and unwrapped a short barreled pistol, polymer handgrip, lightweight. I tipped it into the light. It looked new. HK V9 9mm x 19. The magazine held fifteen. I pulled the rail to chamber a round. If it couldn't be killed in fifteen, then it couldn't be killed.

I hefted the weapon in my hand. "Not cheap."

"New. No trace. Gloves to load it. Jacketed hollow points. Try not to hit my girl."

I nodded. "You know the mayor of Chicago blames Indiana, the whole damn state for the carnage in the city."

"This ain't from Indiana." Drumming his fingers on one leg, he said, "I don't like this at all."

I flipped the phone open. No calls incoming or outgoing, his burner number programmed. Fully charged and transmission bars five by five. "You don't have to like it. Nor do I have to be here.

We can quit now, I'll give you my data and my kit. You know what your girl looks like. You get her yourself."

"You got me over a fucking barrel, ain't you?"

"No, sir. You can accept the consequences of a life unconventionally lived. You can accept the lifestyle your child has chosen. You do not have to respect her choice, but you do have to deal with it. Or you can let me get on with this filthy business. I hate junkies. I hate everything about their infantile lives." I shook my head and sighed. "Jesus, I'm sorry. Lecture over. It's your kid, no matter what she's done. I will get her out, but if I smell a rat, I make life miserable for every person you know and love. If you think you know who I am, then you know this is not a hollow threat. If I go in there and she's dead, I leave and call the police, then I call you. If she's got security dogs around her, I determine whether to continue or abort. We both have choices and we have to live with the consequences."

"So much for no lectures, huh?" His smile was too tired to sustain.

"We'll meet back here, it's quiet and sheltered. If plans change, I will call." I started the engine and feathered the gas pedal. It idled smoothly, accelerated swiftly, and the muffler was attached.

No parent, no matter their crime should bear witness to a child's slow-ride suicide, yet it seemed to be a popular pastime regardless of color, culture, education, ethnicity, wealth, or alleged intelligence. The suburban wasteland kids were bored, urban plantation kids were bored, kids with no dads were bored, privileged kids were bored. No supervision, no expectations, no consequences, no reason to exist, the ultimate in post-modern nihilism. For Christ's sake, I was lecturing myself.

I turned east on Jordan and killed the lights as I approached the building. No traffic at all. I parked and watched the north entrance and waited.

Two hours passed. By my count, the last ghoul had skittered inside, including my target. I rubbed the smelly grease paint onto my face and neck, and the backs of my hands. I slunk across the street, stepped through the hole in the chain link, and climbed the stairs. The fetid odors of human waste assaulted me as I pushed into the darkness. Gandhi's untouchables possessed a dignity these privileged asshats eschewed in favor of jamming poison into their veins with dirty needles and turning their home into a dirty hole. I was angry. I had to control that anger before it hampered my operational capacity.

I stepped inside and let my eyes adjust to the darkness. I took a deep breath through the mouth, willing myself to calm down. Mine was not to judge, mine was to extract whatever child survived inside that scabbed and shrunken shell. At twenty, with all the recuperative powers of youth, she shouldn't look as bad as she does. Something else rode her veins in addition to street fattened heroin. A few months at the mission had provided graduate level studies in the various ways humans hated themselves.

Night farts, snores, heavy breathing, whimpers, an occasional passing car broke the noxious hush. I stepped carefully, shining my penlight directly on faces. Not one of these squirrels moved, not one stirred. I had no idea where she was, but I counted fifteen ghouls entering the premises in total. Only one entered after my target came home. I searched the rooms along the hallway, not every alcove was filled, thank God. Perhaps this was the urban version of a youth hostel and these were all innocent backpackers from Wichita.

Last room on the left, two bodies sprawled on a queen sized mattress. Quick check with the penlight. Up close, a day's worth of mangy facial hair crawled up his face and down his neck, wallet chain drooped on the filthy mattress from pants to pocket, LA Dodgers tee-shirt, mouth agape, right side of neck inked with a square G and a two-armed telephone pole. Asleep, illuminated by a meek pinpoint light, he looked like any Texi-Cali banger with a thousand miles of road years on him. His arm draped over a pale female. I made positive identification of Taylor from a small beauty mark, a mole, upper lip left. Light bruising on stick arms, too skinny, bones sharp. This was not some shithole country where women had no alternative but whoring. Jesus wept. Did she even eat? I could pull the trigger, take him out, we were isolated, nobody would come looking, the cockroaches would scramble, then I could yank her out. I told all my voices to shut up and concentrate on getting this sack of bones out of here quietly. No more judgment, only action.

Stowing the light in my pocket, I stepped forward silently and crouched down for a pulse at her neck. Bump, bu-bump, too slow, but her heart was beating, she was breathing, and that was enough for me. I slid his arm off her torso carefully, grasped her shoulders, and pulled her toward me like a ragdoll. She muttered and flopped forward, head on my shoulder. I hugged her into me and pulled her to standing. Her breath stunk of yellowing decay, her skin clammy. I whispered soothing sounds. "Got some pretty pony for you, come with me, la da di." One step back, she was forced to shuffle forward with me, a second step, another shuffle forward. "Tired," she whined, "Wanna lay down."

I cooed sing-song noises in her ear as I dragged her with me, stepping back and pulling her. The male skell murmured and rolled into her empty space, left cheek on the mattress. He resumed snoring. I took a third scuffling step back, dragging her, then a fourth.

"Puta," growled the man who no longer slept. I sidestepped to the right pulling the unwilling girl by her spindly arms. I flung her toward the pale light coming through the door of the damaged fire escape. A knife slashed close enough to feel the whoosh of its passage. The force of his trajectory took his hand to the ground, knife tip scraping on the concrete. The whites of his eyes shiny in the feeble light. The man looked remarkably healthy, hunched like an ape, dancing the knife back and forth for my entertainment. He was toying with me. He was the cat and I was the mouse.

Still hunched, he grinned up at me, laughing softly, teeth exposed in a hideous grin. He enjoyed hurting people. This stupid child didn't deserve to be treated like a diseased dog no matter what crimes she'd committed. I reached under my sweatshirt for the stolen gun jammed in my belt. I kept my eyes locked on his, anticipating his next move. His grin widened. I stepped backward, my boot landed on the girl's hand. She whimpered and struggled weakly to free her hand. I dared not look away from the enemy. I couldn't back any farther with the stupid girl behind me. He arced the knife overhand like a bad actor menacing settlers encroaching upon sacred lands.

He lunged toward me, weight forward on his left leg, providing maximum downward thrust. A boom broke the silence, rolling across the relative flatness of the city. War games at NAS or a jet jockey breaking Mach. It could have been an atom bomb. His eyes darted toward the sound then returned to me. He had already committed to the forward motion as I freed my firearm. No time to aim. I stepped right and fired from the waist, barrel tilted upward. His head rocked back, flesh torn from the impact of a single frangible projectile fired at less than five feet. I tripped over the girl, falling on my ass, my head bounced off the concrete. The momentum of the intended assault carried him into me. The knife plunged into my left thigh as he landed on me.

Pain exploded at the point of impact. I pushed my right foot into his shoulder to scoot myself backward. The girl weeping, awake now, drug high eaten away by adrenalin, shoving at me to get at her dead man. The bullet had worked as advertised and fragmented upon impact. She lifted his head, his face no longer the face of her lover, no longer recognizable. Her weeping turned into a high pitched keening.

I wrapped my hands around the knife, praying, and followed the incoming wound path, pulling it out at approximately the same angle as the entry. Not supposed to do that, but I was reasonably sure waiting for a medic would kill me. The pain roared louder than the percussion of the single gunshot. Heavy gray fog moved into my field of vision threatening to blind me. Deep breath, focus on one point, any point. My gardenia. Glossy leather leaves, perfect white blooms releasing an exquisite fragrance, like nothing else in the world. My breathing calmed, fog ebbed, heart slowed.

I pressed both hands, palms down on either side of the wound to assess the damage. The knife struck no bone, bleeding was heavy, but not mortal, no creeping chill or sleepiness. The leg would hold for now. Gangster boy stuck me deeply but missed the important stuff.

I picked up the knife. A five inch blade coated in my blood, handle wrapped with some kind of tape. Dammit. I had to take it with me. My blood was all over the handle as well as DNA from his last victim. I jammed the damned thing in my boot. But the gun, I liked the gun. It was quality and expensive to replace legally. I wiped it clean with the dirty sheet and dropped it next to his body, out of reach of the girl, trusting Steady had kept his own prints off the weapon.

Balancing the weight on my right leg I stood. The left would hold me up, but not well. "Come on, Cindy Lou Who, we gotta go. Now. Cops are coming." I didn't know if they were, but it seemed a reasonable assumption even for this neighborhood. I touched her on the shoulder, she was shaking with grief. She pushed my hand away and continued rocking his head in her lap. "No, he's dead, you fucking bitch – "

Four more unrepeatable words and my anger got the better of my manners. I cuffed her in the ear, knocking away the ugly sounds. I jammed both hands under her armpits and levered her off the floor. Stunned by the blow she stopped struggling. I grabbed her arm and said, "We go now." I was at a disadvantage with one leg weak, but I was angry, and I wasn't a junkie, and I was sick to death of touching her. Why the hell had I risked my life to save this skank. Her mouth would make the devil blush.

Un-boarded windows made a dent in the darkness, beckoning toward the intact stairwell about a million miles away. Not one ghost emerged from their cell as I dragged her down the wide hall, out the heavy door, and down the metal stairs. I took no precaution for stealth at this point. My ears rang too loud to hear much of anything. I hustled her to the car, half carrying her, and wrestled open the passenger door. Ragged and starved, she felt like hot spindles, yet she fought like a rabid bear. Forgive me, Lord, I am about to sin, again. I slammed her head into the door frame, dragged her to the trunk, hoisted her up, and dumped her in. I dug for the duct tape and slapped a strip on the slack mouth. I zip tied her hands, then her feet, and looped three more to connect the trusses. I slammed the lid and limped to the driver's seat. I looped three strands of duct tape around the wound, and pulled my legs into the driving well.

My hearing returned by a small degree, but my head throbbed in time with my heart. I dug the burner phone out of my boot, pressed go and said, "I'm heading to Hernandez with the prize."

I drove through a narrowing field of vision to the rendezvous. Waiting for Steady, I pried the back off the phone, knocked out the battery, pulled the SIM card, and broke all the cheap pieces. Sadly, the phone was newer and nicer than mine. With a filthy sleeve, I wiped down everything I had touched, inside the door panel, turn signal, shifter, headlights, rearview, and seat lever. Funny how many things you touched just getting into a car.

A vehicle running dark barreled into the gravel lot. I limped around and opened the trunk. "She's in bad shape. Like one virus away from heaven's door."

"You put her in the trunk – you fucking tied her up? Goddamit, what the living fuck did you do?"

I held a hand up in a wait signal, and pulled the dead man's knife out of my boot. While I cut her bindings, I said, "She didn't come along peacefully. Her friend isn't coming at all." I left the duct tape on her mouth.

He stooped over the open trunk, wrapped his little girl in a blanket and cradled her like a newborn. I opened the back door of his borrowed sedan, and helped him stretch her out on the seat. He checked her pulse and slammed the door. He looked me up and down, deciding where to put a hole in me. His eyes paused at the spreading wetness on my left thigh. "Whose blood?"

"Some mine, some the boyfriend's. Get me closer to the hospital and let me out. You're on your own after that." While he made fish faces trying to put words together, I climbed in the passenger seat. Vanity kept the groans and grunts to a minimum. My leg was wet, but it wasn't pouring. Nothing major hit, just muscle tissue damaged with a dirty knife. Steady jammed the car into gear and pulled onto Hernandez, hooking a left at the stop sign.

"How bad is it?"

"Me or her?"

"You," he sighed.

"Deep, not fatal, unless infection sets in."

He nudged his head toward sleeping beauty.

"She's a long way down, but she's breathing," I said.

Another sigh, another block closer to the hospital. "Why did you agree to do this?"

"Anybody tell you guys no?"

"You could have."

I shrugged. "Wish I had an answer. But put word out that Junkie Day Camp is closed. I've seen some shitholes, but this is voluntary, none of these people – fuck it. No lectures, I'm starting to get fuzzy, let me out here, between the street lights."

"We're headed to Emergency."

"Not with me in the car. You take care of her." Steady wouldn't identify the body left behind. I doubted the PPD had the manpower to waste forensic work on a dead junkie. Odds in my favor, but I had to ditch the knife, and I wasn't going to trust him with a piece of evidence placing me at the scene. I wasn't too worried about sleeping beauty as a reliable witness.

Holding onto the door frame, I hoisted myself out of the car. I put a little weight on the left leg, and slammed the door. Tires squealed around the last turn to the hospital.

No phone, no car, no ID, no cash, and on the wrong side of the highway. A chain link fence protected an empty lot from looters. Seemed like a good place to ditch the knife. I placed more weight on the injured leg and limped to the fence. Leaning into a pole for balance, I painstakingly peeled the tape from the knife and shoved the wad into my pocket. I wiped the weapon with my shirt sleeve, dropped it on the ground and kicked it under the wire. I hobbled a seeming eighteen miles to the entrance and stepped into the odors and sounds of a busy urban hospital as dawn broke somewhere far to the east. Steady needed to take care of his daughter, not his mercenary. It wasn't personal, it was business.

A chunky security guard bursting out of his uniform groaned his way up from a folding chair. He looked me up and down. "You got any weapons?"

"I wouldn't look like this if I did." He shrugged and waved me through, sighing heavily as he settled himself back into the chair. I walked twenty miles to the desk and waited for a woman in gray to finish a phone call. I couldn't read her name, but the RN stamped on her badge could be seen from space. I had no idea the hierarchy of hospital employees, nor the protocol for addressing the various busy people dressed in a dizzying array of grays and blues. I stood at the desk waiting to be noticed.

The woman dropped the phone in its cradle and looked up at me. "What happened to you?"

"Two guys wanted my stuff, one had a knife. I lost.

"Tell it to the cops. What is your medical emergency?

I took a step back so she could see my medical emergency.

"Name?"

She click-clacked on a plastic keyboard then looked up and asked for my name again.

"Mansfield, Jane"

"Alright Ms. Mansfield, take a seat."

She missed the joke, but I caught none of her instructions as I plodded to an empty chair and collapsed. I closed my eyes for a moment.

"Are you passed out?"

I blinked up at her and shook my head.

"Then fill this out." She dropped a clipboard into my lap.

Without argument, I picked up the pen and began a short fictional memoir. Avoiding disagreement with service personnel yielded better service. God knows what this poor woman has had to deal with already. I knew what mess had come through a half hour before my arrival, and judging the gallery sitting in the noisy waiting area, a whole lot of patients had arrived before I dropped in.

Another trip to the desk. My leg had stiffened. It was more of a lopsided lope across the tundra of dirty linoleum. The busy nurse was on her phone again. Gray scrubs to her right leaned over the desk and said, "I'll take that." Stethoscope draped over his neck, a stack of laminated tags clipped to a pocket. He scanned my fiction and leaned over the desk to see what could be seen. "What happened?"

"Mugged."

"How long ago?" He typed almost as fast as the other nurse. I wondered if it was a super power they all had to master.

"About an hour, maybe more."

"And you're getting here now?"

"Long story, long night, no wallet so no cab. It hurts and I'm pretty tired – "

He interrupted, "Who brought you in?"

"I walked. If this is gonna be a while, let me use the phone. I'll call somebody for a ride."

"I'm supposed to call the cops for domestic violence."

"It's not domestic, and I don't need cops. I was in the wrong bar at the wrong time with the wrong crowd. Plain old garden variety stupidity."

He exhaled loudly. "Go. Sit. I'll find someone. It's been a long night."

I was tempted to walk out the door, but the fog returned, reminding me I wouldn't make it a block. I could ill afford the scrutiny passing out in public. Risky enough being in the same Emergency after little Miss Junkie arrived. I prayed for her continued health, at least another couple of hours so I could escape before her giant father-of-the-year found me or the police arrived.

So I sat. And brooded and dozed. The noise didn't rise above the volume of the television bolted to the wall, but the place was busy enough for a Thursday with the weekend just getting started. Maybe it was Friday …

I snapped awake feeling well enough to make it out the door, maybe another block to find a phone. The doors weren't far. Weak morning light challenged the drab florescence. I stood, bearing the weight on my right leg.

"Hey, hey, Mansfield, you're up to bat," a voice called. The male nurse stood next to a man in none-too-fresh blue scrubs studying a clipboard. The nurse aimed a come-along gesture my way. I stepped toward the exit and my leg buckled, dumping me on the filthy tile with a thud.

"I got her. Where do you think you're going?" Blue scrubs tucked his hands in my armpits and lifted me upright.

"Foley. Not so busy."

"You're funny. Big rush here is over. We'll get you a nice table with a view of the patio. Darryl, help me out here."

"I'm good. Honest. Bleeding's stopped. Just a flesh wound. That other nurse said she wouldn't give me any drugs so I'm wasting my time hanging around here."

"Ma'am, that's a lot of blood." Darryl got an arm around my waist before I laid down on the cold tile. I wasn't pouting, I was tired.

"She's pale," said my new friend in the blue scrubs.

"My normal color. Whiter shade of pale." I chuckled at myself. I was pretty funny and my leg didn't hurt so much. The two men walked me into an exam room. Blue rummaged through drawers.

Darryl asked, "Can you take off your pants?"

I unbuckled my belt and wiggled my jeans over my hips.

"All the way off, ma'am."

I leaned against the exam table, and tried to push the pants down further. "They're stuck to me."

"For God's sake." The nurse put his hands around my waist, plucked me off the floor, and plopped me on exam table. The paper crinkled under my butt. He pulled off my right boot, taking the sock with it. He gently maneuvered the left off. The sock was glued to my foot with my own blood. He glanced inside the boot and grimaced. He straightened and pulled a drawer open, laid wicked looking scissors on a tool cart. "We'll have to cut the pants off. They're dried to the wound."

"I'm not going home without pants. Too many questions."

Blue man leaned around the nurse and said, "We won't let you go home without pants. My promise." A smile flitted across his face. I tried to smile back.

Darryl snipped and tugged. He held up a strip of duct tape and shook his head. He worked until my pants lie in a heap on the floor. He let me keep my underwear. Another of mother's maxims floated into my fuzzy head, something about always wearing clean underwear in case of an accident. Couldn't remember if I had donned clean underwear this morning. It was a million days ago.

"Why didn't you just make shorts?" A wordless glance of exasperation passed between the two medics. Darryl cut around the fabric stuck to my skin. He piled new things on the tool cart while the other man bent over my leg, analyzing the mess.

Blue man snapped on gloves and placed something cold and wet and stinky over the denim covering the wound. "This is gonna hurt. A lot. We have to get the material off the wound." He pried and lifted, moistened, pried and lifted some more. It hurt a great deal. I kept my mouth shut and showed no reaction other than involuntary sweating and an occasional shudder, also uncontrollable.

Medical terminology passed back and forth between the medics, which I did not understand nor care to. I laid back on the crinkly paper to let the men work, and wondered why the damn curtain was wide open. Some new government regulation meant to humiliate a patient even further.

The doctor lifted the last of the denim from the wound. "Rhonda was wrong. We will give you some drugs. Not a lot, just enough to get this cleaned and sutured. First, I need to know a couple of things. You said you were at a bar, did you have a lot to drink? I don't smell alcohol."

"Who's Rhonda?"

"Nurse at the desk."

"She doesn't like me."

"No, she doesn't. She sent Darryl here to assist because you worry her, which is why the curtain is open – for your safety. Can't have a vulnerable female alone with two big men"

Darryl chimed in, "You're supposed to have a female in attendance, but our only available female appears to be afraid of you. Now can you answer the question? Have you been drinking?"

"Vodka."

Blue scrubs cupped my chin and tilted my head toward the light, peering into my eyes. "Bullshit. You'd sweat out the alcohol. It leaves a distinctive odor. Did you take anything else? Pills? Snort? Smoke?"

"No."

He stuck the stethoscope inside my sweatshirt and listened. "So why were you in the wrong bar at the wrong time with the wrong people?"

Questions were problematic. Pick a simple lie, add a couple of details, and use silence to advantage. "Because I am an idiot. I was looking for a guy who owes me money. His friends didn't like me."

"Hmm. Shocker," opined Darryl. The other man used his little pen light on my eyes again, then shoved a wooden stick down my throat and shined his light looking for God knows what. He pushed up my sleeves looking for scabs and holes. He peeked between my toes. I said nothing while he did this. More medical gobbledee-gook between the two men. A needle materialized and jammed into my arm. Darryl handed me a plastic cup containing a tiny white pill and a large capsule. He held my head up so I could swallow them.

"Can you understand what I'm saying?" Blue scrubs asked.

I nodded.

"I'm Doctor Tannenger, and today you get stitches and a band aid. You just swallowed tramadol and amoxicillin. The shot was for tetanus. Your own doctor will remove the stitches in seven to ten days. If the area gets hot, puffy and red, or develops streaks radiating out from the wound site, head to Emergency immediately because the infection will spread quickly and kill you. I'll send you home with ten days of oral antibiotics. Take them all. Keep the wound dry. Move around as little as possible." He shook his head. "That wound is too damn deep to be an accident."

Darryl asked if he needed to call the police. The doctor paused his stitching. He looked at me, but spoke to Darryl. "Is this incident likely to be repeated, Ms. Mansfield? Will we see you on the morning news?"

"Not likely." I responded. He sewed, and then sewed some more, layers of stitches. He clucked his tongue a number of times. I felt pressure and movement deep within the tissue, but it became less important as the second hand of the clock revolved ever so slowly. Hmmm, the doc was cute. Strike that, handsome, but in a boyish way. Hair short, brown, graying a little at the temples. Nice smile, tired brown eyes. He seemed a little tightly wound. He needed more bedside manner, less smart aleck. I drifted away on my happy cloud of pain medication.

"You still with me?"

"Hmmm."

"Is this connected to an assault that came in not long before you did?"

Alarm bells clanged in the distance, disturbing my mellow. "I had an accident due to bad judgment." Darryl made a coughing noise eerily similar to the word bullshit.

The men finished their work, dropping gloves and sundry in a red bag marked with the universal biohazard symbol. They talked to each other as if I weren't in the room. The nurse had his back to me, shunning me, but I could read the laminate blue scrubs had clipped to his shirt. Jacob Tannenger, M.D., a bunch of other stuff unknown to me. Shiny pins stuck through the plastic badge. The doctor looked down at me, as if to speak, shook his head, and left the room without another word.

Darryl ordered me to wait for a tech to move me to another room. The doctor wanted to check on the wound in a few hours, make sure I didn't have a reaction to the medication.

I was not moving to another room. I was going home. Too early to call Oscar, but Bear would be awake. "Yes, sir, but I need to make a call. I gotta let my boss know I won't be in."

"You don't have a phone." He seemed incredulous

"That disappeared, too."

He pulled a large thin phone out of a hip pocket, checked it, punched in a key code and handed it to me. "It better be local."

"It is. Promise."

I stared at the virtual keypad trying to remember Bear's phone number. Too many digits dancing in my head. Who else to call? Hannah? Visiting the dreaded Emerald Isle. The stupid cat couldn't drive. Angela? She'd take me straight to the psych ward. The only numbers to assume a cohesive pattern were Bill Thornton's. He was the last person who needed to be made aware of my foray into criminal foolishness. The drug was wearing off and I was depressed. Pity party next stop. I hit the home key and returned his phone. The nurse raised an eyebrow in question. I shrugged, and turned my head away from him.

I slept through the move to a multi-bed dorm, and awoke hooked to an I.V. drip. I closed my eyes and let hospital chatter drift into my thoughts, separating the voices, guessing at their notch in the food chain by the tone of their words. A familiar voice drew near. "You're awake." It was Dr. Tannenger, dressed in jeans and a white button up. He tossed a Wynn-Dixie bag on the trolley-table next to my bed. His eyes were red ringed and his skin looked grainy. Stubble covered his chin.

"I can't believe you're still here," I said.

"Double shift, my second this week. We're short staffed and the rage virus is spreading rapidly. I don't usually see this much action on a weekday." He raised an eyebrow and gestured toward the blanket covering my lack of pants.

I tugged the blanket away from my leg. He pulled on gloves and peeled the bandage back, made an hmmm sound, and pressed the pad back in place. "It's swollen. That's normal. It's warm, normal as well. I'll have someone change the dressing before you're discharged. It's gonna leave a scar."

"It'll match the other ones."

He tucked the blanket back in place, and leaned a hip against the bed rail. "Accident prone?"

"Lucky, I guess. I need to get home. Any reason I can't go now, except for the no-pants thing?"

"We take your pants if we think you won't pay." He pulled a rolling chair close to the bed, and dropped into it with a sigh.

I had slept enough to recover some sense. He was on a fishing expedition. Why else was I getting the extra attention? I asked, "What happened with your assault? You still looking for a villain?"

"Darryl chewed my ass about that, but the timing of your intake seemed coincidental. I can't tell you about another patient, but she sure could use a hero. At least one who isn't a giant outlaw biker."

He'd been up all night, and he smelled tired. I caught underlying odors of soap, hand sanitizer, and something else, not cologne. It was laundry softener. His street clothes had been laundered by a female. That was sexist think, punishable by law, but I'd rarely met a man who remembered those goofy dryer sheets or that chuckling little bear hawking miracle fabric softening qualities. I glanced at his left hand. Empty, but a lot of folks performed labors wherein they would not wear jewelry. It didn't make them cheaters. Dr. Tannenger didn't strike me as the type, but I had been stoned during most of our acquaintance.

"I have no medical reason to keep you. I could order a psych evaluation, though."

I waited. His eyes were dark caramel with little flecks of gold near the pupil.

He pushed out a pent up breath, stood, and shoved the chair away. "We're running out of beds over in the bird tower. Unless you eat the blanket, you're good to go."

"I'll bite. What's the bird tower?"

"Psych ward. Kind of surprised you don't know." He snatched up the bag, tossed it in my lap, and walked out of the room.

Sweatpants, men's large, and a UWF sweatshirt, extra-large. They smelled of disinfectant, but the faded gray fabric had been laundered so many times it felt like cashmere.

A nurse, very harried, very pissed, and very female charged to my bedside, peeled the tape from my hand, unplugged the IV, and bent my arm to an uncomfortable angle, ostensibly to stop any bleeding from the harpoon's exit. She wrapped a pressure cuff tight enough to cut off blood flow, and stuck a thermometer in my mouth.

"Let's get you discharged." She pulled open the door of a cardboard cabinet. "Your boots survived the cupboard. Normally anything not nailed down walks out of here. I've got paperwork for you to sign." Beeping stopped her. She looked down at a box clipped to her belt and scurried out of the room.

I replaced the old sweatshirt with the clean one, the one without the blood and tissue of two other people soaked into it. I tugged on the donated pants and swung my legs over the side of the bed. Sliding down the side of the mattress, I carefully put weight on my left leg. Pain shot through the top of my skull, but the leg held me up. I slid feet into my boots with a grimace. The left tacky and rough with blood. I limped out of the room, and tracked my way to billing, stopping long enough to shove the soiled clothing into a public trash bin.

I asked the clerk if she could send the bill to my husband as I had no identification, no wallet, no credit card. Sadly, Mr. Mansfield had separated from Mrs. Mansfield, and asked her to leave their recently shared domicile.

"Fine. What's the billing address?"

"1060 West Addison, Chicago."

The harried woman at the desk looked up sharply. "And he'll pay?"

I nodded. "I'm on his insurance. If he doesn't, my brother will beat the daylights out of him."

"Must be nice to have a useful brother." A smile almost pursed the clerk's lips.

I scribbled an illegible signature, thanked her, and limped my way downstairs where I located the dispensary, waited for my bottle, gave the clerk my fictitious husband and address, then limped my way up dirty stairs, emerging into bright daylight pouring through the glass doors. Too much light. I shielded my eyes and waited for the automatic doors to let me out.

Large men clustered, talking and smoking, at the far end of a long row of motorcycles, no doubt all of them Harleys. The shiny chrome was shooting laser rays into my eyes. The men all looked alike. One broke from the herd. As he approached I recognized Max, my fellow Marine and soup kitchen buddy. He shook out a cigarette and offered it to me. Grateful for the nicotine, I took the smoke and let him light it.

"Taylor's in bad shape," he said.

"She had another week, maybe two. There's something else wrong with her besides the heroin." I blew smoke into the morning, watching it dissipate.

He looked me up and down. "How bad did you get hit?"

"Nothing that will kill me. Tetanus shot, antibiotics, a couple of stitches. I'll live. But we're –"

"I know, we're all done. Cops showed up at the squat, found a dead banger." He took a deep breath and blew it out, looking out toward the road. "Seems like our kids got the most fucked." He flicked his cigarette away. "You're owed. Remember that."

"So long as I only have to see you on Thursday mornings."

"You still gonna come, all cut up like that?"

"Seems my atonement is yet out of reach."

Max snorted, and accepted my answer. The rumor mill churned the waters of the seamy undercurrent running through both our lives. It was surprising our paths had not crossed sooner.

"Ms. Mansfield?" Dr. Tannenger stopped five feet from me, squinting into a daylight he hadn't seen much of this week. "Are you all right?"

"Enjoying the sunshine."

"You find a ride home?"

I looked at Max. He shrugged. I did not relish the thought of riding pillion in the chill air behind one of his minions. Or him.

"Not yet."

"Would you like a ride home?"

"Yes, thank you. Save me the cost of a taxi." I limped behind him. He beeped the locks to a recent model sedan, sedate and safe, no dents, only a couple of door dings. I slid butt first into the passenger seat and swung my legs in. The pain returned and no one had thought to provide a party pack of painkillers. I pulled the door shut and latched the safety belt, hissing through clenched teeth.

He cruised past the honor guard and turned out of the lot. "I can't make Wrigley on one tank of gas."

"I moved here recently."

"So I would guess. Too bad about Mr. Mansfield."

He kept his eyes on the road, hands at ten and two, checking the rearview mirrors regularly. He looked used up. I had served my own double shifts. I survived, as would he. There was always a pint of adrenalin in reserve for the miles to go before the sleep.

I gave him directions to the shop instead of driving me all the way to the island. He didn't know me, he didn't need to know where I lived, and I hadn't yet figured out his angle. He had suspicions, obviously, but would that warrant personal attention?

He turned south onto Pace. I marveled at the amount of open space available for development. The view was dotted with fenced in lots, empty except for garbage or an overgrown foundation. Empty storefronts stood next to functioning businesses, car lots, rental places, gas stations and palm trees. The open space and industrial destruction was the result of bad decisions made by stupid politicians during our suicidal force reduction years. I leaned my head back and closed my eyes, noise of the world locked behind the glass, the movement of the car lulled me to sleep.

I snapped awake and sat up, blinking away the confusion. We were still on Pace, and the landscape had dropped from moderately depressing to criminally negligent. "Thanks for the ride." I stifled a yawn.

"Not every day a man gets to meet a world famous pin-up girl."

"I suppose not."

"No offense, but you don't strike me as a sex-goddess."

"I can understand that might be a stretch."

The silence lasted until we drove through Warrington. "Okay, I give up. Are you a secret agent?"

"No." I shook my head and shut my eyes.

"I'm too tired to play twenty questions. The girl gave you up. She claims a woman matching your description kidnapped her, beat her, tied her, and locked her in the trunk of a car."

"I had a busy morning."

"And shot her boyfriend."

"If you follow 292 to the island, you'll find a particularly mean constable who would love to drop me in Raiford and throw away the key. Assault, kidnapping, and murder should finally do it."

"The only thing keeping that girl alive is the resiliency of youth. I can't speak to your many felonies, but she would not have survived another five days out there."

Too tired to care, and too tired to lie. The good doctor would keep my secret. It was his ass on the line for not requesting police presence. Or maybe that was television nonsense.

"To what end?" I asked

"You saved her life, gave her a second chance."

"You and I both know she'll end up back on the dragon before spring."

"So jaded for a film star."

"You're supposed to say I'm jaded for someone so young."

"I don't think you're that young anymore."

"Fair enough." I dozed a few minutes. Grease from the fryers of ten fast food joints stirred my stomach. The gigantic Walmart at the intersection toward above the flat land. I lifted hundred pound eyelids, and pointed him to the driveway over which an unwieldy sign stood guard, gifted me by my cranky neighbor Frank, a man who petitioned the county to make me go away when I first arrived. The sign read Gardens on Sorrento curved over the top of a ficus in bas-relief. I hated it and loved it and was embarrassed by it and teased mercilessly because of it by my small cadre of friends. Friends whose phone numbers I could not remember.

Angela's sedan squatted alone in front of the building. Tannenger turned into the lot and drifted to a stop. I took the man on faith. Maybe the truth would set me free. Some of the truth. "The girl's father asked me to find her, bring her home. It got a little dicey."

"What's security supposed to do about the motorcycle gang blocking half the parking lot?"

I took a deep breath and blew it out. "Pray the girl doesn't die before you get her moved out." I stared out the windshield, embarrassed how close to tears I was. Adrenalin drain had left me weepy.

"I owe you. You didn't call the cops, you patched me up, brought me pants, and drove me home. Thank you."

A smile crossed his face, lighting up tired eyes. "I interned at Detroit Receiving. Not too much surprises me." He stared out the windshield toward the building, his face registering shock. I followed his stare to witness Angela barreling across the lot toward the car. She made an impression even when she wasn't running.

I gingerly stepped from the car. "Thank you for the ride and the bandage. I promise to send a check for the bill." I looked toward the approaching Valkyrie and back at the doctor. "Hey, don't stare. Angela started life as a man and is still a little self-conscious." I slammed the door and limped toward my friend.

09 TRAVELING PANTS

I heard the shift into reverse and kept walking. Angela raised an eyebrow in query at the departing vehicle. "We've got a problem," she announced.

"Who is we?"

"You, me, Bear, the feds, the Coast Guard for all I know. Bear mostly. The FBI arrested him this morning at his house. For terrorism. Early, before daybreak. They think he blew up his own marina."

My head throbbed and my leg hurt. "Angela, what the hell are you talking about?"

"Where have you been? I've been calling and calling, and so has everyone else. You checked out of the world. Who was that man? Is he the reason you aren't wearing pants?"

Her voice had risen in pitch signaling a level of hysteria that I was unprepared to deal with at the moment. I limped inside, levering myself around the benches to get to my office. I riffled through filing drawers looking for pants, found bourbon instead, and poured two shots into dingy mismatched coffee mugs. She stomped into my office, visibly upset. I held a dirty mug her way. She shook her head but took the cup. She shot it back, slammed the porcelain mug down, and glared at me. I waited for her to calm down.

"Where are your pants?"

"Can we assume that sometimes pants are sacrificed for the greater good? I think Bear in custody is a little more pressing than the location of my pants."

"Your pants are a curious aside. Anyway, Bear was arrested this morning, in a raid. According to Bill, they kicked in his door. They – "

"Who are they?"

"For goodness sake – they, the cops – not the local cops, the feds."

"You mentioned the Coast Guard, the cops and the feds. It's a fair question. Why was Bear arrested for terrorism?"

"The marina blew up. Not the whole dockage of course, that's poured concrete, like an airport, you couldn't really blow that up. Part of his building, or maybe all of it blew up. I don't know for sure. They – the local police – have the road to the marina blocked. The county is still in the loop so Bill is getting a little information. And he's looking for you."

"Would you make some coffee? Please. It's been a long night, for everybody it sounds like."

She busied herself with the brewing of the coffee and asked, "Does your long night have anything to do with your driver, maybe related to the location of your pants?"

"Something like that, but don't get your hopes up, he's married." I poured another shot in my mug awaiting the coffee. "Let me get this straight. Bill Thornton, island precinct captain, functionary of the law enforcement community, is feeding you information?"

"Well, no, he can't, but Oscar can."

Dr. Oscar Gunnar, aeronautical engineer and all around horn dog. The man could bug NORAD. Legend was he did just that after force reduction rumors had escalated tensions on both sides of the Iron Curtain during the waning days of the Cold War.

"How did Oscar get involved?" I asked, dreading the answer.

"Bear sent him some kind of SOS, then Bill called me, then, shit, sorry. Bear got some kind of message to Oscar when the police arrived. He hid his phone so only Oscar could find it. Bill called me looking for you. Said he went to your house, nobody was home, but your truck was there. So? Is your driver part of this?"

"Completely separate incident."

"We, Oscar and I, snuck over to Bear's. It's taped off and the door is boarded up, but the back door they just propped up. No guards or anything. And you know his neighborhood. Oscar located Bear's cell phone. Do you guys have a plan for how to handle raids? Like leaving clues or something? Oscar's at your house working on it now. He said you have tools. I'm no use with all the super-secret spy stuff so I came back to work on the orchids."

"You were with Oscar? What time was this?"

"Is that relevant?"

"Yeah, but not, oh, for fucks sake, not you and Oscar. What time did Bear send his SOS?"

"Around six this morning. Reporting on the explosion is sketchy, but the news said the time was twenty after four this morning. It was so loud half the city called the police."

She poured steaming coffee into my mug. I stuck my nose in the fragrance. The boom that saved my life. It wasn't a jet jockey spiking the sound barrier out over the gulf. It was the marina. An explosion. Five miles away. Late at night, no storms, nothing much to stop the sound from rolling across the city. Oh Lord, the destruction of Bear's marina provided me the half second necessary to avoid being dead.

"Where are they holding him?" I asked.

"Downtown. Oscar's calling attorneys. He's worried they could drop him down some homeland security hole and we won't be able to find him. My God, Jess, Oscar said there was a photograph of man hanging on the fence inside the marina. I don't know what it means, but I told him no more unless there was something I could do. I dropped him at your house."

Her voice broke. She was close to tears. This was not the Angela we all knew and loved, apparently Oscar more so. Sheesh.

I poured a half tipple of whiskey into her coffee. "We can't do anything right now except wait, so mostly we are doing nothing. Can your mom help?"

"My mother? She's not part of any law enforcement power structure, she's a psychiatrist for God's sake."

"I thought she worked with the cops."

"Civilian stuff, psych evaluations, post event counseling, that kind of stuff. Do you ever listen when I talk?"

"I'm tired. I forgot. Forgive me." I bypassed our familiar argument by sticking my hand out and asking for her phone. "Mine's at home." I punched in Bill's number. The taxpayers funded the latest in cellular technology to him, but the man was on-call twenty four hours a day, seven days a week.

Bill's voice, anxious. "Have you found Archer?"

"Yes, she's on the phone."

"Goddamit, where have you been? I'm with somebody right now. Are you home?"

"No."

"Go home, wait for me. I can't talk right now."

"No, I will not. I'm going to get a guy, who can get to another guy, and then we are going to spring Bear."

"You won't get near him." Male voice in the background, maybe the someone else he mentioned. "Jess, I've got the guy who knows the guy, okay? I can't talk right now." He disconnected.

One friend was in danger of being redacted by an unregulated department of homeland security, and my other friend, as stoic as the first, had tears running down her face. I hobbled over to Angela and tugged on her shoulder. She resisted until I wrapped my arms around her and hugged her tight. "We'll get him home, Ang, even if your mom can't help us. I promise."

She pushed me away and told me to grow up. "Do you have any ideas?" She asked, wiping her face with a paper towel.

"Not yet, maybe something. Did Oscar tell you what was on Bear's phone?"

"No, I just assumed it would exonerate him."

If the feds got hold of that phone and figured out how to access his storage, he'd be in Super-Max before midnight. Innocence be damned.

"If Thornton calls again, tell him I'm home, as per his order. And I will be if you'll run me down the road. Maybe I can catch Oscar, figure something out."

She flipped the closed sign, motioned me out the door, and locked it. She missed her calling as a Daytona driver, turning into Hannah's drive almost before we left the nursery.

She asked, "Is this thing with Oscar going to be a problem?"

I shook my head. "No, it's me, I'm tired and I'm worried. What you do with anybody isn't my business. It's just, you know he's kind of a player, right?"

She pulled a key to the house off her keyring and handed it to me. "What makes you think I'm not? Go on. I'll tell Bill you're home. Make sure I get my key back. Get Bear out of jail."

"We'll get him." I hugged her and hauled myself up the stairs. No one was sleeping on the couch, nor in my bed, nor lurking in the linen closet. Relieved, I gave the cat a piece of bread, grabbed a clean towel, and maneuvered through a shower without soaking the bandage on my leg.

Bill was parked at the table when I got out of the shower, a mug of coffee steaming in front of him. I nodded his way and fled into my room hoping to find clean pants magically ironed and hanging in the closet. I found a pair of jeans fermenting in the hamper. I located clean underwear and pulled a musty tee shirt over my head. Oscar had been in and out of my room leaving no sign but the ghost of his cologne, which was very expensive and very masculine. My super-secret spy tools were nestled within their tool box, a battered aluminum briefcase, the possession of said tools guaranteed to piss off the feds. Maybe put me in a Super-Max cell next to Bear. Linguistically, pirating, hacking, the words were interchangeable among the chattering classes whose vocabularies never rose above pop culture ignorance. Professionally, that ignorance provided a great deal of wiggle room when situations required a more fluid reading of the law.

I took a deep breath and stepped out to meet the Sheriff's anger. Jeez I hated him. Bill, not Oscar. I didn't hate Oscar. I didn't hate Bill either. I was mad because he still had the power to make me feel like a gawky fifteen year old full of angst and hormones and pretending the massive crush under which I had long suffered was a passing fever. I was too tired to feel like this, and too damned old.

I poured myself coffee, brought the pot to the table, and refilled his mug. I took a seat opposite and waited for him to yell. The man was two beats away from cuffing me.

"I been trying to get a hold of you since 0600 this morning. Where have you been?"

I blew steam from my mug, sipped, and burned my lips. Hannah's coffee maker brewed a much higher quality cup than the rummage sale drip machine I kept at the office. I blew on the coffee again. "Been a busy week."

"For Bryant, yeah. Second call out for the coroner, in what, five days? He runs a busy damn port."

I tried levity. "At least it's not on your island."

"Not today, Archer, goddamit, not today. You were at the scene. Moreno told me you were right in the thick of it."

"We've been over this. And your deputy is a gossip. I was not right in the middle of it, I was reporting for work."

"What work? You drove into the middle of an active crime scene."

"Work as in labor. Bear's fixed my plumbing half a dozen times. I owe him. And I parked outside the gate so I would not contaminate the crime scene."

"You should have turned around and left."

"But I didn't. Never leave a brother behind."

"Don't start that brotherhood shit with me, you ain't in the service anymore."

"Marine Corps, Sheriff, remember? You all thought it would be the best thing for me."

"I am stating for the record I was wrong. It made you worse."

"It provided a purpose for my life, and a family. Something I lost. Violently. Through no fault of my own. You convinced Hannah it would be best. And it was."

"For Christ's sake, you want to argue history? How about current events? What the hell is going on at the marina?"

"I don't know. What I have, I gave you."

"Not all of it."

"You're right. Yell at me if it makes you feel better." I stood to fetch a laptop from my bedroom. He stood as well, tensed and ready to detain me. I held a hand up, "I'm not running away, just give me a minute." I ducked into the bedroom and grabbed the battered HP with the modified engine. I grabbed a blank disc and set the machine on the table.

I powered up and waited while it ran through internal diagnostics. "I'm going to give you the rest of it."

Bill stood over my shoulder, too close. I held my fingers over the keyboard and waited.

"You know I can't steal your password as fast as you type." He covered his eyes like a child.

I dropped the disc in the drawer and dragged two large files to the burner session. "It'll take a few minutes. They're in original format, date, time, location, everything intact. The image quality isn't great, but it's good enough. Put the disc in your computer and double click the first file. It's a series of stills, but it will playback like a video. Then you'll know everything that I know, that Bear knows. And it is not much."

He glanced at his watch, a gift from his late wife Sarah. She had been kind to me when I washed up on this shore as a teen, orphaned and de-incarcerated from a prison overseas. While Sarah hadn't been old enough to be a mother to me, she had been a patient and invaluable friend. God took her home way too soon. My eyes welled with tears I refused to shed at her passing. I was tired and the seams were fraying.

The machine finished burning information to the shiny silver disc. I opened the drawer and held it out to him. "This is all we know. Everything from his security cameras. The pictures I gave you come from the second file. It clears Bear from any involvement in the murders."

He tucked the disc into his jacket pocket. "It may clear him from Sunday, but Homeland Security wants him for the explosion. What fucking kills me is no one is asking about his cameras. I got a bad feeling Bear told the feds that the cameras are dummies. If those morons noticed the cameras at all. I tried to talk to the SAIC, tell her it made no sense from any angle, not insurance, not security, not any damn thing." He leaned back and barked a laugh. "She suggested I help out with the coffee and leave the analysis to the professionals."

I shut the machine down. The protocol I used to access those files would only work from the IP address I created to transmit the files into the so-called cloud. Any attempt at access from any other address, any other key, would send a kill switch to the storage array. Bill possessed the only physical copy.

"They're never going to sweat Bear."

"They think they can." Bill looked at his watch again. "As much as I love our little coffee chats, we gotta go. Grab a jacket, we're going down beach, if the son-of-a-bitch shows up."

I shoved cash in my pocket and snugged the holster through my belt. No more amateur hour with the damn thing jammed into my waistband. I stowed the .38, shoved the phone in my pocket and pulled a sweatshirt over my head, tugging it down over my belt. I had a hand on the doorknob when Bill poked me in the back, right above the gun.

"You got a permit for that?"

"You're my permit."

I took shotgun in the cruiser, pulled out my phone and dug through the contacts looking for Johnny Dominquez, attorney to the underworld, and the one man Oscar might not think to call. I pushed send and held a hand up for silence while listening to the outgoing voice mail directive.

"You called me. Leave a message," followed by a short beep.

Bill pulled out of the drive way with enough force to lash me around the bench seat. I ignored him and tightened my seat belt. Johnny D used an answering protocol, grown in my lab, so callers didn't get dinged by the minutes munching robot voice providing too many options, all of which amounted to the same thing – he ain't home. Many of his clients either called from jail or used burner phones like mine. After the beep, I spoke into the phone. "Robert Bryant is currently held, possibly not booked, at Hayne Street, but with potential federal implications. The detention follows the second event in five days involving the marina to which he purchased title. Sunday, approximately 0700, four bodies were discovered, three burned beyond recognition, a fourth body, displayed separately, throat cut ear to ear. Approximately 0420, Friday, his marina exploded, I have no data as to the extent. Bryant was arrested at his home before 0600. Please advise Mr. Bryant that his droid is safe." I closed the phone. Oh so cleverly, I had asked him to pass a message to his client, which was technically illegal, but so was detention without a writ regardless of the agency.

Bill floated the car into the gravel lot of the 'Bama without breaking and with minimal fishtails, skills acquired through years of backroad swamp running during his youth. He had an incorrigible youth, as had I, but he hadn't forgiven mine. I spotted a row of chrome twelve deep in the side lot. Bill's dust drifted that way. Good maybe there will be a rumble, Sharks and Jets style, dancing and jabbing. Oh fuck, I did miss the fight. It had been quiet for too long, and it made me restless. The self-revelation of my shallowness was not surprising, but it was disappointing. I lacked not the intellectual rigor for introspection, but the discipline.

Bill hissed, "We have got a massive clusterfuck involving everybody and their goddam brother. I called you, several times and you ignored me. You should have called me Monday."

I was done being his punching bag. "With exactly what? I knew nothing. You knew where I was. Instead of talking to me, you panicked Angela. Thank God Hannah's not in town. Did you know she's sleeping with Oscar?"

Bill turned the key, shutting down the roar of the abused interceptor. "Mz. Hannah's doing what?"

"Hannah's out of town. Angela's sleeping with Oscar."

"And that matters to me why?"

"I thought she had better taste."

"Jesus, Archer, I thought you meant Mz. Hannah. You got somebody in mind for Angela?

"Maybe an accountant or a plumber. I met a nice doctor, almost not married, age appropriate, single gendered, no kids, gainfully employed."

"Give it a rest. You're not her mother."

"No, I'm not, but she's, I don't know, not one of us, not compromised, not dirty."

"I resent the hell out of that comparison. I showered, put on cologne, was supposed to be on a date. Instead, I am traipsing around my island, as you call it, trying to get some asshole from the DEA to fess up. He's laying low, on administrative leave, AWOL if they do that kind of thing. My bloodhound spent three days tracking him down." Bill shook his head and laughed, "Dirty, shit, get your buddy off the pedestal. She's one of us all right, she just happens to look like a super model. That's your problem, she's too pretty. Unless it's Oscar. You got a crush on Dr. Gunnar?"

I slammed the door hard enough to rock the big cruiser. "No, Mr. Know-It-All, it's mother hen syndrome. I'm worried. She's my friend. I've never had a female friend before. I don't know how to act."

"She's not a child, although she is nuts working for you. Wish you'd worry a little more about the rest of us." He pushed his way through the weeknight locals with me on his tail scanning for friend and foe. I recognized few friends, fewer foes, and followed Bill up the worn wooden steps to the deck overlooking the dance floor. Best position for spotting targets. Clothes lines draped from the ceiling swayed heavily under the weight of thirty years of brassieres tossed in celebration of alcohol. Oddly, the colorfully decorated lines did not impede the view. In the short time I'd lived on island, I had not gotten myself drunk enough to toss my dainties. The night was young, but the company was too grumpy.

Bill stepped to the bar and ordered two beers. He drank from one bottle waiting for me to pay. Chivalry was not dead, but Bill had beaten it to a pulp. Of course, I wasn't the date for which he'd primped and preened. He did indeed smell nice. I paid for the beer plus a generous tip. We assumed post at the west wall with a one-eighty view of the deck and main floor.

"What are we looking for?" I asked.

"All I got is a description from the guy who set up the meet. Early forties, blond hair, five foot ten. Said he doesn't look or act cop, said he's got a solid reputation, which is why everybody panicked when word leaked it was his partner dead."

"And he has intel to share? My friend's freedom is on the line."

"Our friend, he's our friend. I like Bryant. He pays his taxes and treats me with more respect than you do."

"He doesn't know you like I do." I spotted two of the color guard from the vigil for the biker baby at the emergency room. Nobody was wearing colors. Glad for once of dress codes. The rough trade was not tolerated because it chased off tourists and locals alike. Bill and I sat in silence scanning for his friend, drank our beer, and listened to the evening's entertainment tune their guitars.

Bill broke the silence. "The stack of charred dead were personas muy importantes."

"Skip the spanglish. How important?"

"Two Guatemalan nationals, one percenters, and one DEA agent, who was this guy's partner. No line yet on the fourth and uncooked male. No obvious connection to the three. Approximate age around twenty five based on the coroner's preliminary report. He's the only one not identified, and his body wasn't barbequed."

I swallowed hard to keep my beer down. "For Gods' sake, Bill, have some decency. Those people died hard, but they died with honor. I've never seen anything like it, not on this side of the border."

"For all I know, this fed might be part of it. And I do not plan on getting caught up in the middle of some central American drug war."

"It's already here," I mumbled.

Bill ignored my comment and continued his rant. "My gut feeling says Bryant himself is incidental to all this. I'm thinking it's the marina, symbolic for something, maybe. Who could have known that particular place would suit his needs? Bear bought that marina free and clear, his record is clean, but it may have been an import point, or maybe the location of the kill was convenient. But it smells like Mexican cartel shit. Big power vacuum left when they popped the head of Chiapas, a lot of gangsters vying for control. And contrary to your opinion, I am not some backwoods hick. We managed to get a lid on this shit before, hell, we got the station funded from the proceeds of our last party. If we have to, we'll do it again, but we can't avoid the feds this time."

"I haven't said you were a backwoods hick, not recently. But Feds or no, I will not stand idly by while Bear gets torched as collateral damage because Washington has its head up its ass."

"Neither will I. I'm all for using the National Guard to chase this filth back across the Rio Grande, but nobody cares what I think, so we do what we can with what resources we have."

Unfortunately for Bill, I was one of his resources. I would boldly go where no uncorrupted law enforcement agent could go. Bill stood, grabbed our empties and went to the bar. He was mad because he was right about the mess we might be in, he was more mad because nobody was listening. Boots on the ground reported more and more gangs coalescing inside the upper forty-eight, marked by their tattoos, their scars, their utter lack of humanity, allowed to practice their brand of culture unchecked. Bill's hands were tied and his legal resources spread too thin among the home grown crazies to tackle the imports.

Bill returned from the bar with two more beers and a tail that moved in close and quick. "You Thornton?"

"Yup." Bill set the beers on the ledge, laid his hands flat on either side.

I snuck out the .38 and held it hip level, letting the dim bar light play off the metal. The new guy glanced at the weapon, shook his head, and stepped back. "I'm Vincenti. I got a decent description of you from our mutual friend, but I don't know your friend." He looked at me then back down at the weapon. "You really think you can get me before I shoot your boyfriend?"

I stood absolutely still, gun aimed at the man's hip. Bill laughed. "She'll shoot you in the dick before you can pop the safety."

Vincenti took another step back, tucked his weapon inside his jacket, and stuck his hand out to me. "I apologize. It's been a shitstorm from the start."

I chose to be petty, ignoring his outstretched hand. I lifted my sweatshirt, holstered my weapon, and dropped my hands to my sides, fingers tapping against my thighs, keeping a good rhythm.

"Gonna be like that, huh?"

Without warning, Bill turned and grabbed the lapels of Vincenti's cheap suit and pushed him back. "That's better."

"Fuck you people. I don't have to be here. It was my partner got killed." He was haggard, eyes pouched, dirty blond cowlicks swirled uncombed, cheap suit rumpled, mingled sweat, cheap motel soap, cigarette smoke, whiskey. The man's nerves were frayed, whether in grief, fear or both. He pushed stale air out of pursed lips. "Let's go somewhere quiet, talk private, you can bring your watchdog. I'll feel safer if I can see her."

"Nowhere more private than right here. And safer. She won't shoot you in here unless she has to." Bill winked at me and said, "Honey, would you grab a pitcher?"

"Sure darling, how about martinis? Or maybe a nice sangria. I'll ring for the sommelier."

"Fucking comedians," Vincenti said.

I ordered a pitcher of beer. Bill commandeered a bar table sandwiched between the wall and the overlook. He dragged a third stool to the table, and positioned Vincenti so his back was to the public. I poured, drank, waited. Bill did likewise. We could afford to wait, this was our territory.

Vincenti broke the silence. "Fuck it. Our mutual friend said you can be trusted. Those pictures hit the wire and all hell broke loose. One seriously high Guatemalan ministry actor, his lovely wife, and one agent, my partner, dead, burnt up. The other guy is, was, an assassin for hire."

"Why weren't you with your partner?" I asked.

"Fuck you, lady."

Bill shook his head. "Wrong answer."

"She's asking the wrong question."

This man was hurting. In a softer voice I asked, "What happened? Why was your partner in the warehouse without you?"

Vincenti rubbed at his eyes. "Because Ramirez fucked up, that's my partner, was my partner … Dave, he fell in love or had a bad case of the hots, I don't know which, but the mission went balls up four months back. We landed the biggest of white whales, chief deputy to the Minister of Agriculture. We offered safe haven to them and their kids, boy and a girl, in exchange for names, routes, accounts, all that shit. Some seriously high level ministry involved in the trade, as in presidential level catch. Then something happened. Maybe they got made. We didn't have any credible threats against the family, but when she called, the wife called, she said to get them out now, or they would run. Middle of the night, we commandeered a spook jet, got the folks and their pups out with nothing but a couple of bags, stashed them in a safe house, then filed for permission."

I refilled his glass and waited for him to drink.

"We underestimated the threat, whatever spooked her. They got cash, a lot of it, or had it, hell I never checked their bags. Within hours we're running across a goddam dirt field in the middle of the night to catch a flight. It was Dave's contact, a goddam Gulfstream, probably some drug dealer's jet. I don't know how the hell the pilot got the damn thing on the ground, but it was damn close getting back out. We didn't have anything set up for them, not even fake identities, that was how fast we made the extraction so there was nothing to watch except them. And we blew it, we lost them. We were both sanctioned. Last week, outta the blue, the wife calls Dave, says she's gotta see him, she'll get her husband to turn over whatever we want, but she wants out, out of all of it. Who the fuck would leave their kids? Maybe it was a ruse to get old Dave running, maybe I misunderstood how goddam hooked he was."

"Where was the meet?" Bill asked.

"In this city, west side. They were living mean considering where they ran from, but still okay, nice middle class neighborhood. Even registered the kids in parochial school under the name Reyes, claiming diplomatic status, and waiting on paperwork. I'm mad as hell, but old Dave, he's panting like a puppy needing to pee. Goddamit. Can I get something besides this piss warm beer?"

Bill raised an eyebrow at me. I nodded and held out my hand. I didn't have enough cash for whiskey. I had plenty of time to scan the ever growing crowd, while I waited for the order, noting who was where, who was wearing what. A bra flew high in the air and folded itself over the clothesline. Seemed kind of early for it, but the natives were content and it was Friday night. I watched Bill. He was asking questions. Vincenti's shoulders slumped. He scrubbed his face with grubby hands.

The girl at bar had returned with half empty bottle of Evan Williams. "Donny said you can have the bottle cuz it's the Sherf."

"Thank you. I appreciate it." I had no clue as to the identity of the generous Donny and why it would be okay to take an already opened bottle instead of hopping up and down every time a glass emptied. I left her an extra ten for her trouble. It was the Sherf's money, not mine.

I poured drinks. Vincenti took his in one swallow and coughed, color spread up his neck and out of his dirty collar. He pushed his glass at me for a refill. "Thanks."

"So Dave says we're going to dinner down here. So I'm asking, where's here? He says Pensacola, Florida. Long long long fucking way from Sacramento, where we'd stashed them. So me and Dave, we argue about how goddam stupid this is. I wanna call in a team and lock them up, what we should have done, what I should have done. I'm mad as fuck they disappeared on us and he's dressing up for a dinner party. So we get on a flight and get down here by Happy Hour."

Bill refilled his glass and asked, "Operational security? Any back up?"

Vincenti shook his head. "We mostly operate as separate units, like cells, we're autonomous. Makes it harder for the bad guys to find out who we are, where we are, where our informants are kept. We learned a few lessons from the 80's, like too many layers of hierarchy gets you killed. So we fly across the fucking country, and she's all Susie fucking homemaker, new minivan in the drive, dinner on the patio, kids at the sitter's. Did her fucking husband know what his bitch was doing? I don't know, maybe he didn't care. Maybe he was keeping the kids and getting rid of her. We set the pickup at 0500 Saturday morning, still dark, safest time. We shoulda taken them immediately, but hell, they seemed safe enough. And the kids weren't there, and – fuck – shoulda shoulda shoulda. A whole line of should haves."

I offered the bottle. Vincenti shook his head, reconsidered, and held his glass out. "Me and Dave, we go back to the motel. I'm up half the night with the trots, felt like my guts were coming out. Told Dave no way I can go. He laughs at me, says no problem. It's a milk run, take them over to Tallahassee, it's like, what, a couple three hours? I go back to bed, sleep a little, wake up mostly okay. Empty but operational. I call Tallahassee, they haven't seen nobody, asked me what the hell I was talking about. His phone is off, no lo-jack on the rental car. I got nowhere to start looking. I can't call it in hot without breaking cover, and it's Saturday, man, trying to get a search started? I call my chief tell him the short version, and by Sunday evening, I'm on administrative lock down, pulled into the Tallahassee office and read the riot act. They got a team together, tore the house apart. Found a lease for the rental house and the van, fake shit for the schools, but there's nothing on the wire with their names, fake or real."

Vincenti continued. "You gotta understand this was major, like the largest potential bankroll ever seized. We're looking at a political coup in a moderately stable country, at least by South American standards. Elected officials in the executive branch, all the way to the top, judges, ministers, all involved in money laundering, drug trafficking. And we had them. Fucking Dave. I get it, she was something, but shit, when we were grooming them, she kept going on about how she's some Maya princess, and how she could never sell out her own people, on and on. The Mrs. didn't make a real secret of leaning on Dave. Maybe that was the power play all along, suck us in so we get them out, then she runs."

I'd had enough of his bellyaching. "So to be a super-secret white hot drug task force agent, you gotta be amazingly gullible."

Bill stepped in. "Stop it, Archer. She led him on, he bought it, they got them out, they disappeared, now they're dead. And we have no clue who called the hit. That about sum it up?"

Vincenti nodded. "Mostly. The kids, boy and a girl. Quiet, well-mannered, like I said, they bought ID somewhere to get them into school. Renting the house, the car? Shit, cash alone will get you that. But papers for the kids? That was good quality shit, immunization records and birth certificates and passports. I got one friend left who's willing to feed me data. So far no leads on those kids, not in school, not since Friday. School claims to have no knowledge of the kids being picked up by anyone other than parents. We, not me, the team was interviewing at the schools, trying to get a line on who their friends might be. Hitting some walls. Administrators at both schools demanding warrants. I thought you couldn't pick up somebody else's kids without some kind of paperwork?"

Bill glanced at me, but I wouldn't meet his eyes. Maybe he finally figured out who his deputy's house guests were.

I kept my eyes on the agent and said, "No kids at the marina, just four adults. But what about this second assassin? Adult male. 20's, Latin origin, I heard rumor he was a heavy hitter for the Chiapas cartel."

Vincenti banged his empty glass on the table. "You tell your girlfriend everything? That is not public data. I don't appreciate the leak."

"Your war has come to my neck of the woods. I need to know what we're fighting."

"So you got any intel on those kids?"

Bill shook his head. "I don't know about any kids. PPD and county are on a need to know basis. Feds took over the operation and it sure as hell wasn't your DEA."

I cut in. "What's on the sign underneath the hanging man?"

Vincenti glared at Bill. "Who the hell is this woman?"

"She's someone I trust to put an end to this mess because I don't see it happening any other way. She's got more resources than either of us and no restrictions. If she asks you a question, answer it."

"Fuck it, somebody has to do something. That sheet, the sign? It's called a narcomanta, a narco message. They've been popping up in Michoacán, Sinaloa, Jalisco, Juarez, Tijuana, and it's headed north. We got two redacted events on our side of the border marked just like this. And the cartel responsible is getting stronger, giving rivals no choice but to ally. They are without morality, without mercy, and scare the ever loving fuck out of everyone, including us. Chiapas is in chaos, assholes fighting to be top dog, not paying attention to this Cártel de Leon Nueva Generación. This Nuevo Leon cartel looks like they're going to eat everybody alive."

Vincenti held out his empty glass. I obliged. The man was putting back the whiskey, but the anger was burning it out almost as fast as he poured it in. Vincenti played with his phone, swiping down several times and stopped. He handed the phone to Bill who studied the image and passed it to me.

Morning light did nothing to soften the impact. The killers had painted their message on a white painter's canvas, tied it to the fence, and hung the surviving marina assassin to weight the message against the gulf breeze. I enlarged the image and skootched it around until I found the square G and a double-armed rod. Same fucking mark burned into the neck of Taylor's boyfriend.

"I don't do Spanish. What's the message?" I asked.

Vincenti grabbed at the phone. "Here, let me see it, I don't have it memorized." I fumbled with the phone, it was too big for my hand, and it clattered to the floor.

"Jesus, lady."

"I got it, sorry." I ducked down and retrieved the phone, brushed it off, and handed it to him.

He fingered the screen until the image reappeared. "It's kind of a pigeon mix of gutter and Spanish. "En muchos lugares clebramos que Leon vea esto en vivo, para que sufre lo que sufremos cuando esta en el poder. Tendremos los niños. Ningún daño vendrá a ellos."

He took a deep breath, pushed it out, and emptied his glass. "This translates to 'In many places we celebrate that Chiapas see this live, so that it suffers what we suffer when it was in the power. We will have the children. No harm shall come to them.' Essentially, they want those kids. Identification came in quick for our hanging man. And yes, he was a contract killer for the Chiapas, their best. And see that?" He enlarged the display and held it toward Bill. "This symbol painted in the lower right corner? It's been showing up more often. It's a signature for the

Leon cartel. And they didn't use paint. That's blood. That's all I got, that's all she sent."

"She?" I said, "So you don't hate all women?"

"I don't like you."

Bill interrupted before a fight broke out. "She gets that a lot. Don't worry about it. This mob wants the kids. Why?"

"I don't know, maybe leverage, maybe revenge, doesn't matter, we'll find them."

"You and your partner got their parents killed," I said.

Vincenti tangled his foot in the stool trying to get at me. Bill grabbed him before he and the stool went over. "Goddamit, sit down. She's got nothing, she's my" he looked at me then back at the rumpled agent. "What'd you call her? Watch dog? That's exactly right. I appreciate you coming in. I promised I'd trade anything I find and I will, but I don't have anything. Jurisdictional squabbles take precedence over police work. But you came through and I appreciate it. If and when I find anything, I'll give you what I have. Quickly. Quietly."

Bill stood, signaling the end of the meet. Vincenti didn't seem to want to go. He'd been cooped up for days, shunned by his own people, grubbing about in the underbelly of federal bureaucracy to salvage his job, maybe his honor, but he would never get his hands on those children. That was my sacred vow. I stood as well and held out my hand. Vincenti stared at it for a long pause, and decided not to be petty. His hand was clammy.

"Thornton, this is your town, your people, your fight. I'm in a shit load of trouble, but I owed our guy a favor. I gotta warn you though, if this is a cartel war, Leon doesn't fuck around. They make new recruits eat their first kill, they ambush cops and judges alike. They have absolutely no fear of the military or the government of Mexico or anywhere else." Vincenti ran a hand through his hair and sighed. "I've done what I could, you've been warned, but my favor is done."

Bill's eyes targeted something behind me. I turned. Max stood eight feet away flanked by two hairless apes wearing black vests with no insignia.

Max nodded at Bill. "Hey Archer, you gotta sec?"

I raised a hand at Bill, telling him to stand down. Vincenti stood his ground and stared at the men. Max stepped forward while his men stood guard.

"How's your friend?" I asked.

"He wanted to say thank you. It's gonna be a long road, but," he measured his words carefully in the presence of law enforcement, "but they are on it." He looked at Bill and held out a hand. "Sheriff."

Bill shook the man's hand. He knew the men, they were local, but they were criminals no matter how much money they raised for Shriner's Hospital during bike week. "How's it going?"

"Good, real good."

"No trouble tonight." Bill said.

"No, don't think so, not here anyway. Come up to talk at Archer."

"You hear anything going on? Maybe Mexicans or something like that moving in here, into the city?" Bill asked.

Max shook his head. "Not much, rumors, nothing actionable. Did pick off some Thirteens for probable cause, but they were pretty far outside their playground, no back up. Doubt anybody'd miss em."

Bill nodded, torn between sworn duty and the benefit of having another unbridled asset on the ground clearing out the filth.

"Can we catch up later? We'll flip for bathroom duty." I asked.

Max nodded, "Just wanted to make sure you're okay. The company you keeping and all."

"Thanks. All good, all clear."

Bill watched Max, followed by his enforcers, leave the balcony. "I don't even want to know."

I smiled. "Yes you do, it's killing you. Consorting with known criminals and all."

Vincenti cut in, "I get it. You're connected. You hear about those kids, you get to me right the fuck away. I need those kids. I'll start dropping your name in Tallahassee and see if they want to pick you up."

I had tolerated his whining long enough, grief or no grief, this agent had lost his charges and gotten half of them killed. Thornton had to put up with a certain degree of garbage from this asshole because he had a career to think of. I did not. I stepped in close and whispered, "You lost those children, you got their parents killed, and you have the audacity to threaten me? Buddy, you call in your fucking cavalry if you think they can make it through my line of rolling thunder. I will bury you."

Bill pushed between us. "You better go. I don't have a leash on her." We watched Vincenti walk down the stairs. He'd left an inch in the bottle. Bill filled our glasses. He handed one to me and said, "Cherryl ain't gonna let those kids go. Not when she gets wind of what happened to their folks."

"Does Bobby know what they are, who they are?"

"Yeah. He figured it out real quick when he saw your pictures. Nobody knows who these kids are except us. I can't put protection on them without letting our little secret out."

"So what are we looking at, a full scale cartel war here? On U.S. soil?"

"You were always given to the dramatic."

"Odd that because I am always right."

"I don't think the Mongol hordes are about to overrun our tranquil little slice of the hillbilly Riviera just yet."

"For Christ's sake, we've tore down the gates and welcomed cannibals that make Mongols look like Canadians. Jesus, Bill, you have been on-island too long." Bill tried to interrupt, but I stopped him. "Max and his crew ran cartel enforcers out of our little nirvana, and what, four months back, how many Kings did county pick up? The barbarians are already here."

"We took three illegals with alleged ties to cross border drug trafficking."

"Alleged my ass, those tattoos don't lie. It's not alleged, it's a vanguard."

"No. It was an open opportunity. Running shit to and from Chicago for your friends most likely.

"For God's sake, this is way past distribution points and penny-ante drug running."

Bill swallowed the last of his glass. "Enough. I am not Elliot Ness, and neither are you. We deal with the knowns and the known unknowns and we call in the federal boys when we have to."

"Ness got himself a name, but he made a mess of Chicago."

"And you've got outlaws owing you favors. You never change, Archer, I really hoped the Corps would beat that out of you."

I finished my drink. "We've been over this already. Unless you're coming upstairs when you drop me off, you probably don't want to know about my new friends."

"You can walk home." And he left me at the bar. And walk home I did. But first I needed a drink or four.

10 CRIMES AND MISDEMEANORS

I woke wet and sandy, hot elephant dung clogged my throat. My eyelids ached. I shifted my legs. A growl rose over the thumping in my head. I opened an eye. Ralphie the stray cat had been asleep on my feet. Stupid cat. I sorted through my hangover checklist: Pants, yes. Underwear, check. Company? Just the cat. And the reek of whiskey, surf, and clothing in need of laundering. My damaged leg had stiffened after the long walk home. I peeked under the covers. No bleeding, no new bruises or contusions. I successfully bid farewell to the festivities before I could toss one of the few bras I owned.

I'd slept past breakfast, a self-service affair this month with Hannah traveling the length and breadth of Ireland of all places. According to Hannah, Ireland was the state-sponsored spawning ground of peasantry in the colonies. Personally, I hoped the island would tip over. They killed my parents and I held the entire island responsible. I had not outgrown fits of irrationality in the intervening decades, not where my folks were concerned. Nor had I outgrown getting myself sufficiently soused and hosting a hangover pity parade.

I tromped to the kitchen and stared at the travel itinerary taped to the refrigerator. She avoided Heathrow on the flight out, but decided to spend a few days in merry old England after six weeks touring the Emerald Isle. Return date from Britain open. She liked traveling to exotic locales and mixing with the locals. She carried a Nikon instead of an M-4, which made the natives less suspicious of any nefarious intentions she may have held. I hoped she'd return for Christmas. Spending Thanksgiving at the Waffle House was okay, but not Christmas. The cat tore past me on turbo charged happy feet. While I slept, someone had broken into my house and fed the cat methamphetamine.

I reached to open the sliding door as the cat ran into the glass. He flipped ass over tea kettle. He struggled to his feet, sat, licked a paw and rubbed his ear. Stupid cat, I saw you run into the door. Not cool, though I did sympathize. I'd run into a few doors, usually after lapping several circles chasing my own tail. The cat and I shared a few traits. I opened the door and told the fuzz ball to go forth and pounce.

The stupid cat tore down the stairs and chased beach treasures carried by the morning breeze while my coffee dripped. A leaf, a shadow, cigarette cellophane. My best friend was in jail and I was standing on the deck envying a neutered cat the luxury of chasing the ephemeral.

I checked my phone. No word from Oscar this morning. The good doctor had been parked on my couch when I stumbled in last night, my laptop open, notebook by his side, no doubt performing illegal digital acts in effort to spring Bear. I nodded at him, threw up in the bathroom, passed out on my bed. If Oscar were planning a jail break, he would have left a note, or maybe had his girlfriend call. I don't know why this ate at me so much. Angela, not unlike Hannah, seemed normal, as far as my notion of normal stretched. My normal did not involve carnal relations with Oscar. Or maybe it did. Or maybe the odds of my ever meeting a man with which to have carnal relations were so astronomically high that I was a little jealous. Maybe a little more than a little.

I scooped up the cat and tossed him into the house. He promptly jumped on the couch and began his morning bath. Hannah allowed me on the couch if I were freshly showered and dressed appropriately. The fur ball had been granted far more privileges than I.

I pulled on my boots, locked the front door, and trekked west on the shoulder of the 292, forcing myself into a trot after two long blocks, leg be damned. The only reliable remedy for a hangover was a full on fried breakfast with several proteins in meat form, potatoes fried in bacon fat, coffee, milk, fresh juice.

Winded and limping, I pulled the door open and flopped into a booth. A waitress arrived balancing a carafe of coffee, large glass of ice water, and a stone mug. Oscar tapped on the window. I caught the empty mug, and the waitress caught the coffee, saving me another trip to the emergency room. I made a note to leave a sizable tip for her heroic actions.

Oscar sat opposite in the booth and smiled at the server, who immediately brought more water and a second mug. She returned his smile like a love struck teenager. She took my order as an afterthought. Skirt steak rare, eggs scrambled, hash browns, bacon, orange juice, coffee and milk. She swished to the kitchen to put in the request.

"Dammit, Oscar, you gave the girl a heart attack. How did you know I was here?"

"Process of elimination. Nobody at the house. Truck in the drive. Hannah out of town. I knew you would seek feeding elsewhere. And it's walkable."

"I like to walk. It's healthy."

"Looked to me like you were trying to double time it. Running is said to burn out a hangover. I, however, practice moderation in all vices. You trot like a drunken sailor that lost his peg leg. Anyway, Johnny D called me, said he found a barracuda with a hard-on for the government's ongoing abuse of minority members of American society. She refers to her clients as the Voiceless Color Brigade. Do not give me that look. I don't care what she calls herself or anyone else if she springs Bryant. She said she'll file charges for false imprisonment if they don't book him or release him in the next forty eight hours. She can't talk to him yet, told the police she knows nothing of his phone, which they didn't find in their search, which she claims was illegal to begin with. We have made significant progress."

"Angela told me about the 'we' part."

"Is that a problem?"

"No. Just don't run her off. Or send her to the looney bin."

"Her mom's a psychiatrist, she'll get top notch treatment for free."

"No, dammit. She's my friend. A real live person, not a mercenary, not a lunatic, not a cop, but the closest thing to normal I have in my life."

"On behalf of Miss Hannah and myself, we are offended."

"And you both are certifiable."

The waitress brought our plates and a fresh carafe of black coffee. I tore into the steak. It was bleeding rare and perfect. We plowed through our plates quietly and efficiently, leaving nothing behind but the porcelain. I leaned back and sighed contentedly. "You tracked me down. You could have left a message."

"I dropped Angela at your tree shop, the industry to which you have pledged your life and fortune, yet she seems to be the only person working. She didn't want breakfast, but I was starving." He jiggled his eyebrows in a poor imitation of Groucho. "Long night."

"She wanted the damned orchids, she can deal with them."

"And the tourists, too? What if a customer mistakenly wanders in?"

"Unlikely. What do you have?"

"The phone liberated from Bishop's Row has yielded interesting results. We'll head to yon abode, securely access Skynet, and find out which agency is trying to jam up our friend."

I gratefully accepted a ride back to the house. I let the cat out and put leftover coffee in the microwave. Oscar fired up his own laptop and logged into my network. I offered him use of a simple masked router application for his humble abode, but he declined, saying he preferred only one of us arrested for breaching secured networks, and it would be better if it were me. He felt I had a better chance of not being lost inside Super Max because I was a girl. I told him he was an idiot.

"When the bank finally surrendered title, Bear installed Intensified CCD's as opposed to the standard IR. Because he could. Contracting has its perks. Each camera transmits to an offsite server…" I tuned him out. I created the program and helped Bear install the stupid system. Oscar jacked the outside cameras into city power via the light poles. Three poles, front gate, back lot, and dock. Bear daisy chained four infrared cameras inside the building. It was how we had gotten the images. The good doctor liked hearing himself hold forth, even if the audience was just me, and I already knew this shit.

Oscar droned on until he got to the sub-net section of his lecture. I tried to stop him. "You realize I set up this protocol, right? Bob's EZ router Dark Web application? The very one you and Bear abuse?" I got up and poured nuked coffee into mugs while the hourglass spun.

"I do not abuse it." Oscar clacked at the keyboard, fingers bouncing harder than necessary to complete his task. "I don't know why Bear was rousted. Worse, by a para-military force normally reserved for larger and superior threats."

I set a cup of coffee next to him. He ignored it and said, "I sped through the files from 05 November. The images were poignant. None of the doomed flinched or begged. It was heroic. The third prisoner was in love with the woman. Husband and wife? Lovers? Siblings?"

"Husband." I abridged events of the last few days, omitting the retrieval task in which the explosion heard round the city saved my life. I told him of my meeting with Thornton and Vincenti. "We got a song and dance from this agent about being the dead man's partner, getting the family out ASAP, about losing them. He gave us as little as possible, and he didn't do it for free, favor of a favor to a mutual acquaintance of Thornton's. And you need to see something."

I pulled the laptop my way and opened a new browser session. It took three attempts before gaining access to the offsite storage area. Hard to remember keystrokes through a hangover. I double clicked on the single image file and pushed the machine toward Oscar.

"I accidently dropped Vincenti's phone. Somehow the image transmitted to the cloud. That man hanging on the fence is the second assassin from our original event. This man was the only person to leave the building alive. He killed the smaller assassin." I enlarged the image so he could see the brand on the narcomanta. "I think he spared his partner the funeral pyre out of respect, but look at this mark on the sheet. This is the same shit I saw on a dead drug dealer. It wasn't just a tattoo, it was raised, like a brand."

He frowned as he read the message. His grasp of languages far outweighed mine. "Holy shit. What children?"

"I wandered down beach Sunday afternoon to unwind, get a drink, and I ran into the Ellis family plus two underage houseguests."

"I am vaguely familiar with the family. The missus is quite comely, redhead no less."

"Yes, Oscar, she is. And she is married to Bobby Ellis, island deputy. They have three starfish of their own and two foundlings, boy and girl, about eight and thirteen. Latin, porcelain skin, Queen's English as a second language. Cherryl said she picked them up Friday after school with her own brood. Nobody at their home, no one answering their phones."

I switched to the playback of the original file and sped through until I located the woman. "The girl child bears a striking resemblance to this woman."

Oscar stared at the screen and whispered profanities, then opened another file, pointed at the screen and used the forward control to speed through the images Four hours of moths, night creatures eating the moths, gentle sparkles illuminating ripples on the water in the bayou.

"Watch. No activity until Friday at 0337. South dock camera, two men approach in a watercraft, then two minutes later we see two men climb the ladder, each laden with a large pack. That seesaw motion? They are prying the door." Oscar moved the mouse over a file labeled 091124x12 ISW, the internal bubble eye camera covering the south west quadrant.

We watched them enter the building three seconds at a time, diverge to the outer walls, place boxes the size of field radios on the ground, and exit the building. Oscar said, "I told him to get new cameras, those older IR's are fine for regular folk."

"It wouldn't matter, not with the masks." I said.

Oscar opened a second file and shrunk both sessions to fit side by side on the monitor. He synced the time stamps. The last internal image was white due to the explosion, then the feed went dark. The dockside camera went dark as well.

He leaned back and said, "We have useless images of two men and we've got the exact time of the explosion, which knocked the cameras out and killed the transmission. I could have opened the gate camera, but what's the point? They all went off line."

"We've essentially got a whole lot of nothing."

"No, we just don't know what we have. The feds are pissed because they can't find what the cameras fed into, but they didn't look until after Bear's arrest, not until Thursday did anyone order a thorough sweep of the marina."

"We all forgot. Except Bear. We pulled stills, printed them and I slipped them to Bill."

Oscar stared at the monitor. "I wondered about that. Identification magically appears for the husband and wife, the agent, and I kept hearing the word assassin, then multiple assassins. The feds are throwing around a boat load of cartel names, well, not a boat load, there are what, two or three major players left? And that sign is the signature of a recent breed out of

135

Nuevo Leon, they call themselves the New Generation. Originally an enforcement squad for Chiapas then dumped when they got too big. They gathered power scooping up the remnants of smaller families running from Chiapas butchery. This New Generation curried favors with the peasants by wiping out roving gangs of enforcers referred to as Zeta, called themselves Zeta Killers for a while, then spread like cancer throughout Mexico and down through central America, including Guatemala. Kind of explains our dead family. The husband was Alejandro Vasquez de Vaca, first deputy under the Minister of Agriculture, his right hand man."

"I know you've bugged Hayne Street, but when did you get to be such an expert on drug cartels?"

"I have not bugged the precinct, I have friends. As for the antics on our southern border, the aeronautics division has expanded to encompass the use of the almighty drone. I am old enough to enjoy touring the world without getting dysentery."

Silence spun a web in the room as we both thought our own dark thoughts. Mine ran to that damned mark connecting my junkie's deceased boyfriend to the Leon cartel. I shook my head. "Burn me a disk. That fucking agent knows a lot more than he is sharing. For all I know he set this up, got his partner killed. Wants the kids for some kind of leverage, exchange, bribe, something. None of this smells right. And according to Agent Vincenti, it is worth billions."

"Hundreds of billions. You want me to provide physical evidence proving you are in possession of knowledge of a federal crime?"

"Several crimes actually. Pull it down and strip the meta data. It's not going any farther than a single viewer. I'm going to find Vincenti. He's all we have at the moment. We've got two cartels in the city, like a fucking convention, and those children are at the heart of it. We secure those kids, get Bear sprung, and then turn everything over to Bill. He can decide what to do with it. This isn't about Bear. None of it."

"Kids first? When did this nesting instinct set in?"

"Bite me, Oscar. Kids first. Only you, me, Bill, and the family Ellis know what they are. If it gets out, we might as well plan the funerals now."

Listening to the whirr of the drive burning the data onto a disc, I leaned over to make sure Oscar was using my protocol. He rolled his eyes and opened a session of Tetris.

My phone dinged with an incoming message from Max. "Found our boy." I had asked him to put a tail on the agent.

A second message with the name of the roach motel and room number accompanied a generous offer. "Need an escort?"

"Not today. Thanks."

I slid the disk into a plastic case and left Oscar to amuse himself. Although I doubted he would find much humor anywhere this evening. Bear incarcerated, narco-cartels hunting children. Another day in paradise.

Thirty minutes into the city. I located the Ambassador Inn squatting in all its dilapidated glory just west of the army/navy surplus in Brownsville. I parked at the tavern next door. The old Chevy blended in with the local vehicles. The agent's window was the fourth from the east end of the building, ground floor. The window was backlit by a television screen flickering behind flimsy curtains.

I banged on the door like a cop, stood to the side, hand on firearm. A shadow darkened the gap under the doorframe. The door opened a crack. I stepped back so the light hit me.

"Goddam it. Archer. I been waiting for somebody, not for you."

"For what? A hooker? Pizza?" He backed away from the door and let me in. Not a non-smoking room, which was fine by me. I lit a coffin nail and asked for permission to sit. It cost me nothing to be polite considering how our first meeting had gone. He rubbed me the wrong way and I behaved peevishly. I wanted to

137

like this guy. I felt bad for him. I'd been in the hot seat a number of times and it hurt.

Vincenti opened the conversation with an offering. "Your boy was headed for processing last I heard."

"He's innocent, he shouldn't have been arrested in the first place. You all know damn well this shit has nothing to do with Bryant."

"His arrest had nothing to do with me."

I took a deep calming drag. He was right. He'd already been benched when Bear was arrested. Cheap whiskey covered him like body spray. I took some small pity on him and offered him a cigarette. "So you're AWOL?"

"Now I am. I left the office without permission to follow your man after the execution and haven't been back. Can't show up without something to offer the brass. I know your friend's not involved in either incident. As for trafficking in narcotics through his import license, I got no clue, but the message on the fence put paid to his release. And it ain't a show for the media, there's a blackout on the events of the last week punishable via criminal contempt. Plus your boy is DoD, he's untouchable. He coulda blown up 1600 Penn and been offered kisses from Vestal virgins."

I had information to share, which Bill promised regardless of my growing contempt for this idiot. Maybe he'd be more cooperative if I bought him a pizza. "You eat yet?"

"Not a lot of four star dining establishments on this side of town."

"You requisition a laptop when you disappeared?"

He stared at me like I'd spoken Urdu. I pulled the disc out of my pocket and held it up. "I've got information to share per your agreement with Thornton. I am the agent of said agreement. Billy boy is busy fetching coffee for the feds."

He reached under the bed and retrieved a backpack. He opened a laptop and logged in. "No free internet here," he said, handing the machine to me. "I can use my cell phone."

"Motel's got satellite for pay-per-view porn." I slipped the disc in the drive and pulled up the files. I didn't need connectivity yet, but he didn't need to know that. I waited for the images to decrypt.

Vincenti sat down next to me. He was ripe. "You need a shower before I buy you dinner."

"I got nothing else to wear."

"Just go shower, turn your underwear inside out. Were you never a boy scout?"

He muttered words no gentleman should know and slammed the bathroom door. I waited until I heard the water, then opened file manager and scrolled through his files, looking for the login scheme. The destination and protocol was stored in plain text. For the love of Christ. I spawned an aliased login using the unsecured protocol and pinged the motel's satellite to see if I could use it. Ping back within acceptable failure rate. I could log into his machine whenever I felt like it.

Oscar had deconstructed the feed loops to strip identifying data when he moved them to the disc. I opened the first folder using a slideshow and sped the images to one second bursts. The faster movement made the actions on the screen no less horrifying. I set the machine on the bed while the rest of the images unpacked.

I poured the last of his whiskey into a plastic wrapped paper cup. The paper wouldn't hold the liquor long, but long enough for my purpose. Vincenti stepped out of the bathroom rubbing his hair with a flimsy towel, dressed in the same rank clothing. "Did you finish that?" he asked, nodding toward the whiskey bottle.

"Saving you from yourself, one glass at a time. You wanna see this then decide if you want to eat." I patted the bed next to me and handed him the machine. "These are single stills loaded into a slideshow. Right click to halt."

Vincenti watched without expression until the larger man pulled the mask from the woman. The color drained from the agent's face as the smaller assassin slit the woman's throat from behind. I handed him the cup of whiskey and watched his face. This woman meant something to him. He tensed as the men stacked the bodies, and doused them in gasoline.

"I lost several bursts of footage, over a minute until the cameras adjusted for the fire. A couple of the interior shots light those boys up."

"Oh Christ. This was … it was live? Were you watching it? You didn't stop them?"

Vincenti coiled to attack and I was on the wrong side to retrieve my weapon. I spoke in a whisper. "No, sir, I found this after the massacre. I would never have allowed this to happen regardless of any crime those people have committed. This woman suffered, as did they all, but she kept her honor, she did not beg. Hold on to that. Hold it tight."

He lurched into the bathroom and slammed the door. The sound of his retching leaked through the paper thin wall. It was not his partner who had compromised the mission, it was him. Vincenti was in love with that woman. What a clusterfuck. I smoked a second cigarette, debating whether to ask about this turn of events. My prurience served no purpose other than inflicting more pain on this man. His lover would still be dead. Those orphan children still hunted .

He emerged from the bathroom wiping his face with a threadbare towel. He sat next to me and muttered an apology. I nodded and handed him the laptop. He played with the arrows, stopping at the only clear image of the larger assassin. Vincenti pointed to the larger man, "Our man on the fence. This is Carlos Roberto Navarete Morales, employed exclusively by the Chiapas cartel. He was untouchable, a ghost." Three seconds pass, the two men appear farther away from the fire. Three seconds later, two silhouettes appear to be talking. He clicked forward the next several images. The next burst shows the smaller man on the ground, face down. "He killed his own Sicario, that's an assassin."

"In the Latin, sicarius, a dagger man, the plural is sicarii. As in two paid killers made it through our non-existent border and murdered an American law enforcement agent. I don't need a Latin word for filthy murderous animal. They are the same in all languages. They kill for profit."

"Spare me the lecture. Tell me why Morales killed his contractor." Vincenti said.

"Cleaning up loose ends." I reached over and opened the next file, which Oscar had amusingly dubbed Number Three. "This is the footage from Friday morning. We've got a two man crew dropping their bags. They wore masks. This is from the pole camera on the dock side."

"Your friend paranoid?"

"Prudent. He bought the marina for a song. Some jerk wad at SunTrust got his panties in a bunch overextending the bank's money, found a way to make a lot of money and keep the shareholders off his back. And like you said, Bear is DoD, even if he is retired. He builds shit the government sometimes buys in case they want to overrun the citizenry. Most of it is for rich hobbyists who bitch about billable hours." I clicked play. "This is approximately twelve minutes after they left."

One second of interior then a blinding flash. "The explosion took out the interior cameras, the external cameras weren't fried, but they were knocked off-line. At some point they dragged your Carlos out of the boat and strung him up on the fence with their linen message."

Vincenti stood and paced. "Or there was more than one team. What's the angle on your prudent friend's cameras?"

On the motel note pad, I sketched the outline of the marina, and shaded in the areas covered by the cameras. He snatched the sketch and studied it.

"Leaves a lot of gap," I said. "Bear doesn't have the cameras watching who comes in the gate, just who parks inside."

He paced and muttered, trying to work out who was killing whom and why. I smoked another cigarette. I held the pack out to him as he swept past in his twelve foot path. He shook his head, and resumed his semi-private monologue. I sat on the bed and watched him pace.

He stopped in front of me. "I gotta have this. The originals. I need unimpeachable time stamps."

"Not until Bryant is home, boots off, drinking margaritas."

"How about I get your friend back in custody, both of you go down the rabbit hole?" He said, looming over me.

The laptop lay on the bed. I leaned over, ejected the disc, broke it in half, then again in quarters. "Get your judge. These images won't do you any good. They've been stripped." I stuffed the pieces in my back pocket. "You promised cooperation with Thornton, you held up your end, and I did the same. Exchange over."

A cornered man was a dangerous man and Vincenti was cornered. He had watched the woman he loved viciously murdered and set on fire, along with her husband, and his partner. I blew out a pent up breath and spoke slowly, patiently. "You're missing the big picture here. I can make all this disappear, poof, gone irrevocably. You said Bryant was untouchable, so he walks anyway. Or I can turn all the data over to the feds anonymously."

He closed his eyes, clenched his fists. He was armed, I was armed. My hand closed around the butt of my firearm. I waited for the one question he had not yet asked.

"Do you know where the children are?" His desperation painful to hear.

I scooted over, and stood.

He locked eyes with me. "Are the kids safe?"

"What kids?"

He lost the staring contest, and looked away. Guilty. Dammit, I tried to like this guy, but his greed broke the last of my pity. He wanted those kids, and it wasn't for their safety. They were a medium of exchange. I have committed morally questionable acts as a civilian and as a Marine, but his was a bar below which I would not crawl: You did not fuck with children. I stepped around him, toward the door and said, "We're done. No more cooperation."

He glanced at the gun in my hand. "I can't threaten you, can I? Just what is it you do for Thornton?"

"Annoy him, mostly." I closed the door quietly and retrieved my truck.

If I were a better woman, I would have swallowed my anger, grabbed a pizza and a bottle, and sweet talked more information out of him. But I was not a better person, and I never pretended to be. Hannah felt that my issues stemmed from the eighteen months I spent involuntarily in Ireland, her current culture and travel destination. If she traveled to the motherland for information on my mom and dad, she'll be sorely disappointed and possibly sent home in a pine box. And she'd deserve it. She had no business meddling in graveyards best left forgotten. The Irish knew how to hold a grudge. They invented grudges. Since half of my genetics came from a second generation mick, I, too, could hold a grudge. Every damned Irishman involved in tossing four sticks of dynamite under my parent's rental car discovered that I could hold a grudge.

I put no stock in lineage. I would never be a hyphenated American. I could not fathom the need to dwell on a past that wasn't mine. I could not change the past. I could only plan the future. And prepare to have those plans dashed on the rocks of fate while the gods laughed.

I needed sleep, my maudlin was off the charts. I dialed Bill, got his machine. "I got the data to Vincenti. We've got two narco-cartels fighting over those children and Vincenti wants them for bait. I don't trust him, I think he fucked this whole deal up and is trying to buy his life by turning those kids over to somebody. Get the family out of town now."

Bill would do as I asked immediately. He would spirit the Ellis family plus two to safety. He and I were arch enemies, but that was vanity. Protecting the family was a matter of honor.

The house felt abandoned with Hannah abroad, traipsing about winter meadows across the sea. I put cream in a bowl for the cat and sat on the edge of my bed. I plugged my phone into the charger. I'd missed a message. It was from Bear. One word. "Home."

11 BUSHWACKED

Pounding on the front door jarred me out of bed. I grabbed the gun from my nightstand, and tripped over the cat. I regained my footing and yelled "Who is it?" The hammering continued. "Identify yourself." Last time I heard pounding like that, two goombahs from the Region had arrived to kill me. One left in a police car, the other in the coroner's wagon.

I crouched low, pressed my ear to the door, and caught faint sobbing and shushing, weathered boards creaking under multiple feet. I yanked the door open and jumped back. Cherryl stood in the light of the porch, five children huddled behind her. I killed the light and opened the screen door. She pushed past me without a word. I waved the kids in. I stepped out onto the porch and saw that she'd barreled up the driveway and left the van blocking the turnaround.

"Give me your keys." I pulled my truck forward, and backed her van behind the line of palms I'd planted months prior in an effort to hide my own vehicle. I parked my truck in front of her van, blocking any view from the road. I tossed both sets of keys on the counter. "What's going on?"

The children huddled on the couch. Five sets of eyes widened in fear watched Cherryl stomp back and forth. "You want to know what's going on?" Her voice was shrill, all professional control gone. "What's going on? Two men attacked us. I'm afraid to go home. We've been hiding for hours."

The oldest, Bobby Junior, caught his mother and folded her into a hug. "It's okay, mom, you did real good. And dad's out with Uncle Bill trying to find those guys, right? It's okay, it's okay." She struggled for a few seconds then gave in to the comfort her son offered.

Cherryl was a trauma nurse, accustomed to dealing with armed gang-bangers and jacked-up hillbillies. She was not given to panic.

I said, "Hey, Bobs, you guys wanna hang out in Hannah's room while I talk to your mom? It's way bigger than mine and a lot cleaner. And she has a giant television."

"You don't?" he asked.

"She let won't let me get one. Says I watch too much already." A sentiment he could understand – parental units denying children more television. "You go on in and I'll bring some blankets. You can make a fort or something."

Four silent and hollow eyed children followed their leader into Hannah's room. I grabbed the comforter from my bed and rummaged through the linen closet, locating more blankets and sheets. Bobby had found the remote. The comforting sight of a yellow talking sponge and his best starfish filled the screen. "You all need anything, you holler. You know where the bathroom is." I pulled Bobby Junior into the hallway and said, "You're on sentry. Keep me posted if you see anything, okay?" He nodded gravely, eager to do his duty. The job gave him purpose. He was an Ellis all right. Duty above all.

I turned to leave. He touched my arm and whispered, "I hit the guy with my bat, Aunt Jess. I had to, he was hurting my mom. I hit him hard. He went down." The boy was near tears.

"You did just right, Bobs, you protected your mom, your family."

He hitched a breath. "They wanted Lily and Xavy. That's what the one guy said, they just wanted to take the kids to their folks. But mom said no, that she'd take them. The man was lying. I know he was. I think something happened to their folks, but I ain't said nothing about it. I grabbed my bat and I climbed out the door and I hit the man. He had her by the throat. Lily bit the other guy, the one who was trying to pull her out."

I put my arms around the kid and held him until the shakes passed. "You did real good Bobby. Real good. I'm proud of you."

"I won't get in trouble, will I?" He wiped tears from his face.

"No. You won't get a parade, but you should get a medal. Being brave is hard."

He swiped tears from both eyes with the heel of his hand. "I'll keep watch. Thanks Aunt Jess."

How the hell had I become an aunt? It must be some kind of appellation applied to vetted adults. Hannah was supposed to be an aunt somewhere back in our bloodline, or maybe she wasn't. I never gave it much thought.

I left the bedroom door open a crack and found Cherryl in the kitchen, crying at the stove. I hugged her. She struggled for a few seconds. She cried herself dry and pushed me away. "I'm okay. You're armed, right? Do you have any more weapons?"

I led her into my room, spun the dial on the safe, and laid out my meager wares for inspection, including my personal good luck charm, the little Smith and Wesson hammerless .38. She picked up the Taurus 9mm. She expertly dropped the magazine, then racked the barrel to eject the chambered round. She tossed it on the bed, and looked at the Hi-Point. She repeated the safety check. She put that one down and claimed the Taurus. Only my personal firearm had been obtained legally but none had been used in the commission of reported crime.

"I can't believe you keep them loaded." I said.

"They're not much use empty."

She rolled her eyes and said, "You don't have kids." She stuffed the 9mm in her back pocket.

"Can you tell me what happened?"

"Two men tried to – we've been driving for – oh shit. I am not okay."

"Come with me." I had handed an hysterical woman a loaded gun, and then I was going to pour a large drink and make her finish it. I shuffled through the liquor stock and located brandy. I held the bottle out. She shook her head.

"Yes, you will." I poured two glasses and led her out to the deck. I motioned towards a chair. "Sit. Drink. You're off duty."

She perched on the edge the deck chair, took a large swallow, and grimaced. Her hands shook. The liquid sloshed, but did not spill.

The night surf rolled out to sea, ebbing its way to dawn, creating a hypnotic white noise. I waited for the brandy to work its magic. I pulled a chair close to hers. "Start at the beginning."

"You people. Goddammit, you people. Those kids. Their parents. They're dead. Did you know that? Of course you know. And a DEA agent, and some other guy. Bobby's out chasing Bill there and yonder, running in circles." She cursed me, cursed Thornton, and cursed her own husband. She railed at the dead parents until she ran out of venom.

"It was eight or so, I don't remember what time exactly the movie got out. I'd gotten everyone herded into the van and then a car stopped in front of us. A sedan, beefy, like an unmarked police cruiser. Right there in the parking lot of the picture show. Just pulled right in front of me. Two men got out and walked up on either side. I locked the doors. The man on my side rapped on the window, told me he was sent by Mr. Reyes to pick up the children, bring them home. I yelled at him to show me identification. He held up some kind of badge. He was smiling, pleasant, humoring me. Oh God, I pulled the lock up on my side and got out of the van. I got out to see the badge closer, it looked legitimate, but Bobby always told me never ever get out of the car." She finished the last of her brandy and held the glass out for more.

I refilled her glass from mine. Each unique situation dictated the method of interrogation. I wouldn't need to water-board this one, just gently lead her through the event. Adrenaline and brandy. She would sleep soon.

"What did the badge look like?" I asked.

"I don't know, like an FBI badge you'd see on TV, but I knew something was wrong. And I got out of the goddam van. "

"It's okay. You're here. You saw the badge and then what did he do?"

"I asked if I could see it closer, he said it was not necessary, that he was sent to collect the children. That's when I heard the slider door on the passenger side open. The other man had opened the door and was trying to pull Lilia out. She was in that seat, closest to the door. All of the kids were yelling and screaming and – Jesus, when you hear your own children scream. I took my eyes off the fake cop and he grabbed my throat and slammed me into the van. It seemed like forever, but it was only seconds. He was hurting me, and then he fell. I didn't see Junior come around the van. He'd gotten his baseball bat and climbed out the back gate. That dang bag is always in the car. The man didn't move so I kicked him. Bobby was yelling at me to get in the car. The other man had backed out of the sliding door holding his arm, yelling, but it sure wasn't English. He was bleeding heavily. I didn't know why, but the kids said Lilia bit him, took a chunk right out of him. She was covered in blood from her nose down, the front of her shirt, in her lap. Oh shit." She covered her eyes. "My head hurts, my throat hurts. God, I almost lost them. How come the kids acted smarter than me?"

I refilled her glass a third time, and motioned her to continue. "I threw the van in reverse and tore out of there. I drove north until I passed the state line, up past Flomaton, for God's sake. I don't remember the drive. Dammit. Bobby got Lily cleaned up with baby wipes. I finally stopped at one of those self-wash car places, with the hoses hanging all over? It was dark, empty, like it was abandoned. We parked in a stall, hid out until an hour ago. The kids ate all the stale candy from Bobby's baseball bag. My God, I can't believe this is happening."

"Cherryl, have you called your husband? He's gotta be worried out of his mind."

"No. And I didn't call 911 either. Bobby's out chasing Mexican drug runners, and two yapping thugs try to abduct my kids. No ma'am, I called nobody. That guy with the fake ID. He had a funny accent, like he was trying to talk American, but it didn't sound right. So no, I didn't call anybody. I woulda sat in that damn car wash until morning if Bobby Junior hadn't suggested that you could help us. My son thinks you're some kind of goddam super hero. Why? Why? Why would he think that?"

I refilled my glass, ignoring hers. "Because people gossip and kids hear it and get the facts all jumbled up. I don't know, maybe Bill told him that I was a Marine. I used to be, it's nothing I hide, but it's something I would never discuss with a child."

Or maybe her thirteen year old heard rumors. Or maybe he asked to see my gun, and I ran him through a safety check. Told him that guns were tools, not toys, and never point a gun at any living thing unless you had to, that guns were the last resort when people wouldn't agree to stop hurting each other.

Or maybe little Bobby was peeking through a keyhole when his mom and dad were gossiping about the incident leading to my having met them both, separately, but each in their professional capacity. They were a nuclear family cliché. Mom a nurse, dad a cop, mini-van, camping, baseball, apple pie. For a kid on the edge of puberty, gossip was more exciting than the day to day grind of being a kid.

"God, what a night." Cherryl said. "I took 41 south through a whole lotta nothing and made it to 87 which is even emptier. I wound through the city hoping they, whoever they are, wouldn't find me. Praying the city cops wouldn't pull me over. Bobby Junior smeared mud on the license plate before we left the car wash. How would he know to do that? Christ, I'm glad I filled up the tank this morning. Those kids haven't eaten. How am I supposed to say their parents are dead?" She folded herself over and put her head between her knees as if to throw up.

I found my still soft voice. "I'm glad you came here. I swear by all that's holy I will keep you and the children safe. You stay as long as you need, but don't tell the children, not yet. They might know already. You know how kids are."

She sat up violently. "What? Kids are what? You don't have any. You don't know what it's like." She called me names, but I'd been called worse and deserved it then, too. She'd been through hell and that anger had to be released. Through sheer good luck, driving skills, the providence of the Almighty, and two brave children, she got her tribe to my home safely. And she was right. I didn't know a damn thing about children. I would never know.

She slumped back in the deck chair exhausted. "Oh, God, I'm sorry. I didn't mean any of it, I just – "

"You just got the wits scared out of you, yet you got everybody home safe. You rail all you want. It's the brandy talking."

"No, it's me being a bitch."

"Then you're in good company. But why didn't you call Bob, or Bill, or the National Guard?"

"You know why."

"He's your husband. Not that I have one of those either, but he's gotta be worried sick, and he's a cop."

"I didn't call 911 because somebody found those people and killed them. Bobby told me that Reyes laundered money for a drug cartel, got scared, and ran away. Somebody found them and killed them and now those killers want their kids. He also told me about your friend's marina, finding those bodies. Then somebody blew it up. Then somebody tries to kidnap my children. Somebody is leaking information. I call anyone on the job and the whole damn county gets alerted. They found us once, I won't risk it again."

She was right. Either the bad guys planted a mole, or a good guy had turned rotten. If I had any sense, I would herd them all into the van and run to New Orleans. I had money coming in, I could afford a few days at a decent hotel with a pool and a playground and room service. I debated with the voices in my head until a tiny snort broke up the internal argument. Cherryl had fallen asleep. I rousted her carefully, pushed her into my bed, and pulled the covers up to her chin. The cat hopped up on the bed, blinked at me, and curled up on her pillow.

I checked on the children. Bobby Junior was leaning against the wall, all but asleep on his feet. Four children draped the king-sized bed. I gently skootched little Elizabeth closer to Lilia without waking either girl. I leaned down and brushed the dark hair from Lilia's cheek. She looked so much like the beautiful woman caught forever in black and white. I convinced Bobby to lie down. "I'll take this watch. Your mom is laying down in my room, right across the hall." The boy rolled onto his stomach and went to sleep.

After the last home invasion, Bear and I installed a steel frame, steel door, and a proper deep-tongue dead bolt. Kick proof and ram resistant. If the enemy showed up with an RPG, we were in trouble. I wedged a chair under the door handle, closed the curtains, dropped a broomstick in the sliding door track, and killed the lights. I pulled a chair into the living room and sat in the dark, weapon in hand, my thoughts darker than the room.

Demons chased screaming children through wet caves illuminated by torch light. As fast as I ran I could not save them. An onyx death god belched fire as he rose from hell. He pointed at me, marking me, mocking me. I ran and ran and ran, but the earth had knitted shut, forcing me to run deeper into the earth. At some point during the night, the gun slid off my lap landing gently on the carpet.

12 BREAKFAST AT TIFFANY'S

The smell of coffee, vibration of movement, feel of morning sunlight brought me back to reality. I pried open my eyes. Bobby Junior stood in front of me, furtively glancing toward the kitchen. He held my firearm down at his side. Index finger stretched safely along the rail. He motioned me to take it, and whispered, "It's okay, Aunt Jess, nobody saw."

I'd fallen asleep on duty and dropped my gun. I should face a court martial. Instead, I faced a smiling young man who forgave my trespass. I shook my head and smiled at him. "Thanks," I whispered, "I owe you." The other children were lined up on the couch staring at the television. A spritely young woman wearing an unfortunate pink dress informed me that the I-10 was backed up into the city. The nasal drip in her voice made me grateful for the mute button.

Cherryl scurried about the kitchen, fridge to stove to counter scrambling eggs in a ceramic bowl, pouring milk into glasses. "We've got eggs, a lot of eggs, we need protein. Milk, cheese, cream, bread. I got what they had at the Thumb. Got bacon, too, a couple pounds, and coffee."

I acknowledged her efforts with a nod and escaped to the bathroom, brushing my teeth and avoiding eye contact with the mirror. Cherryl was too damned energetic after three brandies, four hours of sleep, five children to look after, and did she just say she went to the gas station and bought food? Maybe moms should be Marines and the rest of us run support. Cherryl's ability to adapt to a fluid situation should be taught in a textbook. I was still trying to shake off the vapors from nightmares in which ancient gods stuffed children into their stinking cavernous mouths.

"I brought you the paper. Bobby Junior is watching the news to see if we show up. I don't have the heart to tell him that our skirmish was a private one," Cherryl said when I stepped into the kitchen. She had three burners going, bacon in the oven, toast in the toaster, and fresh butter on the counter. Would this have been my life if my parents had lived, maybe followed a more conventional path? Good God, it was too early for thought. I poured a cup of coffee and refilled Cherryl's.

"How did you," I started, looking around at the groceries, "How did you get all this? Better yet, why?"

"Children have to be fed and your fridge is empty. Lily and I walked down to the Tom Thumb and bought the place out. Bobby Junior stayed with the kiddos. He was wide awake and acting squirrely. Said you put him on sentry duty last night and he was ready for another shift."

I wasn't ready for conversation, but with no choice I strung words together. "Cherryl, I gave him a job. It made him feel better after what happened. He's what twelve, thirteen? I didn't make him a soldier, I just, well, I gave him a purpose. He thinks he's in trouble for hitting that guy."

"In trouble? Hell, if I could afford one of those fancy televisions, I'd get him two. I told him he wasn't my little man any more. I cried. Can you believe that? I cried. I told him he's a fine young man. Christ, I'm going to cry again."

"Adrenalin depletion."

"Motherhood."

I laughed and leaned against the counter and watched the troops wiggle on the couch, trying to share the cat, trying to be quiet. Hell, even I knew that silence was an unnatural state for children. A race to the shoreline and back up the stairs would help.

Pounding on the front door. Bam, Bam Bam, three in a row, cop knock. I motioned Cherryl against the far wall and ordered the children into the bedroom while the pounding continued. "Who the hell is it?"

"Officer Bobby Ellis. My wife's van is here, let me in."

I looked at Cherryl to gauge her reaction. She shrugged and turned her back to me, whipping mercilessly at yet another bowl of eggs.

I stuck the gun back in the holster and unlocked the door. Bobby Ellis, Escambia county deputy extraordinaire, looked extra tired, uniform wrinkled, hat pushed back, face puffy with lack of sleep. "Bobby," I said, then holstered my tongue and stepped back to let him in.

He rushed past me and confronted his wife. "Uh uh, no way, how long have you been here? I been lookin for you all night. Where's your phone? I called a hunnert times. Dangit Cherryl, what's going on?"

"Breakfast, then talk." Her mom-tone made it clear she would truck no dissension. All five children, Deputy Bobby Ellis, and I stood to attention and lined up for mess. A great deal of chewing and clattering silverware and polite requests for more, please. Within minutes, plates were licked clean, glasses drained, pans scraped and stacked in the sink. I could offer to wash up while they took the children down to the shoreline or I could let the grownups talk privately while I ran the kids up and down the beach. Decision made. The troops and I were going on a walkabout.

I yelled, "Who wants to hit the beach?" The Ellis children, inheritors of their mother's amphetamine-style energy, tore out the sea side door and pounded down the stairs. The two strangers hesitated, staring at me with large brown eyes. I squatted down to Xavier's height and told him to go on down, that I'd find him a bucket to collect shells. The whoops and hollers drifted up to the house, but these two waited as statues while I rummaged for the promised bucket. I handed it to Xavier. I took a tiny hand from each of the children and led them out into the bright blue morning. The boy dropped my hand at the bottom of the stairs and lopped across the sand to the others, banging the bucket against his legs.

Lilia held my hand and walked with me, every few steps looking over at me. She needed to say something. I was afraid of what it might be.

"Mi Madre, she is gone, she is dead, Yes?"

"Lilia, we don't know that."

"Buluc-Chabtan came to me last night. He told me I would rule the Jaguar kingdom. I must avenge mother's death, or he would come next for me. I knew yesterday when I held that man's flesh in my mouth, I knew my mother had gone to the Dark House."

While her god told her to seek vengeance, some fucking demon chased me through hell. She didn't need my help, she needed a priest, maybe two, maybe some thorazine. I fought to remain calm. She stared at me, waiting.

"I'm sorry for your loss. Have you told your brother?"

"No. Buluc must come to him and tell him of his father. Secrets share only with the holder of the bloodline."

"Of course."

"Buluc told me Ahulane would come to you and you will fight, you would lead a war, and it will be near big water. You are not of my blood, but of another tribe, but this does not matter. He would tell me no more."

I stood in the clean morning sun cursing whoever infected this child with these horror stories.

"You must tell no one, Lilia, people will not understand." I yanked her hand, and resumed walking on the high tide line while the others ran and splashed.

"Buluc Chabtan showed me the fire. Huracán will not allow mother to climb in Chicnauhtopan if I do not avenge her."

The child stood in front of me, back to the rising sun. She stared at me, fighting back tears, waiting for an answer. She was a child, and she was delusional in her grief, and, and, and, and I wasn't but a year older than this child when my parents were murdered, an event that sparked a war, my private war. My father had been targeted by a loyalists, or separatists, or whatever the fuck they called themselves. Labeled a spy, but for whom I never learned. We were tourists, on holiday, in a lovely city with a lovely river. Vaporized on a lovely cobbled street in Derry, Ireland, half a block beyond a lovely bakery. Had I not dallied to eyeball the sweets in the window, I would have died as well. In the end, the motives of the bombers had not mattered one bit. Dark gods possessed me, allowing me to locate and end every last one of the bastards, their associates, their livestock, and anyone attempting to stop me.

I prayed I was not this child's future. Was she my past? Was she my chance to atone for past bloodshed? I was an Old Testament kind of girl. There walked the God of vengeance. I liked the New Testament, but I wasn't entirely comfortable with love and peace as His Son instructed.

"Lilia, I will fight for you, that is my duty, but I will not murder. Your Booluk Chavton is not my god. Murder is not my duty. Do you understand the difference?"

"All things serve the purpose of the gods."

The recipe for wholesale murder throughout the reign of man. From the fall of Rome, to the rise of Mohamed, all the way through the 20th century madmen, Stalin, Mao, Hitler, Castro, Pol Pot, Chaves. The list was long. I was tempted to belt the little brat, asking a grownup to avenge her mother. She was spared my anger when Bobby Junior came tearing down the beach pursued by his siblings. Even Xavier was running in the surf. The girl touched my arm and said "Thank you," as if I'd accepted her demand. She ran to join the others.

Bobby and Cherryl walked the high tide line holding hands, Bobby's wrinkled uniform out of place. "Jeez, Archer, I didn't sleep at all and you look worse than I do."

Bobby was a good man, but I doubted his skills ran to supernatural possession by other people's gods for the purpose of bloodletting.

"Goose walked over my grave, I guess."

Two hours of chasing the children in and out of the surf, collecting shells, peeking into the big buckets of the surf fisherman, each child taking a turn to pet the fish placidly waiting their turn to become dinner. We spotted a late season pod of dolphins heading west, jumping out of the water. A tanker far out in the gulf rode the curved blue line of the horizon. My little Maya princess kept me in sight at all times.

The nightmares filling my few hours' sleep had killed my appetite. I'd choked down a piece of toast this morning, but gave the cat the strip of bacon I couldn't push into my mouth. Ralphie grabbed the offering, growled at me, and ran under the couch to enjoy his catch. I was starving. I knew nothing of children, but growing up with Marines, we were always hungry. I had a hunch these little monkeys were as well. The flags of the 'Bama rippled in the breeze.

"Hey, anybody hungry? Cokes, fried things, Bushwackers? Chock full of vitamins and milk and rum."

"Jess, they just ate. You want a drink, go get one, but –" Cherryl said.

"But nothing," yelled Bobby Senior, running across the sand. The children followed their father and protector up over the boardwalk and through the screen door. Cherryl gifted me with an evil eye and followed her brood.

We took over two tall tables on the upper deck. Lilia sidled next to me and climbed on a stool. "Are you angry still?"

I glanced around to make sure no one could overhear what would undoubtedly be a bizarre and terrifying conversation. "Do you understand what you ask me to do?"

"Yes," her dark eyes stared unblinking into mine.

"Do you understand the difference between duty and murder?"

"When you do your duty, it cannot be against the will of God. A priest told me this, at home, in Cayala, I asked him of our soldiers who kill men to protect our home. 'It is their duty,' he tells me, 'to protect,' then he tells me to go and play, to stop vexing him with nonsense. He was old. He did not like my questions, but he obeyed his duty and indulged me because of the importance of my father. You see, everything serves the gods, even an old mad priest."

I blew out a heavy breath and silently repeated a prayer for guidance. Demons, mad old priests, and bloody sacrifice. Two servers bearing wide trays saved me from further madness. Baskets of fried everything and plastic cups full of rum, chocolate, and heavy cream, all whipped up and topped with a cherry.

"Are you out of your mind? You are not giving my children alcohol. " Cherryl was off her stool, blocking the waitress from setting the drinks on the table.

The woman raised an eyebrow at Bobby's grimy uniform, but addressed Cherryl. "Ma'am, the white ones are virgin. The red cups are for you and Jess. During the day we have to let the kids in, that's the law, but we sure don't give 'em liquor." Bobby looked at his white cup in disappointment.

Cherryl sipped a white cup, then a red. "I'll be damned."

The eight of us consumed enough saturated fat to refuel and relax, the contents of the red cup softening the edge of my worry. A refill might dampen the fire entirely.

Bobby's phone rang. He stalked off listening to the caller. I caught a significant glance between Lilia and Bobby Junior. They knew they were on borrowed time. These kids were not stupid. They understood that there was far more in heaven and earth than in the philosophy of their adults.

Bobby returned to the table and announced, "We gotta go. I got my marching orders. Party's over. Bill's gonna meet us at your house, Jess."

"Let's go, let's go. Let's get to the house." He led his brood down the stairs and down to the shoreline. Our merry band marched the mile and a half back to the house without incident beyond shoving each other into the shallow surf. Except for Deputy Ellis. He was in uniform.

Captain Thornton angled across the sand toward me. When he got close enough, he said, "Christ, Archer, this is your idea of hiding? You are not hiding anybody with half a dozen cars in the driveway, and two of them prowlers."

"Thank the county for graciously providing security." I marched past him and up the stairs. I assumed the house was clear as Bill was here, but I poked my head around the rooms just in case. The noise of three adults and five children climbing the stairs scared the cat into the bathroom.

Cherryl yelled, "Feet. Clean. Now." I assumed it was an order for the kids. I grabbed beach towels and tossed them to the older children. After appropriate grumbling and fussing in the process of removing sand, Cherryl herded the children into Hannah's room for another round of cartoons.

When Cherryl returned, Bill said, "We're getting everyone out of here now."

"In what? They found Cherryl in her own car." I asked.

"The cruiser?" offered Deputy Ellis.

"They know who you are, Bobby, they know your family. By now they know where you live," I said.

"And you know this exactly how?" Bill's anger was barely contained.

"Deductive reasoning. No one has landed on my doorstep since the attempted abduction. Two women, five kids, if the bad guys had a team ready to roll, they would have attacked. Consider the fact that they've had all week to pick up the whole damn family, and nobody has. The bad guys didn't know who they were looking for until last night. Cherryl described a two man scout team, not a strike team. Those men were stupid, they should have continued surveillance until the rest of their team arrived. But how did they find her at the movies? They got data from somewhere. The school? Downtown? Our bad guys have unlimited resources with which to buy information, but I think they got lucky. And I checked the van, I didn't find a transponder. If someone let slip the name of Ellis, any twelve year old can find the number and track the phone."

Bobby stared out at the sea through the glass doors. "She's right, Chief, we had those kids all week. They been going to school just like they were home with their folks. Somebody's a rat."

No one spoke. Cherryl loaded the dishwasher, and set coffee to brew. She pulled clean mugs out of the cabinet.

Bill broke the silence. "You trust your friends, the ones who met us at the bar last night?"

I nodded. "Yes. They don't want this kind of action down here either. It's not safe, and it's not healthy."

Bill told Bobby, "Keep everybody inside. Don't answer any calls unless it's me. And if someone comes to the door that you don't know, shoot them. Do not hesitate. We're gonna take your van." He nodded his head at me and said, "Let's go. Head to long-term parking, stash the van. You're my bait. The bad guys don't know where the kids are right now, but they know the mini-van. I'll follow in the cruiser. If I see something wrong, I'll pull them off you. You get to long-term parking and meet me at the guard shack. If we don't have an escort, I'll pick you up outside Departures."

Bill had a plan. I felt two percent better than I did ten minutes ago. I maneuvered the Ellis family transport through the sand and led the way out to 292. Bill followed in his prowler.

I made one call on the way into the city. I needed two things. I was told to stand by for reply. My phone dinged with directions by the time I pulled the family van into a parking lot off Tippen.

I caught the parking shuttle to the departure terminal. Bill picked me up. I gave him the ticket. "Don't lose it. I don't want to buy them a new minivan."

"Like you could afford it."

"I got a little coming in. I sold some software."

"Do I want to know?"

"No, but on the plus side, I found transport for the exciting Ellis Family Adventure."

"You think I'm wrong to send them away."

"I think it's the smartest idea anyone has had since this mess started." I gave him directions to a club property west of the airport and kept my mouth shut.

Bill pulled into an auto-repair lot lined with gleaming chrome, shiny horses of the apocalypse. We waited in the car listening to dispatch until Max stepped outside. He nodded at Bill, handed me keys, an envelope, and said the van was around back. "Guy named Jenks, under the bridge. I'll get your check to him. Vig is 2C's for the rental."

"Two hundred dollars for the van?"

"Naw, van's on me. Two hunnerts interest for the cash. He'll take your check to the bank as soon as it opens. It better be good."

"It is. What about the van?"

"Get it back here Friday or you'll think the cash is a bargain."

Ten percent for clean cash seemed fair. I thanked him and returned to the cruiser. Bill inched around the bikes, and into the alley behind the garage.

The Ellis Adventure Van was a Big Ford Econoline with seating for eight and cargo space and a clean plate. I asked Bill to follow me to the Wal-Mart. "I'll fill the tank and get supplies. Will you help me? It will go quicker." I hated groveling, but I needed his help. I wanted the family out last night, but that didn't happen. Now I wanted them out before sundown. The reasoning was based upon the shaky logic of darkness providing cover for the bad guys. They might not expect a daylight run.

Max was good to his word. The van ran well and smelled pine fresh. I filled the tank and pulled next to Thornton's cruiser in the parking lot. Within minutes we gathered seven cheap sleeping bags, three cases of water, assorted snacks and protein bars. Bill added two cases of assorted cans with ring-pull lids. "Kids will eat anything out of can."

"They need underwear. The adults can manage, but those kids are going to ripen badly." We stared at the racks of children's underwear. "For goodness sake, you get the boys, I'll get the girls." Two of everything, socks and underwear. I grabbed a three pack of Haynes for Cherryl as well. Bill came back with two packages of boy's briefs, but nothing for Bobby. "Go buy your deputy some boxer shorts."

We didn't fight over the tab. It was part of my atonement for not moving sooner. I had known those children were orphans for days.

We stacked everything in the back of the van. "I've got one stop to make, under the bridge."

Bill wasn't happy. "I'll give you fifteen minutes. No longer. We've used up our luck."

I turned left on 292. He followed me out of the parking lot, flicked on his light bar, and roared past.

I turned down Canal and backed into a spot next to a utility pole. A hairy bear-man emerged from a dusty and dented cargo van. He waved me over. I handed him the envelope Max had given me. He read the note, nodded, and climbed back into his van. He emerged with the same envelope, made heavier by cash. My banker was the guy who sold shrimp out of the back of a big yellow van under the bridge.

I backed the rented van down the driveway, right to the bottom of the stairs with six minutes to spare. Bobby heard the heavy engine, and came down. I handed him the keys, and asked where Bill was.

"He'll be here in a few minutes. He's getting stuff at the station. Hopefully he'll get some weapons."

Cherryl had made fresh coffee, pouring me a fragrant mug while I incapacitated the GPS on Cherryl's phone, and on Bobby's department issue phone as well.

"The problem is everybody and their brother can lock onto the signal and grab your location." I took apart a quick charger and plugged his phone into my laptop. I installed a dialing protocol to bounce the signal around before making a connection. I handed him back his phone and showed him the Jolly Roger icon. "You need to make a call, use this phone. Press the Roger once to engage, tap it again to turn it off. See how it goes gray? That means it's disengaged."

"I get it, Jess, I ain't stupid."

"No, but Bill is going to kill both of us if he sees this on your phone. It's company issue. When you get back, I'll delete it."

He nodded and stuffed the phone in his pocket.

A heavy engine rolled up the driveway, followed by the tromping of heavy boots on the stairs. Bill came into the house carrying a duffle bag that looked too light to hold a grenade launcher. Inside were grimy looking ball caps advertising an assortment of alcohol, a location transponder, and two ancient Motorola hand held radios. Bill tried to show Cherryl how to use the radio.

"You do remember Bobby's been a deputy over ten years. I think I remember how to use his radio." She fiddled with the dials and stuffed it in her pocket.

I caught Bill's eye, glanced at the transponder and shook my head. He tried to stare me down, but lost. He'd never figured out how I cheated. I gave him one more menacing glare followed by a head shake and a finger across the throat. I went into the bedroom and retrieved the Hi-Point 9mm, two empty magazines, and a full box of brass hollow points.

Discussion ceased when I stepped out of the bedroom. Three sets of eyes on me. "What?"

Bill started. "The problem is two women and a car full of kids. Everybody knows Bobby wouldn't let his wife go off alone with a couple extra kids wearing a bounty on their heads."

"Me and Cherryl, we take the kids. Jess if you want to come along, that'd be just fine, but we'll take them, maybe south to Corkscrew or something."

Bill rubbed his eyes. "Goddam it. Ya'll shoulda called me this morning. We could have come up with something less haphazard than this."

Cherryl responded. "No, sir. I did not call Bobby because I don't know who's leaking what. I explained all this to him this morning. Somebody is telling tales." Seeing the look on Bill's face, she softened a bit. "Not you two, don't be ridiculous. But somebody is telling the wrong people something. They found me in my van coming out of the movies. Who knows how to do that kind of thing? Cops, that's who."

"Or bad guys, Cherryl, these people have money to buy information, not millions, but billions." Bill said.

"So maybe they buy cops, too."

"That's enough, Cherr," Bobby yelled.

"It is not enough. They want those kids and they found us."

Bill spoke slowly, in his calming-the-witness voice. "Cherryl, who called you to pick up the kids last week? Was it their mother?"

"Yes, Friday, the charge nurse sent a runner to find me, to take a call from the desk."

"You're positive it was her?"

Cherryl shrugged. "We had some screamers on the floor, but it sounded like Isobel. She asked if I would pick the kids up, that they had people coming in for dinner. I yelled yes over the noise on my end. I got to the school and her kids were outside standing with mine. I didn't think twice about it." Cherryl was quiet for a moment, staring into space. "Seems odd she didn't call my cell phone. I mean, she has the number, kid stuff, homework, pick-ups, we've had them over for dinner a couple times."

Bill turned to me and said, "Round up them kids. Now." His carefully crafted veneer turned bayou when he was angry. Or scared. This time it was both.

I stepped into the bedroom, and closed the door on his barking. The television was off and cold. Five children sat in a circle on the bed holding hands, eyes closed and heads bowed. I stood silently until Elizabeth, the littlest Ellis, peeked an eye open and gave me a tiny smile. I returned her grin and held a finger to my lips, quieting her until the prayer concluded.

"You all are going on an adventure. There may be danger, and there will be hardship, but there will be food roasted over fire. Come on, head 'em up, let's go."

Lilia let the other children pass. She stopped in front of me, drawing herself up. "But you must fight."

I grabbed her by the shoulders and gave her a hard shake. "No, I must nothing, sweetheart, but you must do as you're told. This is not a game or a story. You took a chunk of flesh out of a man and Bobby Junior gave another man a concussion. Somebody wants to hurt you and your brother and we – the adults

– are not going to let that happen." I pushed her toward the door. I would truck no more nonsense about gods and devils, snakes and jaguars.

I followed the children out of Hannah's room and said, "They're not gonna expect a daylight run. They'll be waiting for cover of night. The van is clean, no tracker unit. Those men got lucky. They won't find you this time."

Bill led the way out the sliding door, down the stairs, under the house, palms shielding the rag-tag parade from prying eyes. Bobby stripped off his uniform blouse and pulled a tee shirt over his head. He handed shirt and hat to his boss. I handed the scrounged ball caps to each child as they climbed into the van. "Push your hair up under the hat. No, Xavier, not you, you don't have long hair."

Lilia climbed onto the van deck and turned, grabbing my arm, "You begin now, war begins now. You are Ahulane."

I shot past anger into rage. "Stop this, Lilia, you are going to scare Mr. and Mrs. Ellis. Do exactly what they say and you and your brother will be safe. No more fairy tales."

"But we will need you tonight. Buluc tells me." The child was in tears. I pried her fingers off my arm, and pushed her far enough inside the van to slam the door shut.

Bobby climbed behind the wheel, "I don't like this at all, feels like running, but I ain't gonna argue. Who do you think is tattling, Chief?"

"Not you or me, and that narrows the field down to forty five feds in on this clusterfuck. I don't think Vincenti is part of it. It was his partner got killed, he wants blood and he was willing to share what he knew. I made it clear the kids were off the table, he accepted it." Bill looked at me to see if I would challenge his description. I made it very clear to Vincenti, but Bobby was Bill's deputy, not mine.

"I know, I know, as soon as we get somewhere, I'll call," Bobby started the van.

"No. You keep going until you hear from me." Bill leaned in the driver's window to give Bobby private instructions.

Cherryl had her back to me, barking instructions at the children. I touched her on the shoulder through the front passenger window. She jumped. "Cherryl, turn your phone off, pull out the battery and leave it in the glove box. Do not use it."

I handed her my Smith and Wesson and a half a box of ammunition. "Keep that in your lap. Where are the others?"

She pointed to the door pocket and the center console. I nodded and asked, "Do the kids have phones?"

"Hell no, we ain't that kinda people." She said and turned away from me.

No, they weren't those kind of people. They talked to their kids and taught them to return the favor. I stood back under the porch, praying our idiotic plan of hiding the family in plain sight worked.

Bobby waited until Bill was out of sight in the west bound lane, then followed as if they weren't together. An hour north, and Bobby could safely cross the western Alabama border. If he crossed the western bridge, he be out of Florida in six minutes. He could be sitting on Decatur Street, drink in hand, by sunset.

I climbed the stairs wearily, holding onto the railing, pulling myself up in a fit of self-pity. Sleep beckoned. I rinsed coffee mugs and stacked them in the sink. The table was clean, all signs of intrigue removed. I shut the sun out of the living room, pushed the cat off the couch, and fell asleep as soon as my head hit the cushion still warm from his nap.

Voices near, speaking quietly, male. So much for new doors and locks. I sat up, rubbing my eyes, yawning largely. If the interlopers had meant me harm, I would have been dead, not wondering who filled my head with cotton. Footsteps approached, and a presence loomed over me. "Hey sleeping beauty."

I stood and hugged Bear. He smelled clean and fresh after his days in captivity. He was free, and the family Ellis on their way to safety. Both needs satisfied, I had slept the sleep of the innocent.

I checked the coffee situation. Cherryl had re-provisioned the cache. I was anxious to hear from them, to know they were safe. Lilia spooked the living daylights out of me. Stupid kid. Speaking of stupid, where was the cat? I called, "Here kitty, kitty."

Oscar grinned at me over the top of my laptop and said, "I let him out. Somebody gave him speed." I scrubbed through a quick shower and brushed my teeth, yet again avoiding the mirror. My friends didn't care what I looked like so long as I wore pants. I found the necessary clothing, but had no weapon. I'd donated my three to the Ellis cause. Bill brought at least one unregistered weapon and plenty of ammunition. I smiled at the thought of the hell that would rain down on anyone who tried to stop the Ellis Road Trip.

I sat down at the table. Oscar poured me a cup of coffee and said, "You smell better, at any rate."

The cat shot by me at break-neck speed. "Thought you let him out." The sliding door was open a crack, large enough to admit a tiny fur ball. "Great security guys."

"Who's gonna break into a house where bears live? Real live giant bears. You gotta see somebody about that snoring. Maybe quit sniffing glue, Cap." Oscar said.

"Don't call me that, Skittles." Years back, Oscar earned the nickname, referring to the multi-colored sugar bombs he'd snuck into his mission bag, which, oddly enough, saved our lives one dusty day when we were set upon by pint-sized mercenaries bearing Kalashnikovs and machetes.

Bear interrupted, "Kinda surprised they ain't picked you up yet, Archer. You got an alibi for the rapid and unexpected disassembly of my marina?"

"I mastered aviation ordnance, not dynamite or Semtex or whatever the hell those frogmen used. Huh-uh, my nerves aren't steady enough for things I hold in my hand that go boom at will."

Oscar chimed in, "You haven't answered the question. Do you have an alibi for the explosion?"

"Yes, but it's not for public consumption."

"Something to do with that cute little limp?"

"Section 918, Article 118."

"You bailed out another biker baby."

"Good deeds pave the path to righteousness."

"And sheer boredom builds the highway to damnation."

Bear looked at me over the top of my laptop and said, "Sweetheart, you need a hobby. Get a dog, buy a dress, find a boyfriend."

"All in that order?"

Oscar cut in, "Can we go to tape now? I am catching Bear up on the data we have right now."

Oscar narrated as the images looped, Bear new to the horror of what had become of his marina. I showed him the image of the hanging man, the late Chiapas assassin.

I said, "Vincenti thinks this is part of the war between Chiapas and Leon cartels for supremacy. These guys make him long for the days of the Cocaine Cowboys. This new crew is bad, as in evil, no mercy, no prisoners."

"From Cocaine Cowboys to Heroin Whores." Oscar smirked at his own wit.

Bear rolled his eyes. "You just come up with that, Skittles?"

"I've been savoring it a while, seemed like a good time to try it out."

"It's apt, Oscar, I'm sure it will be the next Big Thing. Anyway, Vincenti thought the original hit was Chiapas taking out their puppets for insubordination." I said.

"Which means they got somebody else all lined up to do the paperwork?"

I shrugged. "Probably. The guy on the fence, Carlos Morales, he planned and executed the barbeque. Vincenti identified him as an assassin for the Chiapas cartel. And somebody took him out. Again, Vincenti is our only source. He says that sign, he called it a narcomanta, is a staple of the Leon crew. As in the state of Leon, Mexico. Up and coming in the power vacuum left by the apprehension of the head of Chiapas. One of the dead on Sunday was Alejandro Vasquez de Vaca, chief deputy to the Minister of Agriculture, Guatemala. Chief Deputy. Think about it, Bear, your marina is a legitimate import hub under the auspice of the United States Department of Agriculture. Coffee, cardamom, etc., all perfectly legal."

"Yeah, and all going out to those funky hipster grocery stores. I know this shit, it's why I bought the marina. Money coming in that I don't have to make room for, don't have to do much for. Leaves me space to rehab the rest of the property. Got a guy from FLUSDA who checks off the boxes and dots the I's and gives me a copy of the manifest documentation to file with the feds for each shipment upon arrival. Stuff goes out within forty eight hours. It doesn't run itself, but I don't have to do much except pay a guy to run the forklift and keep the mice out."

"Don't you think the bank agent, what's his name, Steve somebody? Why was he so angry at unloading a property the bank owed money on?" I asked.

"He managed the property, sure, and he was pulling in something like fifteen thousand a month for the bank, to service the note and pay a management company who made sure the shippers could store their wares until they were picked up. The remaining note was too large for the property income. I told Steve to eat that debt because I wouldn't assume his bad decisions. That's what riled him up. But old Steve signed on my offer after the board threatened him for his profligacy regarding the defaulted loan. I mean this isn't exactly a boomtown anymore. Banks will take pennies on the dollar to get the losses off their books."

Oscar and I waited for Bear to finish his thoughts. I refilled coffee cups and eyed the liquor cabinet. The cat, now exhausted, hopped into my lap and snuggled down for a nap. I stroked his fur. He was warm and sandy, the purring engine under my hand calming.

Bear stopped mumbling. "The warehouse is huge. I was rehabbing one quadrant at a time, updating the electrical, fire suppression, fresh water. The southeast quad was sealed better than the others for humidity control, but I shut down the refrigeration unit, man, it was too expensive. I reduced the traffic, kept dry shippers to make rent. They didn't need anything special except quarantine and low humidity. The shipments were small enough to use a single forklift to shift the pallets once they swung up on the dock."

"How long did you operate before you reduced traffic?" Oscar asked.

"Eight months. Took that long to winnow it down to two a week. Product coming in and moving out of the warehouse like clockwork. Import manifest always cleared. I never had an entry bill challenged, I mean it's Customs, right? They check the cargo because it's through the Department of Agriculture, right? I'm not stupid, the agent would have to be on somebody's payroll."

"Is it normal not to have challenges, as in none at all?" Oscar asked. "Inspection for international importation is technically under the cloak of Homeland Security."

"I don't know if it's normal. I made the bank an offer and took over existing traffic. Nothing hinky turned up in the background check. The facility had no liens or debts outside letting the previous owner take out a second mortgage on the property."

Oscar and I waited quietly while Bear drank his coffee, scratched his chin. "The site has been in full compliance for the last thirty six months according to the paperwork. Bank got it sixteen months ago … I haven't been audited … They wouldn't … I let that little fucker … " Bear fell silent, contemplating how badly he'd been played.

"Steve What? What is his name?" I asked.

Oscar remembered the name. "Sounds like cough syrup, Robason, Steve Robason. I made discreet inquiries and discovered he'd taken a leave of absence ten days prior to my inquiry. Apparently with his nineteen year old personal assistant."

Bear wasn't listening. "Jesus, I could be R.I.C.O.ed any minute, take the marina right out from under me, all the feds have to do is show that this was an ongoing operation and I am cooked. That son of a bitch. Old Steve is doing this under my nose. I'll rip his damned head off."

I interrupted his rant. "I won't tell you to calm down, big man. I hate it when people say that shit, but on the plus side, no one knows except banker boy, and now you, and the exporter. I doubt the shipping firm would risk their own freedom for this hub. You said you kept two contracts? Did you snoop at all?"

Bear was typing at the keyboard. He pulled up the manifests and turned the laptop. "Hell yes I snooped, imports from a central American country? Yes, I snooped. Nothing even remotely hinky or stinky. Got a little gal from PPD to bring her K-9 over once in a while, doing her part for national security." Bear smiled. "Anyway, the last palettes dispatched Thursday previous at 1600, can't read the signature, but it matches the others."

Oscar asked, "When is the next scheduled dockage?"

"Was. Was scheduled. Not until Monday, they get their trucks loaded Wednesday, only way it would work, scheduling them in-out before the second shipper arrived. Like I said, only that one bay open for safe storage."

I reminded Bear, "You were conducting legitimate business based on the advice of a sweaty cracker who called you a carpet bagger. But you checked out both remaining firms, both out of Guatemala, both cleared with their agricultural department and ours. Did you have any idea Guatemala was going to be in play in the next round of the Mexican drug wars? No, you did not."

"Not gonna help in court, Archer."

"It's not going to court. You got a message to your dockers that the marina is closed indefinitely due to terrorism. Whether they are legit or skanky, they'll run away. Let Biloxi deal with them." I said.

"Your import roster might explain the out of town traffic concerning our favorite drug enforcement agents, dead and alive." Oscar said.

"Bullshit." Bear was angry.

Oscar's smile told me that he was going to lecture. "We've got enforcers from cross-border gangs showing up. Fortunately, they either get arrested or they disappear. That's the good news. The bad news is we got a new stripe in town according to my source, and it is exponentially worse than the strays from Chiapas. Local cops picked up a dead junkie in a squat house on Davis. Body had the same marking on his neck as your narcomanta. Feds call it a Zeta brand, but I have my doubts about that being right."

"That was my Article 118," I said. "He was the new king of Parker Field, less than six months. Biker baby was one of his whores."

Oscar typed for a few seconds, turned his screen toward me, and pointed at an image in upper right quadrant. A square G and a two-armed telephone pole. "Their buddies burn the skin, like a cattle brand. When it heals they tattoo it. Pretty gruesome."

Bear's voice was barely above a whisper. "And they are here in my country playing their filthy games. They ain't seen nothin yet. Buncha goddam barrio rats. They are all the same."

"And they all bleed …" Memories from Ago fluttered in my head.

Oscar filled in the next line. "And they all beg for their mamas when the sword descends."

We fell into an old and familiar patois of our former lives, our former selves, when we were paid poorly by Uncle Sam to break things and kill people in defense of our sovereignty, our honor, and our flag. God help me, I did miss it. The mission provided purpose, direction. Now I rescued the voluntarily unclean to fill that emptiness. No more. Biker babies were officially on their own, but the drug dealer, the message, what could they possibly have in common? The memories spun about, and tumbled to a stop on one word: "Kaibil." I whispered the name aloud.

Oscar laughed. "Guatemala, right? You were sent to K school? Corps trades teams, and then they had to send a female for some numb nuts reason. Those guys are serious bad asses."

I nodded. "Their version of Special Forces. I spent eight weeks training plus another twelve playing war games. It was my first taste of international tokenism as an enlisted. No worse than Lejeune in the summer. Spiders were a lot bigger, but it went all right. Nobody wanted to play with me, but none of them tried seriously to kill me. They had a motto: Si avanzo, sígueme, si me detengo, insístame, si me retiro, mátame. It took me forever to learn the words. Something like if I lead, follow, if I retreat, kill me. So yeah, they were badass. But when their government got in bed with the communists to stop the narcos, half those guys ended up mustered out, unemployable. Some ended up running security for the cartels, you remember that?"

"Yes I do," Oscar said. "That is the brand used to mark those who'd gone dark side. If your junkie used to be a soldier, the army has lowered their standards a great deal. All of the cartels have an enforcement branch. Some ex-professionals, some skags. Some started fighting the communists, then they either became communists or narco-army. Not much choice down south."

I exhaled and flopped back in my chair. "Did you see a picture of that junkie? I don't think he was a junkie. I have a feeling he was newly in charge of what Bear's banker was bringing in."

The house phone interrupted our little show and tell. I grabbed the handset and pressed to talk without checking the call screen. "Hello?"

A male voice, not old, not young, somewhat familiar. "Is this Jayne Mansfield?"

I held the phone out and watched the information scroll across the screen.

"Is anyone there?" asked Dr. Tannenger, weary emergency room warrior who had pretty brown eyes and an acerbic bedside manner.

"How did you get this number?" I asked.

"I spoke with a pleasant woman at your nursery."

"Angela gave me up."

"She sure did, or he did. She seemed exceptionally realistic."

"She gave you my private home number."

"I asked how long ago she'd made the transformation. I wanted the name of the team and facility to add to my reference binder."

"I bet that exchange was colorful."

"Very. He's quite attractive, but swore too much. Not ladylike."

"She can be downright manly at times. What did you need?"

"I wanted to check on the wound. You haven't been in to have the dressing changed."

"Not yet. I've kept it clean and dry. The leg is stiff, but the wound isn't infected. I'm taking the antibiotics. I appreciate the personal service, but I'm in the middle of something."

"I tried to reach you at the number on your chart. You get a lot of calls up there, but no one seems to know which department you work in."

I remembered the smell of fabric softener, and remembered that he was separated, not single. "Like I said, I appreciate the personal attention. The check will be in the mail Monday morning. If there's nothing else, I'm in the middle of a meeting."

"Something illegal?"

"And dangerous, but I promise not to show up in your ER. I'll ask the medics to take me to Sacred Heart."

"They'll ship you back over. Look, I have a day off and I called to," a heavy sigh rolled down the phone line. "I wanted to ask you to dinner. Nothing fancy."

"Are you kidding?" I stuttered through non-word noises until I pulled a No out of the jumble.

"Blackmail then, or maybe you'd like to know what happened to your friend. And your bill."

Bear convulsed in silent laughter, and Oscar was making kissy faces, daring me to hit him. I mouthed the words I hate you both, and turned my back on the comedy duo.

"Now isn't a good time, Doc – "

Bear reached around me and grabbed the phone. While I ineffectually attempted to take back my phone, Bear asked Tannenger to repeat the offer he'd made, listened without interruption, and made arrangements for dinner. Tonight. "Who am I? I am the lady's secretary." Bear hung up the phone with an evil smile plastered to his face.

"You go meet him. I am not going anywhere." I said.

"Go," Oscar said. "We're just spinning our wheels here anyway. The family is safe and the Bear is sprung from the trap. We've discussed the matter at great length and arrived at a conclusion. You could use a good schtupping."

Bear added, "At this point, even a bad one might make you a nicer person. You been an angry hornet since your Chicago friend went home so you're going to meet that man. If I gotta dress you myself, hog tie you, and drop you off. You're going."

"I hate you both. Jesus Christ." I muttered through my beauty regimen, powder, eyebrows, mascara and pink lipstick. Okay, I had been out of sorts of late, but nobody was getting laid tonight.

I brushed my hair out and tied it back. I came out of the bedroom dressed in clean black slacks with a tee shirt and blazer. Oscar shook his head slowly. "You're kidding. No, go put on a dress. I know you own at least one." He followed me into the bedroom.

"Two, but one is for funerals. I'll wear that one."

Rummaging through the wardrobe, he pulled out a flowery sundress. "Here, wear this one. It looks girly enough. Where did you get this? It's Angela's, isn't it?"

"Yes. It was too big on her. She gave it to me. I am not putting that on."

Bear stood in the doorway of my bedroom and growled, "We'll put you in it. Go have a nice dinner with a nice Jewish doctor. Make your mamma happy."

I grabbed the dress and changed in the bathroom. Oscar held flip flops in one hand and black pumps in the other. "This is it? This is your choice of shoes? And you call yourself a woman? This is just not possible." He muttered and tossed the flip flops into the bedroom.

"I can't wear heels without hose. That's gross."

"Women do it all the time now. You have been liberated from the toxic masculinity of the overbearing patriarchy that oppresses women and imposes hosiery upon our fragile sisters."

"I am not oppressed, except by you two sisters. It's still gross." I rummaged through my underwear drawer and found a pair of stockings. The ones I'd bought for Joey Steps funeral. My only pair. I rolled them on without snags and slipped into the shoes.

Emerging from the security of my bedroom, I stood at attention for inspection. "Whooweee, I forgot you were a girl. Go get 'em, Tiger." Bear said.

I shunned both traitors, grabbed my wallet and stood at the door, staring at the knob, keys in one hand, wallet in the other. I needed a purse. Christ Almighty, this was ridiculous. Did men have to go through all of this? A small still voice inside my head whispered Probably.

I stomped to Hannah's room and grabbed a black bag large enough for cigs, lighter, wallet, keys. I threw in my chap stick as well. I slammed the door on my friends' laughter.

Nick's Oyster Bar overlooked Big Lagoon on the east end of the island. I backed into an empty spot a hundred yards from the building when I remembered I was unarmed. Fuck it. I killed the lights, locked the door, and hiked to the restaurant. I spotted Jacob in the bar sitting at a tall table. He was watching the door. His eyes rolled past me, then back, eyebrows rising in surprise at my appearance. He stood, approached, and escorted me to the table. "Wow, I didn't recognize you."

"Thank you." The thought of bolting through the bar, and hopping in my truck seemed prudent. I had no idea how to small talk. It was not part of my training. Any part.

Jacob broke the ice. "Do I get to know your real name?"

"Jess Archer."

"Good to know. I've always been a professional and family Jacob, but Jake among friends. I am among friends, I hope."

"So far. I'm not good at this kind of thing. My brothers and I were having a meeting of sorts, and it kind of stalled out before you called."

"Brothers?"

"Brothers in arms. We were Marines. Our service overlapped for some years. One by one we all ended up settling down here."

"Hmm. Is that common?"

"Pilots, engineers, marine assault. Some MOS share behaviors, choices. I don't know. I loved Pensacola when I was a kid, and then I came back for training, and my Aunt is here, so, here I am."

The waitress brought drinks, scotch for him, gin and tonic for me. We clinked glasses.

"You lured me here with talk of blackmail and billing." I said.

"Sounded to me like your brother made you come."

I shrugged. "He thinks I need to get out more. So? Blackmail?"

"Your bill has been discharged. Seemed the least I could do, the least the hospital could do. You brought that girl in. She's alive because of you. She dropped enough coherent words to piece together a description, but I'm the only one who caught on. She's under the impression she was abducted by a white slaver."

"Jesus, who would want her? She's a junkie. I don't know that saving her did a whole lot of good in the grand scheme of things."

"Then why?"

"It was a favor for a friend." I hesitated. I had to know if that junkie could identify me. "Is there a doctor-patient confidentiality thing going on here?

"If you let me look at your leg."

"That is the worst-pick up line I have ever heard in my life."

"You were a Marine, how many did you actually hear?"

"True." It felt good to laugh. "Did the police question her?"

"No police. According to our incident report, her father brought her in, and she wasn't capable of answering questions." He picked up his glass, found it empty and set it back down. Instead of ordering a second drink, he asked, "Is this something you do often, rescue people?"

I shook my head. "Hardly ever. Just a favor."

"For a friend, a guy who happens to be an outlaw biker."

"You watch too much television. It's a social club, just like – oh hell, they're criminals. And they have kids, and wives, and jobs, and homes. They're not so much outlaw as not inside the law. And I don't have the luxury of making moral judgements based on a man's line of work."

"Bullshit." He had a nice laugh, and straight teeth, and clear eyes, and no five o'clock shadow this evening. I smiled and laughed with him. The good doctor cussed, he was human. And smelled good. And had a nice smile. And nice hair. And a nice face. Dinner might be nice.

The hostess seated us in the dining room, at a window with a view of the bridge. I asked if a band was scheduled for this evening. She said no. I had reached an age where loud music was not something I cared to tolerate often. Jake agreed that dinner would be nicer without a pounding headache. I wanted to remind him that he had a wound check to perform, but my flirting skills ranked right up there with my personal apparel abilities.

He asked what kind of wine I preferred.

"Both kinds, Red and white."

"I don't get it."

I wanted to slam my head into the table and run away. I was not cut out for chit-chat. "It's a joke based on a throwaway line from The Blues Brothers."

"And you say I watch too much television."

"That's not television, that's a classic movie like Casablanca or Twister."

Jake rolled his eyes and picked up his menu. "You really do need to get out more."

The grouper was fresh, and the pea pods crisp. I ate the vegetables and pushed the rice around in awkward silence.

"Tell me about your wife."

Jake put his fork down, and wiped his mouth. He picked up his glass and took a swallow. "Short version. She decided she didn't like being married to an emergency doctor anymore. She thought I'd have moved into private practice by now. Less stressful, better hours, more money." He leaned back in his chair, and swirled the wine in the glass. "It's not acrimonious. No one is mad at the other. Disappointed, yes. Just not angry. It's a difference of want. Now, we're waiting on the lawyers to finish their billing."

"Who cheated?" I asked

A lopsided grin and a chuckle. "That's the worst part. Nobody. If that were the case, I don't know, maybe we could go to counseling or something, rail at each other, but this is just, hell, a difference of wants. I want to be where I can do the most work, and she wants the gated community, the wine cellar, the country club, and mostly the husband home once in a while."

"What does she do? I don't imagine she's a kept woman."

"Not on my salary. She's in banking. Trust funds, investments. She's good at it. And no, we no longer share a residence, haven't in almost a year. She kept the condo, she'd bought it before we met. I found an apartment. Second floor of an old pink Victorian."

"You do your own laundry?" I asked.

"Uh, no? I use a laundry service. I'm going to regret asking, but why?"

"I assumed you were married because you smell like laundry softener."

"I'll remember that next time I meet a woman. I'll tell the nice ladies at the service to leave out the fabric softener. I can safely assume you're not married. No kids. What else do you do besides search and rescue?"

"I sell trees in pots to unsuspecting tourists."

"Are all your employees as interesting as Angela?"

"She's my only employee. And she's not a man. She's just annoying sometimes. You should ask her out, less visible scarring."

He poured more wine while we waited for the waitress to clear the table. She left unsatisfied as no one wanted dessert.

Jake asked, "Where are you from originally, unless you're a native."

"I came to visit my aunt a great deal as a child, then permanently after my folks died." He stared at me, waiting for more. I had no clue what to share because it wasn't something I did.

"Short version. I spent time on the island getting into trouble, forged my birth certificate, appeared at the recruiting office, signed my life away, worked my way into OCS, got out with my fixed wings intact."

"Wow, that really is the short version. So you're a trail blazer, glass ceiling and all?"

I snorted. "Hell no. I didn't care who did what when, where, how, or to whom. I was worried about surviving day to day. Vanity, not politics, ruled my choices. There was more room for advancement as an officer. Ground combat technically wasn't an option, but being a combat jockey was. Your turn. Why a doctor and why Emergency?"

He leaned back in his chair, buying time to sell me a tale. The question in the back of my mind was Why? Why this much trouble? Why the interest?

My phone chirped. Without preamble, Bill said, "We have a massive clusterfuck. Somebody jacked the family and took the kids. I'm headed to your house, only safe place in the city. There's some goddam irony for you." He hung up.

"I have to go. I'm sorry. I enjoyed this." No coat, no checked bag, no luggage, I pulled my purse off the back of my chair, hiked my skirt, and ran toward the exit.

He called after me, "Maybe we can do it again, when you're not on call. Do you change costumes in a phone booth?"

I was already pushing through the door, good time forgotten. Goddamit. That rental van was clean. The image of a clean table floated into the front of my mind. The table was clean after we'd shipped the family Ellis out on their adventure. I ran to my truck hunched against the strengthening wind, and tore down River Road. My phone chirped. Without checking the call display, I flipped it open and said, "Traffic's light. I am five out."

13 TANGO ECHO

I rolled onto the 292 without stopping, put the phone on speaker, and dropped it on the seat next to me.

"We got activity at the marina." Bear said.

"I thought the cameras were blown out."

"Oscar is pulling the pole units back on-line remotely. The feed is spotty. Interior eyes are toast, but main and rear gate are responding. Gulf Power shut down the marina, but the poles are on the city's dime. And we got movement. A couple of sedans in the west lot. Recon at Hannah's. Man, I love that tub."

I swerved around a Prius, cursing at bad drivers and bad weather. "How the hell did you fit in there? Forget it, I don't want to know. Tell me you've got pants on." I heard his laughter, deep and comforting over the noise in the cab.

I hung up and beseeched God to bring those children home safely.

I drove the truck around the property, illegal and unethical, but the environmental fun police take a backseat to my needs. I aimed the truck toward the road and dropped the keys on the floorboard. Bounding up the stairs two by two, I stepped into a war room that looked a lot like Hannah's former dining room. I hunched up behind Oscar trying to make sense of the pixels flashing in and out. The bottom half of the laptop screen was black.

"Transmitter damage at some point, might have been a power spike from shutting down the marina. I've re-routed the feed from 'the cloud,' and it ain't perfect. Getting more data, but the camera is not responding"

I left him to his keyboarding knowing no data would be forthcoming until he fixed the problem. I changed clothes, tossing my dress over the sleeping cat. I scrubbed off the war paint, pulled on jeans and tee shirt, located socks, and slipped my feet into my boots.

Bear was brewing more coffee. He grimaced at the label. "Bill got a call from Deputy Bobs, some farm off 22, old man let him use the phone. Bill's bringin' everybody here. I guess he don't trust the feds either."

"What the hell happened?"

Oscar looked up from the laptop. "Don't know all. Your sheriff called me, said the family had been attacked, he was bringing them back here, and we were to find you. That's all I know. Bear had a hunch the marina was in play."

Bear poured coffee and handed a mug to me. "Wasn't a damn thing anybody could do. Sounds like our bogies took them professional and without incident. They took the two kids and the van, the phones, guns, and left the family Ellis on the side of the road, intact and alive."

"Where?"

Bear ignored my question and asked, "How was dinner?"

"Fine, great, the wedding is scheduled for New Year's Day. You're the maid of honor."

"Huh, good. I'd like that. It seems to me like our bad guys ambushed the van on a wide spot named Wetappo, lonely country. Don't know why they didn't take them here, woulda been easier than running to hell and yonder."

I dragged a chair around to watch Oscar and said, "It would have been far more dangerous. Scout team got skunked yesterday. The girl took a chunk out of one of their men and Bobs Junior popped a foul to right on the other. Cherryl tried to run them over getting away. These people want those kids alive or they would have wiped out everyone. The children have to be bargaining chips."

"For what? Their folks are dead, no use to anybody. Stands to reason the bad guys installed new puppets in the minister's office.

This particular trade route is shut down. But … " Bear sat down in front of an open laptop.

"Yeah, but?" I prompted.

"We have two players, and neither one is local. Why would they risk all this destruction at my marina?"

The strengthening storm rattled the ocean side windows. Oscar pounded the keyboard in effort to make the cameras work.

I said, "If you break my machine, I'll kill you."

"My warehouse was empty. The last goods had been trucked out before the fire. According to my friend at the station, the feds swept through it. Not even mouse shit left."

"Then it's symbolic. That marina was never an important hub, I mean, according to the books, right? The gross median in the ten years prior was, what did you say? A couple million? Agricultural. Coffee, sugar, spices, coconut oil. You shipped out fabric, paper, what else, machine parts? Recently, you reduced transit to dry shippers." Oscar said.

"Those with the highest yielding returns and least amount of work."

"Heroin is an agricultural product, and you don't need much to make it worth the risk. And if they ship it in white – processed – instead of tar, well hell, it still seems like an excess of bodies for such a small port. Wonder how your boy at SunTrust is doing right now? Why can't I get the comms to ping. Dammit." Oscar stared at the screen, talking to himself.

"Hey, look at this, camera's live." The upper half of the camera feed, which had been receiving, was blacked out, but the bottom half showed us the lot was filling up. Three sedans had pulled in and parked randomly. "That's two more in thirty minutes. I am not gonna be able to dial it in any farther from here unless I can reboot the damned camera. See that? Recent arrivals. Ambient temps still within normal range, wind less than 10 knots … it has started gusting … shouldn't push the camera around too much …" Oscar was talking to himself again, trying to establish a link with the motor to move the camera. Rapid fire at his own laptop followed by passionate pounding of the Enter key. A good pounding made the software run more efficiently.

We drank coffee and waited, listening to Oscar mutter to himself, and pound on more keys. Intermittent rain ticked off the windows creating a melancholy backdrop. The stupid cat emerged from hibernation and stretched luxuriously before tearing into the kitchen hunting for kibble. I fed the cat as he was incapable of fending for himself. I made sandwiches. I cleaned out the refrigerator.

I stood at the kitchen window and watched the lightening fire up heavy clouds over the city. Few cars passed. Hard acceleration caught my ear, but nothing appeared in my limited view until headlights disappeared from the only vehicle on the road, heading west. Roar of engine rapidly decelerating, glimmer of pale light on a car coming down driveway. A large car, the tired throaty sound of an abused police prowler.

I opened the door and moved out of the way. Elizabeth seemed unfazed by the assault and chattered at me as soon as she had one shoe off. Theresa spoke over her baby sister anxious to be heard. A hollow-eyed Bobby Junior preceded his mother into the house. Cherryl herded the kids into the foyer, admonishing them to wipe their feet. In the middle of an abduction, Cherryl worried about muddy footprints. I passed around kitchen towels.

I looked at Bear, he shrugged. I dipped into my room to retrieve a party pack of valium, left over from a more generous emergency doctor. I groped through my underwear drawer and latched onto the prescription bottle. It would help Cherryl calm, but wouldn't knock her out. Bear poured brandy. I tossed the medicine bottle to him and herded the kids into Hannah's room. All three chattering at once about the helicopter ride, and the man's wife who gave them sodas. Bobby Junior wrestled control of the floor and gave me a run-down of what happened.

"Car in front of us put on his brakes, two cars came up on either side, forced dad into the middle of the road and stopped us. Sherf called it a, what did he call it?"

Elizabeth yelled, "A box, he called it a box."

Bobby Junior continued. "So yeah, we're in this box. The men had guns, but they were really polite, I mean, nobody was yelling. Lilia didn't bite anybody. Xavier started crying, but he's pretty little. The men made us all get out and lay down on the ground and three guys got outta cars and got into the van and then they took off. The fourth car, the one behind us, he drove onto the shoulder to get around us lyin' there on the ground. We walked for a long time until we found a house. They let daddy use the phone and his wife gave us sodas."

Elizabeth had an excellent attitude towards the detainment and abduction. "Then Uncle Billy came and got us in a big helicopter. We all fit and there was another man sitting in there and he had a big gun and he sat at the door. They left it open, can you believe they left it open? It was windy. I thought we'd fall out, but we had seatbelts. A man with a gun sat at the open door and said he could take a tick offa deer from the skybox. That's what he called it, a skybox."

I was tempted to drug her, such was her excitement. I turned on a cartoon channel. Within minutes, all six eyes took on a glassy stare and blinks grew longer. I pulled the door shut and glanced down the hallway into my room. Bobby Senior was tucking Cherryl into my bed with a tenderness that caught my breath. That was love. That was what it looked like, acted like, walked and talked like. I averted my eyes and left them to their privacy.

One laptop displayed a night scene, trees, foot path. I pointed at the monitor and asked Bear, "Is that the east camera?"

"Back gate, got a couple of acres of scrub brush and some trees out there, and a lot of wildlife. Oscar got the motor back online so I thought I'd check out the night life. Nothing but a few deer, maybe some panther."

I hoped Bear was kidding about the panther. If the stolen children were being held at the marina, this scrubland would be our best avenue for extraction. I didn't want to save them only to lose them as cat chow.

"I need that route. Is the gate locked?" Bear nodded. "Can I use bolt cutters?"

He nodded again. "It's a U bolt through the latch, it'll be tight. You could scale it, but those kids can't."

Oscar announced he'd gotten the dockside camera functioning.

I asked if we were expecting a naval assault. He shrugged. "Maybe."

"All right. I got the main gate up and running. I can't reposition it but we've got a full screen feed of the west side of the building. We've got – fuck. We've got more cars. We've got a van."

"Can you tell what it is? Is it ours? Where the hell is Bill, did he – " I stopped myself. If Bill did pop a transmitter on the van, we know exactly how the family Ellis was located. I was tempted to pull up the Ping Pirate on the laptop, watch the display in real time as the van containing our quarry rolled into the marina. It didn't matter anymore how the kidnapping occurred. Our mission was to get those children back. When we got the kids back, when everybody was safe, when we buried these bastards out in deep water, then Bill and I would have a long talk about his breach of security, how he put lives in mortal danger by disregarding a direct order.

"He and Bobby went to get weapons. As much as they could pull out of impound. None of us has much more than personal carry." Bear said, staring at the screen, willing it to move.

"Which means my weapons are in the possession of these fucks. Maybe Bill can bring some grenades."

Oscar muttered, "Yeah, you can never have too many grenades."

"Ain't gonna hurt my building much more." Bear tapped the arrow keys, swinging the camera as far as the swivel allowed. "East end intact, southwest worst." As the camera swung west, lens flare obscured the image. Three seconds later, the camera refocused. "They got electricity running in there. Gotta be a generator. Power and light pulled the plug. You can see the light spilling out here." He pointed at the lower right where the spectrum had lost detail due to the light input. "Not real bright though."

Oscar sucked in breath. "We got bogies. Small bogies. Look." In stilted freeze frame, one tiny creature, then a second appeared around the front of the van, from the far side, then crossed in front of the headlights. Three seconds later, the figures appeared farther inside the blown out hanger door. The next image lost them inside the hanger. Two taller figures followed them inside. The camera fuzzed even more as an interior light overloaded the camera sensors. They were gone from the next image.

The three of us were staring at the screen when Cherryl spoke. "You get my children back to me, you hear? This cannot be happening." Pretending a calm I no longer possessed, I put an arm around her and took her back into the bedroom. She was pale, shaken, and glassy eyed from the narcotic and brandy.

"I promise you, we'll bring them home." I stroked her forehead until her breathing slowed to a quiet steady rhythm. Ralphie strolled into the open door and hopped up on the bed, snuggling next to Cherryl. I pulled the door shut quietly.

"Bear, that party pill isn't holding. How many did you give her?"

"None. She wouldn't take any. Afraid she wouldn't hear the kids if they needed her. I refilled the brandy though." Bear said.

Two sets of boots trod swiftly up the stairs. Bobby pushed past me to check on his family.

Bill waited until Bobby was out of earshot. "House is getting full and we got one more coming. I called Vincenti. He's on his way. I didn't tell him about the kids, just that contact was established and I needed his help. I don't trust him, but we need his intel. He knows these players. We don't."

"I'm gonna kill the sonofabitches." Bobby had returned from checking his people.

"No. We go by the book. This thing is huge, we got state, county, local and fucking homeland security up our asses."

I cut in. "Did you happen to bring some grenades? Might be easier to get everybody out of the building if we knocked a few more holes in it."

"No. I do not have grenades. We have rifles. And flack vests and a few flashbangs."

"Can I throw them?"

"Dammit Archer, this is serious."

"Then don't go all high and mighty about going by the book when you've got three mercenaries ready to roll and a rogue DEA agent on the way." I lowered my voice. Bobby had lost interest and was staring into a video monitor while Oscar clicked through the captured images of what was either two midgets or two children being off loaded in strobe time. I pushed Bill away from the table and whispered, "This is his family. Those bastards left them in the middle of nowhere. He couldn't protect them. They took his gun and the two children they've risked their lives to protect. If he wants to be angry, then we use that anger. We know the kids are in there."

"Goddamit, Bill, they got em, let's go." Bobby yelled after viewing the images Oscar had saved.

"Bobby, we don't know that."

"Yeah, we do. Rewind that loop, show the chief."

Bill stepped behind Oscar to watch the replay. Color drained from his face. He closed his eyes and took a deep breath. "Holy fuck."

Vincenti stepped into the house and looked around. "Nice security you got here."

I waved him in and pointed toward the coffee. He'd cleaned up, gotten a haircut, shaved, and slept. He looked like a suburban ninja in black: shoes, knit shirt, golf pants, ball cap, windbreaker. He noticed me noticing and said, "Figured a low profile might be better."

He poured coffee and motioned Bill into the kitchen. I followed.

Vincenti said, "This is not your concern, Archer."

"We have confirmation the children are in the warehouse. Ninety percent surety unless they are auctioning midgets," I said.

"There is no 'we', I'm calling in the cavalry." Vincenti said.

"No, you're not. You all ride in with lights and sirens, those kids are dead. We," Bill said, nodding toward me, "are the cavalry. We stand the best and only chance of success. We've got five trained soldiers and the element of surprise. You can join us or I detain you here. Forcibly."

Vincenti took inventory of our motley crew. "I was a snake-eater, Bravo Company. Spent six years fighting the war on drugs. You think you can stop me, give it your best shot."

Bill stepped within kissing distance of Vincenti, nose to nose. "You want to lead an armored response to this incursion, staffed by the very federal bureaucracies that brought this war to my shore. You want to trade those kids to salvage your career. You think you're a good man. You are not. You are as bad as the men who stole those children and killed their parents."

Bill did not let Vincenti interrupt. He was on a righteous roll. "When we get them out, and we will, you call in whoever you want to clean out your house, but you don't get the children, not now, not ever. You do the right thing right now or you will be removed."

I felt the heat of Bill's wrath, didn't dare look at him lest it turned on me. He planned to lead this expedition, and it would not be stopped. Vincenti reached a decision. He pulled back his shoulders and took a deep breath. "All right. When you get those kids, I call in a strike team. This would be a whole lot easier if you let me call in a team right now."

"You know exactly what kind of destruction will ensue."

Vincenti engaged in a staring contest with the Captain. Bad move. Bill lost only to me and I cheated. Suppressing a smirk, I plucked the phone out of the agent's hand, popped the back, removed the battery, and pulled the SIM card. I tossed the phone on the counter and pocketed the battery and chip. I raised an eyebrow at Bill. Snake Eater my ass. He let a girl snatch his phone.

"Come on, Vincenti. "I'll show you the data whilst the men-folk prepare the assault. Oscar, please show our friend the clip of what might be children or monkeys."

I stepped out onto the deck to make a phone call. The first line of storms had moved on leaving the air clean, but chill. By the time I'd finished a cigarette, my friend sent a return text assuring me of his obligation and readiness for action. I field dressed the filter and stepped inside. I quietly asked Bill not to shoot any hairy guys wearing colors and sporting tattoos. They were on our side and would be utilized on the north-eastern encroach, but they were not entering the fray.

"They are going to cover my entrance, bar anyone from coming or going, and deliver those kids from the battle zone. My friend has guaranteed their safety."

Bill shook his head. "It's better to be alone than in bad company."

"I'll go you one better than the republic's first gangster. How about hypocrisy is the homage vice pays to virtue? For God's sake, can you agree, just this once, that your bad guys might be our good guys? Those men don't want a cartel war in their town any more than you do. It's bad for business."

We made our plans and the gods laughed. Red sharpie squiggles and arrows mangled an aerial print of Port Bryant Marina. Bear would make the approach in one of his zodiacs, drop in at the civilian marina a half mile away from his, silently paddle over and climb to high ground on the south side, inside the property line. Two of Escambia County's finest, accompanied by the chastened Special Agent Vincenti, would drop me on the dark side, the eastern edge outside acres of scrub woods buffering the marina from civilization.

Oscar was to run comms. I may have rigged the software for the camera system, but he alone possessed the skill to make them dance. He doled out ancient Motorola flip phones, with side button radios, and cellular service right at the end of the usable civilian spectrum, limited to two bars this close to the naval station. The radios worked fine. Oscar finished his instructions. "Okay everybody. This is an extraction only. I hear fire, I call in the feds. Right, Bill?"

Bill nodded, held up the ancient phone, and asked, "Where do you get this shit?" Oscar smiled and waved a hand in the air as if they materialized from another dimension. A great deal of Oscar's treasures manifested in this way. Besides communications, Oscar was also charged with keeping Cherryl sedated or drunk, keeping the three kids inside the house, and delivering death to any intruder. He was good with women, and children seemed to like him. He enjoyed removing assholes from the world.

Vincenti and I climbed inside the back gate of the requisitioned transport van. It had some age, a hand me down from the mainland, and smelled of pine disinfectant. The eyebolts for prisoner chains gleamed. Bill kept his toys clean. Bobby rode shotgun and Bill climbed into the driver's seat. He turned right onto the 292 with the lights out. I burrowed through the first duffel laden with borrowed accessories. I pulled off my sweatshirt, dropped a flak vest over my tee shirt, then pulled the sweatshirt back over my head. I held a vest out to Vincenti. He shook his head. I tossed it on the bench.

I pounded on the steel wall and yelled at Bill to turn on the overhead light, then laid out weapons from the second duffel bag. Four semi-automatics, all 9mm, three different manufacturers, two rifles that took the .308 or the 7.62, three Kbar style knives in leather sheaths, and a baseball bat. I selected one of the nines, seventeen rounds in the magazine. I racked the slide and slid the gun into my back pocket and placed everything back in the bag. I pushed it over to Vincenti. Pulling the last duffel to me, it clunked. I zipped it open and marveled at the number of preloaded magazines and boxes, mostly full, of ammunition. This was gear taken from evidence, and it was ready to use. I shook my head in wonder. Island policing was far more dangerous than I realized.

Bill took Pace north at the speed limit and cut west, making lefts and rights, bouncing the big van over ruts in unmarked service trails. I laid down on the floor hoping Toad's Wild Ride would end soon.

Bill rolled the van to a stop, killed the lights, and came around the back as I placed the weapons out for display. Handing Bill a vest, I pointed at the third bag and raised an eyebrow.

"You know Bobby, he can't sit still. He got everything ready." Bill handed me one of the knives. It was well worn, but the blade edge shone with a fresh grind. He knew I hated knives, but a weapon is a weapon and we were outnumbered. I jammed the sheath in my boot and pulled my pant leg over it.

"Take what you think you'll need." He spoke in a whisper, just inches from me. It gave me a chill not commiserate with the weather. He leaned into the van and rummaged around in the duffel that had contained the vests. He pulled out a canister and wiggled it in the pale moonlight.

"No camouflage? You want me to go in blackface."

"I'm not worried about you offending anyone today. I'm worried about your pale face getting spotted and killed."

He stuck two fingers in the pot and smeared oily black gunk on my cheek, spreading it around my face. I felt like a child getting her face washed. Except this was not my mother and he was a man whom I'd secretly crushed upon my whole life. I regained my senses and pushed him away. "I'm covered enough. Christ, I'll never get this stuff off." I finished smearing the oily paint on my face and neck, the backs of my hands knowing it would stain my skin for days no matter how hard I scrubbed.

He smiled and began darkening his own skin. I handed Bobby a flak vest. He shook his head no. "Ain't putting that on. I'm on search only, remember?"

Bill told him, "Yes you will, or I'll put it on you."

Bobby muttered the whole twelve seconds required to add a single layer of protection to his torso. I grabbed the bolt cutters and stepped alone into the darkness of the tree line.

The big truck accelerated west. It was black, and it was unmarked. He'd traded plates with his own patrol car. Illegal as hell, it would mean his job and his freedom, but Bill was that kind of guy. An asshole, yes, and he was particularly an asshole to me, but a good man regardless of my personal opinion. Most everyone else liked him. Maybe I was the problem, but I had my doubts.

Bill was to circle north and approach the marina from Hancock, go lights out three hundred yards from the main gate. They'd wait in the dark until I radioed Tango Echo. Unless gun fire erupted, the Captain, his deputy, and our rogue drug enforcement agent were to provide support only. They were not to engage unless forced. Bear would disable any water craft that did not belong on his dock. If anything happened, they were to evacuate and hail the licensed and credentialed cavalry. I was the only combatant. My heart rate accelerated, aches and pains of battles and aging no longer relevant. I smiled in the dark. That stupid biker was right. I was bored and had been for months. Growing trees in pots was not the most exciting of career choices, but it was supposed to be reasonably safe.

I crept through an acre of trees planted a century ago providing a buffer between the commercial zone and what was then private land. The elms long since died out due to imported blight. The non-native deciduous trees could not withstand the winds and the salt. They were crowded out by hardier and uglier species. Baobab survived in this green desert, sand pine, scrub oak, palm shrub, and numerous prickery weeds thrived as well. This tiny oasis of native ecosystem was protected and maintained by the area's business owners, and patrolled by hungry Florida panthers.

Angela and I had scouted these woods on numerous occasions during daylight hours, which allowed me to avoid the clutches of skinks and spiders. At night, I was at the bottom of the food chain. The moon had risen. It sloped on the downhill side of full, providing intermittent illumination. Referred to as a waning gibbous, I wondered why an ebbing moon was called a skinny monkey. I felt rather than saw the gathering storm, tattered clouds scuttled across the dark sky, distant thunder out over the gulf. My night eyes gradually came online as I hopped from shrub to tree, breaking limbs here and there, marking my trail. I doubted the bad guys had posted a sentry. This felt like a meet and greet, an exchange of goods.

I was making a tactical error supposing anything other than facts in hand. Bad guys, whoever they were, had our kids in that building and it was my job to get them out quickly and quietly.

We'd run riskier missions armed with less data and emerged with our prize and our lives intact. The radio clicked. I held the unit to my ear. Oscar reported four units in motion, compass pointing the building perimeter, a hard four, but they were impatient, smoked, and exhibited little readiness control. Good. If we happened to end a few bad guys, that was aces in my book. The scattershot nature of any recovered ballistics would confuse hell out of a crime lab, if it got that far. Feds would cover the whole thing up. This was their fuckaroo, even though it landed on our doorstep.

The east end of the building was intact, no overt damage visible in the night gloom. The explosion I'd heard was large enough to roll sound across a flat city with few tall buildings, but not large enough to destroy the marina. I cinched the cutters around the latch and strained silently. I pulled the broken lock out, slipped through the gate, wiped the cutters, and stowed them under an overturned boat hull. I ran crouching to the hanger door – not a hanger, a warehouse. This was a marina, not an airport. In the words of the immortal Mr. Bryant, "Words mean things, Jess. Control the words, control the culture." I told the voices in my head to shut the hell up.

The bay doors were rolled down, but the standard door between them stood open, a portal into darkness. Curiouser and Curiouser. Either I faced inept blackguards or somebody neglected to secure the property.

I flattened myself against the steel building, closed my eyes, and listened for movement, felt for vibrations. Far away noises faded out of consciousness and I detected no immediate noise, no movement. Guestimate next eight feet clear. I slid inside the doorway, crouched and peeked. Nothing but darkness. I crawled farther inside, remembering the layout from my months of labor. To the left a wall, to the right a wall, the corridor in which I stood led to wide spaces large enough to hold transport planes.

Noise emanated from the left and far forward. Voices, not loud, but not whispering. I flattened myself along the inner wall and listened. Separate voices, three, possibly four. Deeper sounds, then a loud and deep toned "Ha." Distinctively adult female.

Get the kids, get the kids. I crept farther into the corridor. Weak light filtered into view. Puddles of broken block strewn throughout the corridor hampered my stealth as I slid closer to the center command nest. Feeling my way through the debris, I followed the light. It wasn't strong, but it was steady and grew as I neared. The center of the building housed the dispatch command perch in an aerie squatting over four office cubes, none of which were larger than closets.

The light was brighter on the far side of the damaged quad and it stretched out on the floor. The cube walls must have been damaged as well. I crawled around the far side, wishing I had the eyes of a barn owl. Aging played hell on night vision.

Low murmur, a laugh, male, guttural, stopped my forward progression and raised gooseflesh on my skin. Only one stinking animal made that kind of noise. Oh sweet Jesus. Squirming closer, I heard the boy's whimper, and the fury in the girl's voice, harsh in her native tongue. I moved toward the sound of the boy, spotting him in the remains of the southwest cubicle. His eyes were screwed shut. Tears cleaned tracks down his cheeks.

I prayed these kids had been introduced to Cherryl's signature sound, the preferred method of grabbing a child's attention. Akin to clicking a horse to obey, it was far more civilized than screeching like a banshee at errant children. I crouched behind the broken wall, stuck my head around, and produced the sound. The boy swiveled toward me, eyes wide at the sight of a blackened ghoul. I held a finger up to my lips and made the sound again. He held his hands up, showing me he was bound and pointed at his feet, also bound. I covered my mouth with my hand. He nodded, and nudged his head to his right, my left. The girl was slinging epitaphs even I understood. She wasn't giving up without a fight. The male voice laughed and spoke words too low for me to decipher, but I could feel his evil.

I crept next to the boy, removed the knife from my boot, and cut his binds. I held my hand up for him to stay. He nodded and folded himself into a ball to disguise the lack of bindings. Smart kid. I listened to the pig long enough to determine his exact location. I crouched down, crawled forward, and poked my head around the damaged wall where the light was brightest. The girl was trapped on the lap of a monster, he was rubbing her arms and whispering in her ear. I took a deep breath in and meted it out, controlling the anger.

"Schnick schnick." Lilia did not move her head, but found my eyes. She smiled through her tears. Dredging up insults learned in the past from countries south of Texas, I said, "Ven a buscarme hijo de puta – come get me motherfucker. You like little girls, heh, you ain't man enough for a woman, eres un coño" I remembered little useful Spanish, but the insults never faded.

He wrapped one arm around the girl's neck, smashing her into his chest. With the other hand he pushed himself off the floor and rose to his feet dangling the child, her slender neck clamped in his elbow. His teeth glimmered wet in the white light of the camping lamp. He grinned and backed up, Lilia was twisting her head and kicking her legs, but without enough air to yell, not enough strength to damage this monster. He rolled his head back and forth, the light reflecting from one eye, but not the other, it was dead. For fucks sake, a cyclops. And here I stood without any wine. The monster backed toward the partially collapsed wall, a grinning cannibal with the prize in his arms. He pulled a knife out of his belt and loosened tension on the child, allowing her toes to touch the ground.

The camp light illuminated the scar tissue running from his forehead diagonally across the dead eye, down the cheek. Someone had tried to end him. I would not fail. I caught Lilia's eye and darted my glance to her left. She went limp, drooping, slipping. The boy crawled on all fours behind the madman. The monster took one step, a second, then a third backing away from me. One more and he would run over Xavier. Lilia bit into his hairy, dirty arm with her mouth wide open. His legs hit the boy and he toppled over. His knife clattered on the floor. Lilia, teeth embedded in the meat, followed the monster down. Blood poured from his forearm. He flailed at her, punching and pushing. I dropped to my knees, jammed my knife into his good eye and clamped my hand up under his chin to keep his mouth shut. He must not scream. A count of thirty, his free arm flopped to his side. The flow of blood thinned as his brain told his heart to stop beating.

I stood and grabbed Lilia around the waist, pulling her off the dead man. Her brother crawled to us and whispered into her ear. She thrashed and snorted, her teeth clacked looking for purchase, face shrouded in the blood of her enemy for the second time this week. She calmed as Xavier spoke, his own nose bloodied by his sister's flailing arms. I set her on her feet and knelt down, using my dirty hand to swipe at the blood on her cheeks. She grinned and spat out his flesh. "He will be the Chin of Cizin and suffer for eternity."

She hugged her baby brother and whispered something that sounded like eres mey arrowway, then wiped two fingers of the dead man's blood over the boy's forehead. I turned away and swallowed hard. I had never eaten of my enemy. Holy Mother of God. I put my hand on her shoulder and whispered "We must go now. My friends are waiting to take you to Mrs. Ellis."

The camp light shone upon the monster we bested. She pointed at him and said, "Cisin shall feast upon him. He shall live in the stink of his own death." She nodded as did Xavier. I held a finger to my lips and made a come-along gesture. I wanted out of this stygian tomb. I took the boy's hand, the girl took his other and I led them in reverse through the dark corridor.

My God was a jealous, vain God who smote his creatures from Genesis to the Revelation, but Christ Almighty, this was beyond Old Testament horrors. Or was it? Maybe all gods were vain. Why else would a god create light out of the great darkness then tear hell out of it when his creatures displeased him? No time for metaphysics, I felt the cooler air of freedom before I found it. I stopped the children side by side and whispered, "Wait." I stepped forward into the patch of night thinly illuminated by a skinny monkey moon.

I sensed movement to my left and dropped to a crouch. Something swooshed the air where my head had been and clanged on the steel wall. I tucked my head and launched myself into the body coming at me, connecting with his chin hard enough to take us both over. I saw no stars, but my vision narrowed for a short count of three. My attacker had not moved, my head on his chest, his heart was running fast. He was unconscious, but alive.

He'd swung his rifle at me. He dropped it when I landed on him. I picked up the weapon and felt for identification and breakage. Folding buttstock, large magazine, pistol grip, maybe a Baltic import. No suppresser. Lethal and lightweight. At the angle he had chosen for the attack, I wouldn't have awakened for some time, if ever. I dropped the magazine and slid the bolt to release the chambered round. I folded the stock, took a stance a foot behind his head, and aimed the pistol grip at his temple. The sound was wet and final and jarred all the way up my arms. I scooped up the magazine and looped the strap over my shoulder, not caring what offense he had committed to be exiled to the wasteland. He'd failed to secure his post and paid a deserter's price. I grabbed his legs and dragged him behind the abandoned boat hull, his head bounced on the gravel. He and I were both past caring.

I scrambled back to the darkness of the doorway. "Come come come." Xavier poked his head into the night, eyes searching for mine. I grabbed the boy's hand. "We run. We do not let go and we do not stop. Lilia, you take his other hand. Do not stop for anything. We are going to my friends. They will protect you."

"Your guerreros, your warriors, yes?"

"You go with them, and they will take you to Mrs. Ellis."

She shook with tension. "You must go back. She is inside. She gave me to the filthy pig to prepare me for sacrifice. She said he is Kaibil, but she is the mother of lies, he has no honor. Buluc is happy you have taken another of her men." She nodded her head toward the dead man whose feet poked out from behind the boat.

I shook her hard enough to clack her mouth shut. "Enough. Let's go." I dragged her and her brother through the dark woods following the trail of broken twigs. The child was disturbed and I had chosen violence to silence her. Nice, Archer, real nice. I tightened my grip on the young boy's hand and ran faster. Between us, Xavier's feet barely touched the ground.

I stopped ten meters from the edge of the dark woods. The boy squeezed my hand and tugged me to him. I knelt down to his level. "Men in the room many, but cinco, five, maybe who look important and speak important. "Many guardia – guards, diez. Ten, perhaps more. With the guns. And the woman, muy importante, important. Mi abuelita. She look at Lilia, like, like ..." The boy hissed through his teeth, struggling for words to make me understand. "She look at Lilia like when mi padre wants to own a horse. She did not even look at me, she flicked her hand at me as if to remove a bother. She is la jefa. You understand?"

I wrapped him in my arms and squeezed. "You got good English for a new American, kiddo, and good eyes for seeing."

I stepped forward and flashed two long pauses and one short with my penlight. Within seconds came a welcome response. I handed Xavier the flashlight and spoke to both of the children. "Go with them, they look scary, but they are good men. They will take you to my house and to Mrs. Ellis and they will stay and protect you."

The girl nodded solemnly and took her brother's hand. "You must obey Buluc, you will avenge –"

"Stop it," I hissed. "Get your brother to safety. Whoever the hell you pray to, you pray that my men get home in one piece. Go now."

I watched the thin beam bounce on the leaf strewn path as the children ran toward the iron warriors. Several nerve wracking seconds passed until the little photon semaphores flashed the all clear. My men had secured the children and were ready to evacuate. The acceleration of their pack momentarily quieted the noise of the forest.

I pulled out the stolen radio and held the transmit button for a long second followed by a short burst. TE, Tango Echo, Targets Extracted. Repeat: Tango Echo. I sent the message a third time and waited for a response. I counted to one hundred with no response, then began the trek west through the woods accompanied by the rain and the thunder and the wind and Lilia's demons and the mysterious She, whom Xavier had referred to as the boss lady.

14 BAD DAY AT BLACKROCK

I scuttled forward, tree to shrub, spurred by cold anger, masquerading as honor, pushing me through the scrub, against the rain, toward the rendezvous point outside the fence line. The monkey moon played peekaboo through the clouds racing in from the gulf. I was a dark ghost in a dark night, and my guys would be on watch, if they were there. If they weren't dead or captured. Lilia's Irregulars were supposed to be on recon, not offence. They were to roll out after receiving my message. An acknowledgement would have been nice.

Our targets had been secured. I was cleared to evacuate. Another two hundred yards to their position. Port Bryant was bigger than a football stadium, one of the new ones, the kind I hated. I double timed through the woods minus the requisitioned knife, but I had the rifle I'd taken from the guard, and the 9mm Bill had so graciously provided. No grenades, though. I could end this now if I had grenades. The earlier explosion had knocked the western hanger door off its track. It lay on the ground where the fire department had left it after pulling it all the way off its track.

I spotted one sentry by cigarette glow in the darkness. I dropped into the weeds and watched him walk a lazy route, hunched against the weather. There would be two more sentries unless they replaced the dead guard. The lack of alarm told me they had not. These people were arrogant, lazy, or had been informed they would meet no resistance.

I spotted the transport van, too clean among the abandoned machines. Elbow to knee, I crawled until the weeds ran out. I curled behind a lone struggling tree, and whispered loudly, "I'm at the van, do not shoot."

Too late I heard rustling behind me, no time to raise a weapon. "Dammit Archer, took you long enough." Bill was four feet from me, all but invisible in the night.

"I got no response from the radio signal. The kids are safe and on the move. South sentry neutralized, one internal guard also gone. We got a meeting of some kind in there. The boy, Xavier, he counted a possible fifteen men and one woman. Fuck, this doesn't matter, we are mission accomplished. Let's get out of here."

"Oscar has been chattering like a magpie. Someday you are going to explain to me how he has ears on us. And if he has ears on, who else does?"

Who else, indeed, mon capitaine? I wanted to ask why he worried about transmission interception after I explicitly warned him not to use a goddam transponder on the borrowed van. I kept my mouth shut and followed him. This was not the appropriate time to argue his insubordination, but it would come soon. We stepped into the road. He hesitated, looking back toward the curve in the road separating us from the fight.

Angry voices grew louder as we neared the van. Bill tapped on the back door. Vincenti pushed the door open and hopped down. He had a rifle strapped over his shoulder and a pistol in each hand. He yelled over his shoulder, "No, it's her, she's the one who started this whole fucking mess, she killed my people." He stopped yelling when he saw me. "I'm going in there. You got a problem with that, too?"

I held my hands out. "I don't give a shit what you do. The kids are out and on their way to safety surrounded by a hardcore honor guard armed to the teeth. As far as I'm concerned, we are out of here."

He stepped into my private zone, his face within inches of mine. "What did you say?"

"Step back." I reached for the gun in my back pocket. Out of the corner of my eye, I saw Bill draw his weapon. I dropped my hands to my sides. Son of a bitch would have to back up so I could shoot him.

"Goddamit you've fucked me good." Vincenti grabbed me by my shoulders and shook me hard enough to rattle my teeth. He shoved me backwards. I bounced into the side of the van. He put his hands over his eyes and said, "I need those kids, it's the only way. You gotta call them back. To draw them out. Then we get her, take her fucking head, mount it on a spike, it will stop them all. Then you can have those kids. I swear to God."

Bill did not lower his weapon. "Back away from her, now, Vincenti. Who do we get? Who is She?"

"Wife of Arturo Lopez Medranno, Leon's El Presi-fucking-Dente. Code name El Sapo, the toad. He's old and fat, but she is the queen, she runs the outfit and she runs him. Two months ago, the federals were transporting one of her lieutenants to Guadalajara for trial. She ordered the prison transport taken and every single man on the bus murdered. Guards and prisoners alike, including her lieutenant. They were locked inside the bus and it was set on fire. She didn't have to do this. Her people could have taken her man and let the others go. Her message was received loud and clear: War is on. I gotta have those fucking kids, it's the only way I get out of here alive."

Bill took a step toward Vincenti and spoke softly. "Listen to me. Leave with us now. We call in the professionals, your cavalry, and take down everyone inside. With or without those kids, you cannot negotiate with these people. You've made that clear."

"No. There's no way to fix this. I shouldn't have – I never should have gotten involved in this shit – It should have been me in that fire, not Dave, it was my fault. Oh Jesus." His eyes rolled back and forth, focusing on nothing and no one.

His madness made him dangerous. Bobby had not lowered his weapon. Bill was closer, his firearm was down, but I knew how fast he was. I shook my head back and forth so the men would stand down. I knew what drove this madness, but I needed my men to hear it. I whispered, "Tell me."

He took a deep breath, and looked to the shrouded sky for guidance. "Isobel fed me all this mystical Mayan bullshit, said her abuelita had some book, a popal or some bullshit, that she was from a line of women, like ten generations back, sold to powerful families to rebuild the empire. Jesus, I thought I was too old for ghost stories, but she was so fucking beautiful. And she wanted me – me – to be her white knight. She was frantic to get her children out of the country. She thought they'd be safe in the U.S. She convinced her husband to apply for asylum by offering up his boss. It gave me a reason I could put on a report to get her out.

"Xavier used the word abuelita. What is it?"

"How do you walk upright, Archer? de Vaca, Isobel's husband, was owned by the Chiapas cartel, he laundered billions through the Ministry of Agriculture. Isobel's mother, Bellona Monterrosso Salazar y Medranno, wife of Arturo, is those kids' grandmother. She offered a truce to Chiapas if they bring her the children. For Chiapas, it's a win-win. They get their traitor and a truce. The war is costing them both too much money, too many men. Chiapas is losing power, but Leon isn't strong enough for all-out war, not yet. According to Isobel, that fucking girl was Bellona's key to unleashing the prophesy, opening the door to some underworld. The girl is the Blood Maiden, the sacrifice." Tears streamed freely down his face. He made no move to conceal his grief.

Fuck this fairy tale. The children were safe. I didn't care what happened to this bastard, but I did care about my friends. "You have the heads of two fucking cartels in that building. Get in the van. We are getting out of here now." I said.

"No. I'll die my way, not hiding under your skirt." Vincenti shoved past me, knocking me to the ground. He stopped, shook his head, stomped back, and offered a hand. I took it. "I'm sorry. I really am. I'm glad you got the kids out. They have no business in this mess. Who the hell sacrifices children? Who the hell trades a child's life for a fucking drug route?"

He re-shouldered his rifle. "I'm going in. Alone. This isn't your war. It's mine. Give me fifteen minutes, then call it in." He pulled out his wallet and handed it to Bill. "There's a card behind the shield, call that number. I am sorry for this mess. You don't have a mole. It was me. I needed to lure Bellona here. It worked. Too well. And I – I am sorry."

He turned and slouched toward his high noon. He would sacrifice his own life to finish the mess he'd started. Sometimes when honor came, it came late. Odds were fifteen to one if the boy's intel was correct. I swiped at the wet gravel clinging to my pants and spoke to Bobby. "Up to you, Deputy, they're your kids. We can go now. Let the feds handle this."

He pushed his hat back. "We had a chance to talk, him and me. He's not a bad guy, he got sold a line a goods and he fell hard. Then his partner got killed, says it shoulda been him. He really thought he could use the kids and get them back out. I told him he was nuts. Those folks are bad, bad as in evil, they can't be reasoned with, they can't be bargained with. You gotta kill em, make sure they ain't coming back. That's the only thing you can do with these drug people. They ain't got souls."

"You're talking about murder, Bobby, can you live with that?"

"It ain't murder. It's vengeance for every man, woman, and child those bastards have killed. And will kill if we don't stop them. Yeah, I can live with that. Plus, we ain't leaving Vincenti man to fight alone."

The two men armed themselves from the duffle bags. I had the rifle and the 9mm. The knife was lost besting the beast. Bill raised an eyebrow and twitched toward the duffle. I shook my head. "I've got what I need."

Bill sighed heavily. "We go in fast, fan out, grab Vincenti, knock him out if you have to, drag him out, absolute zero affect. The keys to the van are in the visor. Whoever gets here first, get my van out. I cannot explain losing it. Get over to the Martinique, it's closest even if you have to route through the industrial park. I'll radio Oscar. Stay low and stay out of sight. Mark ten minutes as soon as we cross the gate, then I am calling this in. No more arguments, no more fucking around. We do not have enough men for this war. We get Vincenti and get out. Three taps on the radio, hold, and repeat, and keep repeating."

Bobby's voice low with barely contained anger. "They won't stop, you know that, not until they get what they came for."

"Whoever they are, they got one dead agent under their belt, possibly two if we don't get in there. The best these bastards can hope for is extradition and trial in their home country. The best we can hope for is they get wiped out in the firefight. Either way, they will no longer be our threat."

"You hold by your hope the feds will stop them, not just let them walk? They won't stop these fuckers, and you know that. Goddamit Billy, I'm not risking the lives of my family for these animals again. They ain't right, they ain't even human."

Bill put his hand on his friend's arm. "These people let you go, your family, they let you live."

"Minus two kids. I want them dead. All of them."

"You've got your orders, deputy. Grab Vincenti. Get out."

Bear emerged from the shadows as a darker shadow, speaking low into his phone. He finished and nodded at me. "Oscar counts four sedans, two vans, one of which is the van Archer borrowed based on the transponder Oscar found pinging away. One poorly disciplined watchman at the western wall, marching back and forth, smoking. South and east sentries neutralized and not replenished. No radio traffic as far as he can tell. You okay, Jess? You look a little pale underneath that paint you got on there."

"You were supposed to evacuate."

"So were you."

"Fair enough." I said. "The southwest corner of the warehouse where the blast originated is standing, but roof and walls sustained damage, internal damage around the dispatch tower, where they had the kids. Some rubble, but they didn't work too hard to bring the building down, just damage it. What's the point of that?"

Bear laughed. "Your office is gone."

Bill interrupted, "We're wasting time. We get Vincenti and get the hell out, that's it. If they have him, we leave without him."

"They hurt my kids."

"Deputy, I ain't arguing this."

Bobby hadn't been able to protect his family and he wanted justice. Honor was a bitch and she was insatiable and we were all at her mercy, and goddam if the ride didn't have its moments of sheer joy.

I looked to Bear for help. He shook his head, but one side of his mouth had turned upward in a smile. He stared back at me, raised his eyebrows, and shrugged. "Bill, Archer's point is valid. Why the lack of damage? Bomb squad found traces of HBX, left over from Latin war games is my guess, but not enough to destroy the building, just enough to make a point. But what point? They set up lights, low enough not to be obvious, but bright enough to cast shadows. They set a meet in there, like they knew they wouldn't be disturbed. You boys with me so far?"

When neither of the men answered Bear looked to me and said, "Vincenti is the mole, he's part of this setup. He made sure they wouldn't be bothered. This is neutral ground. I'll tell you the rest later. Right now, we need to get him out of there, if we can."

Bill tilted his head, held a hand up for silence. Distinct pop of gunfire over the weather. One shot, then a second. "War has started ladies, and we are late to the ball." Bill gave the signal to move. Bear and I right, he and Bobby left.

I grabbed Bill's arm. "No. Me and Bear head north, you two into the parking lot. Use the cars for cover, hold out until we come through. I know the way. I got two flash bangs. We flush them out. They'll head for their cars."

"That's not the plan."

"It is now. We're going to herd them out the front and you're going to take them out."

"And if they have Vincenti?"

"He's hiding or he's dead by now, and I don't give a damn. He sold his soul for a piece of someone else's wife and offered to broker her children to dark gods."

"Ten minutes. No more." Bill followed Bobby into the darkness. I'd pay for my public mutiny later, but the butcher's bill was due on these monsters. Bill wanted the same thing, but would not admit it. My insubordination provided a plausible excuse to execute anything moving. I let him keep his timeline. Ten minutes.

The wind stalled, rain poured straight down, the lightning stopped, and we had lost our moon behind the downpour. We were a hundred yards out, behind a soft curve which offered no line of sight. Fortunately, we had Oscar with eyes on. Bear rolled in first and popped up to his knees at the back of the closest sedan, I followed on his heels.

I peeled off from my hiding spot next to Bear and crab walked to the next car, another large four door. South American thugs spared no expense renting luxury cars. Maybe they were the only cars left in the rental lot. Maybe there was a local dealer who rented bullet proof cars made in Japan, shipped to the U.S., then modified for visiting gangsters. My mind lolled in the giggle weeds, winding down in preparation for battle. Bear followed me and pointed toward the sentry. I nodded.

The sentry swiveled left. We followed the darkness around the south side creeping like cartoon spies moving from shadow to shadow. We pressed into the building, feeling our way toward our target. No new sentry posted, no radio checks, no alarm raised. Our bad guys were running a shoddy operation.

I poked Bear and pointed at the feet sticking out from under the boat. Bear smiled, a solid row of white shined briefly. I stepped through the still-open door, using instinct to feel for intruders as I couldn't see my hand in front of my face. Back to back we wound through the maze, looping around, stopping long enough to show Bear the Cyclops who'd been given the task of preparing Lilia for sacrifice.

Bear muttered, "Jesus wept." I shuddered at the thought of what might have been, and I wanted blood. I poked the man's leg with the toe of my boot. Still dead. Still unnoticed. Light pressure on my shoulder stopped me from retrieving the borrowed knife. Bear held a fist up then opened it. He wanted one of Bill's little noise makers. I smacked at my pockets, and located a five inch canister. Enough camp light filtered through the debris to see his hand out, waiting. I shook my head and held up one finger and pointed at myself. He shook his head and waited. I whispered in his ear, "You better not throw like a girl." I felt his laughter.

Bear took the lead, and we crawled through the chute separating the warehouse divisions. Voices bounced around the metal walls, not loud enough to distinguish words. Growing swaths of rubble slowed our progress. Light from camp lanterns filtered through the damaged wall. In between gales of wind and rain, I listened to rapid fire Spanish, male voices, and one definitely female and definitely in charge by the tone. No lilting at the end of a sentence, she made a statement, then another. Then she told someone he was a something something pendejo. She was not happy with whoever she called an asshole.

The voices grew more distinct as we neared the edge of the blast zone. I peeked through a break in the rubble. One man on the left in a folding chair, legs crossed, hair dark, slender build, mid-forties. He was directly facing my hidey hole. The smirk he wore was directed at the woman speaking at him. Her back was to me, she sat erect in a folding chair, her hair tied and covered with a colorful scarf. Stone faced men, pale in the harsh white light, stood offset behind the smirking man's chair. I spotted another guard in the shadows opposite me, a second next to him. Xavier spoke of a possible ten guardias he counted inside. I sighted four, which left six unaccounted for. Based on the boy's number, two opposite, and assuming a mirror image with two backed to my wall, two more guarding the primaries. Unaccounted for, two more guards and two, possibly three muy importante folk. Didn't look like Vincenti had taken out any targets, but I didn't see his body from my vantage point.

A guard, dripping wet, stepped into view. He stepped toward the woman, stopped short by a gesture from a guard. Rain pooled at his feet as he rattled off a report of some kind, short, and judging by his tone, disappointing. She stood, sweeping an arm, gesturing, her aggression cowed him. He stood six inches taller than La Jefa, but stared at the floor in silence as she assaulted him. The man's head rocked from the slap she delivered, the sound echoed above the rain falling on the steel roof. He stepped backward. Her voice rose in anger. She violently gestured toward where he had come from, yelled some more words. Two men marched him out of my view. Two men I had not seen before, climbing out of the darkness like spiders. She had ordered them into the night.

The electric lantern illuminated her face. She greatly resembled her dead daughter, but older, her face more angular, with none of the daughter's humanity. She was beautiful, but like Medusa, her gifts were deadly. Bobby was right. No mercy, no quarter. These creatures were not human. This woman had ordered a fate worse than death for her own granddaughter, a child, a goddam child. She was negotiating with the men who murdered her daughter.

Bear eased his way over and pulled me down to the floor. "She's telling them they get Juarez and some cat named Valencia because they delivered the children."

Bear's voice disappeared behind a roar of anger. My own mother was stolen from me and this bitch had a daughter and a granddaughter and she sacrificed them both. I would personally watch the light die in her eyes, and she would know true horror before sweet death took her. Mine would be the face that followed her into hell. Oh dear God. Pain broke through the wave of blood washing through my soul. I tried to pull away.

Bear's breath hot in my ear. "No. You get that genie right back in the bottle. That rage will get us all killed. We follow the plan. Vincenti ain't in there so now we are gonna herd them out, let the boys pick them off. We got four minutes before Bill calls in the Federales."

I patted the hand squishing my arm, acknowledging the order. Bear whispered in my ear. "She just ordered men outside to look for the missing guards. Which means she's gonna send men to check on the kids. We go on three, be ready, they're gonna scatter."

I knew the drill. Pull pin, throw, duck, plug ears, squish eyes shut. Suckers weren't just deafening, they were blinding. With his left hand he tapped one, two, his arm looped up and over, third tap.

Bear dropped next to me and assumed the position. The canister went off like a howitzer. Even with fingers jammed into my ears, the percussion pushed painfully at my eardrums. Before the echoes died, I pulled the rifle over my shoulder and slid the bolt. This eastern-bloc knockoff had a longer barrel than my pistol guaranteeing more accuracy. I felt Bear move away from me. He took two long steps to the right and crunched over a mound of brick and debris. I ran after him, he required cover and I desired vengeance. Sorry, Bobby, but this bitch was mine.

I slid halfway down the pile scanning for targets. Bodies scattered from the surprise attack. The woman knelt on the floor, hands over her eyes, retching. The man with whom she had been negotiating was flat on his back, not moving. I sighted on her forehead, but shot the body stirring to life behind and slightly to

215

her left. Bellona pushed herself upright. Her eyes were red and ran freely with tears. She'd been close enough to sustain collateral burns, but nothing mortal. Peripherally I watched another guard raise his weapon. He was too shaky to aim, one shot wild, then a second, then his chest bloomed. Her eyes found mine and she spit words I did not recognize, but her tone was unmistakable. She hated me. We women were like that sometimes, loathed each other on sight for no good reason, but I had two good reasons.

The woman held my gaze. She did not look away as she struggled to her feet. She smiled through the smoke. She was unarmed and thought her men would protect her. I moved the barrel a fraction. I lined the rear sight with the sunshine dot. I squeezed the trigger, my own smile never leaving my face.

This woman, carrier of whatever disease afflicted these people, that turned men into rabid dogs, lay on the ground with a hole in her high, clear, aristocratic forehead.

After the boss went down, the remaining men scrambled out the door. I jumped onto the killing floor and scrambled for cover behind a husk of machinery. The slowest two men dropped before reaching the night. Bear crouched behind a section of torn wall and yelled, "We'll be back lit, we can't move."

"You want me to shoot out the lights?" I hollered back.

"Like you could. We go around, get out, let them think we're still here. Leave the lights." I climbed back over the tumbled debris and followed Bear through rubble and glass. My knees and elbows were shredded. Bear's target was the north service door, past the gaping hole where the hanger door had been.

"Lotta shooting out there. You think Bill called in the cavalry?" I wheezed at Bear.

"Nope. They have to yell freeze or some shit. That's our guys holding the fort. I got three down. And two on your barrel plus the bitch. Based on your boy's count, we got bogies unaccounted for. Unless they brought in local muscle we ain't seen."

"Sounds like summer in the Windy city."

"You miss it?" He asked.

"Not really. I don't like being shot at."

Knees to elbows, Bear crawled past the giant hole in the wall and motioned for me to follow. The Ellis Family Adventure Van and a rented sedan provided a blind.

We crouched in the darkness on either side of the man-sized door listening to the melee. Sporadic gunfire, garbled male voices, rain on the metal roof. I nudged Bear and pointed. Fire came from a dark pocket southwest, muzzle flash aimed toward the parking lot, chock full of rented and stolen vehicles. What were they shooting at? No way had my men bunched up. All three served infantry and knew the folly of too tight a target. The noise of lead hitting metal was deafening. For God's sake, they were spending more brass than they could possibly carry. I caught Bear's eye. He shared my smile. He shook his head then pointed toward the closest van.

I nodded. Bear perched on his haunches, ready to run, then yelled in Spanish, "Vamos, bastardos, quieres vivir para siempre?" Firing stopped for a long few seconds while the combatants tried to figure out who the hell was asking if they wanted to live forever.

We skidded behind the borrowed van as fire erupted. "Hold fire, it's us," I yelled. Bobby swung his rifle toward the incoming noise, and swung it back immediately. The shooters were hunkered down behind the sedans.

"This ain't worth shit, got a day scope, can't see in the dark. Bill is out there somewhere, he's pinned down, might be hurt, but I don't think so. Vincenti took off toward the dock." The tremor in Bobby's voice gave lie to his words. He was on the edge of panic.

I touched his arm. "Where do you think Bill is?"

Bobby bumped his head to the right. "We finish this, okay? I ain't waiting here all night to find out my best friend is dead."

"Let me draw fire away, they can't hit me, I'm a goddam ghost." Bear said.

Bobby smiled. "Come on, let's show 'em who they're fucking with."

Bobby rolled right, popped up to a knee and fired in the direction of his nest of hornets, Bear did the same on the other side. I rolled my eyes, dropped to my hands, and followed Deputy Ellis into the void.

I couldn't tell how many were holed up behind the last sedan. Three minimum based on the continuous fire. We leap-frogged around the vehicles. Incoming fire became sporadic Someone was firing at their flank. Sounded like two shooters. Two. Thank God. Bill was alive and well, and so was Vincenti.

Bobby stumbled into the sedan then sank to his knees. "Goddam that hurts." He wasn't covering himself. Bear's voice came from the left. "Get down, Bobby, goddamit, get down."

I rolled out from cover, and flattened myself into the ground. Incoming shots were higher than my ass. I dragged myself to Bobby's position, and pulled him down on the ground. I laid my hands on him. "Where? Show me."

Bobby slapped at my hands and pushed himself back to sitting. "Ain't bad, ain't mortal. Did you get fire from the east side? Bill's still over there pinned down. We got two fire teams. Can't run 'em to ground. Can we herd them together?"

"Bill's damn near at twelve from our position. He and Vincenti boxed them in. I got two guns, more magazines, and Bear. Let me waste the brass to finish them."

He hissed and pulled his arm into his side. "I'm gonna draw fire, you start aiming."

The voice of Bill Thornton roared above the noise. "Fire in the hole." Enemy fire turned toward the sound. Bobby threw his arms around my head and pulled me into him. No time to cover my ears. Bill lit those bastards up. Head reeling from the percussion, I grabbed at Bobby who was no longer on top of me. He had popped up like a demented jack-in-the-box and fired and fired and fired. Targets scattered like cockroaches, I led them until I was sure none of my men were in danger of friendly fire. Tracking three steps then four, then they dropped. I'd lost count, but the kid's number was off by more than a few.

Bobby slid to the ground after emptying his rifle. Either my hearing gone or the shooting had stopped. I felt the rain, then I heard Bobby's labored breathing, then I heard that crazy horse snick sound. Bill approached our position at a crouch. "Goddam Bobs, you went full hillbilly. They're down and anybody not dead is running, but I don't think we missed anything. You're the man." He bent down and grabbed Bobby, pulling his shoulder. "Archer, now, fuck fuck fuck, Bobby's hit. Bad. Aw Jesus."

I dropped to my knees and yanked down the zipper of his windbreaker. Bobby was unconscious, blood pooled in his lap, on the ground, oh shit, he's lost too much. I found his pulse, it was weak and too fast, shit. If he was breathing, he wasn't moving his chest. "Lay him down, we gotta get him breathing." I pulled open the jacket and ripped at the vest straps to free the front panel.

"I'm gonna call an ambulance." Bill said.

"What if his heart stops waiting for an ambulance, or waiting to explain to your Sheriff what the fuck you are doing out here surrounded by a shit load of dead Mexicans and your prisoner van and half the evidence room. No time for What-If. If his heart stops it won't matter if he can't walk or talk or even know his fucking name. He's got a pulse that's not gonna hold unless we get him some air"

I pinched his nose, tilted his neck and clamped my mouth over his and blew once, then again. I knew the latest regulations said forced air wasn't as important as the heart pump, but I didn't trust the testing. I knew what worked in the field. No whistling, lungs intact. I pushed eight breaths when Bill started chest compressions. Footsteps running on the gravel interrupted my prayers, but not my count.

Bear smiled and clapped Vincenti on the back. "Went after the deserters. Couple a bodies over by the dock. "Glad I found you not dead, not hiding, but chasing assholes, just like I thought you'd be." The smile dropped from his face. "I'll get the van," Bear took off at a dead run.

"Ambulance." Vincenti pulled out his Motorola.

"Won't get here in time." Bill was out of breath from continual compressions.

Headlights of the transport van bounced through the gap in the vehicles. I stood and grabbed Vincenti. "We gotta get him in the truck, Bill, grab his legs, Vincenti, hold him steady, don't let him drop." Cradling our man, we lock stepped to the rear of the van. Bear opened the back doors. I climbed inside and pulled Bobby in. Bill followed and we resumed our futile efforts. We lost fifteen precious seconds loading him.

Bear turned the van around and accelerated. The overhead light was not our friend. Bobby was too pale. Vincenti had his hand on Bobby's neck. "Stop. I got a pulse, Bill, let up, Archer, stop, he's going on his own right now."

Bill yelled, "Baptist is closest."

"I got it," Bear yelled and accelerated.

15 VIGIL FOR THE UNDEAD

Bear stopped the van, flung open the back doors, and ran through the sally port calling for a stretcher. I climbed out of the van and recognized Nurse Crabby Pants, she of my last visit, as she came running outside. She recognized me in one hard look and called for a trauma team. Professionals in drab scrubs unburdened us, laying Bobby out on a rolling stretcher and began their healing dance. We had done our work. It was time for varsity to take the field.

Bill spoke to a woman at the admitting desk for several minutes, low enough not to be overheard. She shook her head. He touched her arm and spoke again. Her shoulders slumped and she agreed to whatever he'd asked. The man could be charming when he chose to, but it wasn't his charm that stayed her hand. It was the sight of Cherryl's husband Bobby covered in blood.

Bill motioned for us to huddle in the vestibule. "I'm gonna recover what I can and run the van back. We could be in some very deep shit here." He glanced at his watch. "While I'm out, I'm gonna make up a story for the feds. They can clean this shit up. Archer, you call me if anything happens and do not talk to anyone."

We perched on indestructible chairs engineered for maximum discomfort, drank bad coffee, and stared at walls praying and thinking in silence. My leg hurt, the wound had reopened at some point, but the bleeding had clotted. I wore enough of Bobby's blood to disguise my insignificant problem.

Forty six minutes into our vigil, Cherryl barreled through the doors, accompanied by Thornton. She pushed her way through the pneumatic doors leading into the inner sanctum. Bill sat down wearily. He'd put on a clean windbreaker. He shook his head. He had nothing to say.

Customers came and went unhindered by our presence, but they gave us a wide berth. The noise level in the waiting area remained unnaturally quiet. We waited silently as daylight brightened the dingy tiles. The shadows disappeared, then elongated in the opposite direction while we waited for word of our hero, whether he lived or died. Two city cops arrived with a prisoner requiring medical attention. They took no notice of us.

Night had descended when Cherryl came through the pneumatic door followed by a doctor-looking person in blue scrubs spotted with wet dark spots, and a bandana over his hair. He pulled his mask down and spoke to Cherryl as they neared. The four of us stood at once. Cherryl led the man into to our circle.

"We were able to remove two intact pieces that had not fragmented. The trauma was extensive and his heart may have stopped due to blood loss. We've induced a coma to keep swelling to a minimum. I can't do much right now except wait for his body to recover enough to maybe, maybe look at removing the third bullet. On the CAT scan it looks as if it stopped at his spinal column. The scan is inconclusive as to whether the breach is partially or completely debilitating." More medico speak that I could not decipher. All I understood was heart stop, blood loss, coma, and a goddam bullet was stuck inside him.

The doctor looked at us, eyes resting upon each before addressing Bill. "I know you're his Captain, and since you brought him in, I'm going to plead ignorance when every damn law enforcement agency lands on my doorstep demanding evidence. You take the metal, get it out of here. His clothes, all of it."

The doctor patted Cherryl on the shoulder, looked over our dirty crew again, shook his head in disgust, and disappeared behind the magical doors where we were not welcome.

Cherryl stared after the doctor, her face puffy and blotched from crying, white as a sheet, eyes hard, lines around her mouth etched deeply. She thrust a hospital bag at Bill. "We are required by law to report gunshots, and the city sends over a couple of cops to take statements. In this case, they're gonna wanna send a whole platoon. His doctor put a lockdown on all information saying it's because he's a deputy and we can't risk the shooter finding him here." She looked at Vincenti with watery eyes. "You brought this down upon us. My husband is in a coma because you didn't do your job. You crawl back into whatever hole you came from. Don't you dare let me see you again, so help me God."

Cherryl glared at me and nudged her head, ordering me to follow. Without a backwards glance, she pushed through the pneumatic doors, knowing I would obey. I followed her into Bobby's room. Several machines beeped, one clicked, breathing for him through a thick tube jammed down his throat. The sounds of mechanical life were too loud. Cherryl motioned to a scuffed plastic chair hiding in the corner. "You set right there, and you wait with me. You. You and Bill. Goddam. Both a you, have to right every wrong. People get hurt. People get dead and you two, not a scratch, not one scratch, while my Bobby is lying in this bed."

She gathered in a shuddering breath. "He thinks Billy walks on water. And you. You're some kinda rock star. You know that? Like he missed out not becoming a goddam killing machine, just doing his tour and coming home in one piece, to me, like making a family is not enough." She broke under a tidal wave of grief, soundlessly weeping for a life not fully lived. I stepped around the bed and wrapped her in my arms. She shook with the force of her pain. Her man's blood was on my hands, caked with it, my clothes stiff with it.

Her words bit deeper than any bullet, down deep where my conscience lay, dusty from disuse but functional. After an eternity, she pushed me back and pointed to my assigned seat. She sat vigil in a plastic chair next to the equipment keeping her husband alive. She picked up his hand and held it.

I lowered myself into the seat and prayed. Misremembered lines of prayers from the Sunday schools of my youth ran together with Hebrew uttered in temples in which I'd hidden from the enemies of God's chosen.

We sat in cluttered silence and waited.

The door hissed. I glanced up, surprised to see Tannenger pushing into the room. He registered no surprise at my presence, nor did he look happy. He went to Cherryl, put a hand on her shoulder, bent and spoke quietly in her ear. He stood and motioned me to follow him outside. I shook my head. He stepped within kissing distance, I breathed in his fabric softener and fresh soap.

I stared at Bobby, willing him awake, and said, "Mrs. Ellis needs me."

"Mrs. Ellis, Cherryl, I need to speak with your friend. Is that okay?"

Cherryl nodded without looking away from her husband. I stood, wincing at the stiffened wound. I was alive to feel the pain. Tears threatened. I willed Bobby to pick a side, live or die. This was no way to leave us hanging. You got three, ah hell, five kids who need you, a wife who loves you. Family, friends, a boat. My punishment was to bear witness to the dying of my friends.

I limped to the door and followed the doctor out. He walked several feet down the hall, leaned on the counter of an empty terminal bay, and waited for me.

"There are a whole bunch of uniforms outside. Among them, several cheap suits that look federal. I've got two grandmothers at information, and a retired Navy lifer playing rent-a-cop. By sheer force of will, they are keeping all these people at bay. Half the uniforms are city, half county, but they all hate the feds so that helps. Is this war going to land on my doorstep?"

"Not with my people here. And the deputies won't leave because your patient is one of theirs."

"How about the honor guard? There were eight lined up in the parking lot an hour ago. There may be more at this point."

"Think of them as good guys right now."

"Situation fluid?"

"Yes, something like that."

"You'd better be ready for the worst. He may not make it all the way out. The surgeon said he wouldn't attempt to address the remaining bullet until he thinks the deputy's body can handle the surgery. We can't keep him under long. Even if the surgery is successful, recovery will be long and ugly. He may be permanently paralyzed."

The other cutter hadn't used that term. I would not accept it. "I've called in every favor God owes me. It's in His hands now."

I moved to return to Bobby. Jake blocked me. "I'll ask again, are we in the line of fire?"

Meeting his gaze through tears. "No. It's done."

I pushed into the room where a good woman kept watch over a good man and I prayed, but this time to the Son in the New Testament. I'd read that He was nicer than his Father.

Day sank into night with the speed of a snail across dry sand. Hospital waiting was the quantum opposite of the speed of light. The lever of time moved to full stop. Various scrubbed personnel moved in and out of the room like ghosts.

It was full dark outside when Bill came in to check on his deputy. Cherryl stiffened when he put a hand on her shoulder and said, "I am sorry."

After a long pause, she reached up and patted his hand. She said nothing. Her eyes never left her husband. I stood and stretched, the fabric pulled away from my own wound. I suppressed a scream. I was alive and Bobby was idling in the hallway between life and death. My wound was beyond insignificant.

Bill leaned down and kissed the top of Cherryl's head. I motioned him out to the hall. I led him to the vestibule where I'd spoken to the good doctor.

Without prologue I whispered, "You lo-jacked their van."

His eyes were wet and he looked away from me quickly. "Yes."

"Did you think I was being obstinate or that maybe I know how these things work? Our bad guys caught that signal. That's why I didn't want you to do it. You needed to trust me that I knew what would happen. And you needed to trust that your deputy would get his family out of here without benefit of your spy toy. But you didn't."

"I'll tell him. It's my fault. Jesus. I can't not tell him."

I stepped close to him and looked up into those storm surge eyes. "No you will not. You will not receive absolution for your sins. You will live with your knowledge. That is your punishment. No one knows but me. And yours is yet another secret I will carry to my grave." I reached a hand up to wipe the tears from his cheek. He took a deep breath and blew it out. He pulled me into a hug. I gave him as much comfort as I could. We all had to bear our own crosses, and Bill would carry this one for the rest of his life. Forgiveness only worked if it brought relief to the wronged party. In this case, Bill would lose not only his deputy, but his best friend, and Bobby would gain nothing by this truth but more hurt.

"I have to get back." I reluctantly pulled away, leaving him in the hall alone with his sins. Cherryl took no notice of my return, wiping tears from my eyes.

My eyes drooped. A tachyon accelerator would get us back to before this morning, get Bobby better cover, better yet, lock him in the truck. I knew what was coming. Divert attention, use a goddam grenade, because mass would no longer have weight so energy squared minus momentum squared would equal mass if mass less than zero …

Cherryl's gasp broke my dream. I leapt to my feet, heart pounding. She was sobbing. The machines beeped more rapidly. Bobby's eyes were open. Oh sweet merciful Jesus.

"Ellis, you bastard, you had us all terrified. Oh man. I am so glad you're back."

He blinked, dazed, I don't know if he recognized me.

Bobby came home to us thirty six hours after taking fire. Cherryl had fallen asleep with her head on his chest. She felt his heart change rhythm. A nurse would recognize that kind of thing. A beep sped up, and then a beep or two, nothing drastic, but she popped up and caressed his face. He blinked under the harsh lighting. I snapped off the overhead drowning out the lovely morning light. She spoke to him, telling him he was all right, not to fight the tube, don't move, just blink, she was fine, the kids were fine. All the kids were fine. They were under lock and key and they were safe and her parents were with them. I caught my breath, not trusting myself to talk.

I looked at Cherryl through my own tears. "He is back, then? This isn't a seizure or a false flag?" I reached across the bed for her hand. She allowed one quick squeeze and was back to her husband, talking at him. Tears leaked out of his eyes as well. I limped out the door and waited for it to close, leaving husband and wife together privately, as it should be. Bobby was alive for now and that was all that mattered.

I entered the waiting room and looked at the gray faces of my team, my friends. I held my emotions in check. These guys didn't need an hysterical woman, they needed good news.

"Deputy Ellis is awake and kind of aware. He's not out of the woods, but the forest doesn't look so scary right now."

I collapsed into a crappy plastic chair, wincing at stiffness in my leg. Bill reached over and pushed on the freshened blood stain. "You're bleeding, Archer, did you get hit?"

"No. This was from before."

Bill shook his head and stood. "I'll get the word out. Gonna have to come up with a good story separate from the marina. I don't usually have an island deputy shot up in the city."

Vincenti stood and shook Bear's hand, then stared at me with a crooked grin before extending the same courtesy. "Your friend running the comms gave me some good news. Last count was eighteen down, no survivors. Homeland Security is taking over the investigation. Maybe somebody will look into why two Mexican cartels were able to start a war on American soil."

He waited for my reaction. I gave him none. Homeland Security was a goddam ineffectual monstrosity, but dead drug dealers were a plus in my book no matter who ended the threat. I was too tired to dance around the politics. I stared at the spot between his eyebrows and waited for him to continue.

"I'm glad your friend is awake. I hope he makes it. He saved our asses back there."

I nodded.

"I'm going to lose the paperwork on the family."

I nodded and stared and waited.

"It's the least I can do. They're a good family. They really want those kids."

I nodded and smiled and looked him in the eye. "I'm glad you got a chance to talk to Bobby. They've got something special going on. Those children are theirs, without a doubt, and they'll be raised well." It was his turn to nod and say nothing. He saluted and left me balancing on one leg.

Bear yelled at Vincenti to hold up. He turned to me and said, "I'll run him wherever he needs to go. You gonna be okay?"

"I'm gonna sit for a little while then see if one of those big scary biker dudes will take me home."

I plopped back into my hard chair and avoided eye contact with the professionals manning the intake desk. Somebody had gotten all of the law enforcement personnel to vacate the lobby so the staff was slightly less hostile toward me. Or maybe it was my imagination, maybe the last few days were. Maybe I was in bed having a nightmare. Maybe Bobby was perfectly fine. I closed my eyes for a moment and awoke to the scent of hand sanitizer. I pried an eye open. Jake sat next to me, frowning. He looked refreshed. Probably had gotten some sleep and a shower.

"I understand the deputy is awake. I'm glad. His wife is a special woman." He glanced at my leg. "Stitches didn't hold. Come on, I'll get you patched up so you can resume doing whatever stupid things you were doing to land your friend in here."

I lurched down the hallway in his wake and caught up with him at the elevator. He studied me as we waited. I ignored him. I knew what I looked like, the dirt, the blood, the mud on my ass. I'd lost my hat and my hair band. My teeth felt dirty.

"I won't ask who mugged you this time."

He stopped at the desk and conferred with someone who assigned him a room with a chair and latex gloves. Deep throbbing outraced the aggravation of itchiness from the blood that glued the jeans to my skin. I could not afford to lose another pair of pants. I grabbed a handful of paper towels from the dispenser and waited for a turn at the sink. I worked the wet towels into the leg of my pants until the denim pulled away from my skin. I unbuckled my belt, pushed the pants to my ankles, and hopped up on the exam table.

"I'm running out of pants."

"Maybe you should find a new line of work."

A fresh faced nurse unknown to me stepped through the door and scrubbed up. She didn't raise an eyebrow at the scene, and spoke to the doctor in short cryptic sentences. She cleaned the wound site with precision, but without concern for my discomfort. She dropped the soiled pads into the can, donned new gloves, and prepared a harpoon.

Jake furrowed his brows, his mouth pulled into a frown as he removed the previous stitches. "You popped six of the inner stitches."

While I was distracted by that news, the nurse shot me in the meatier part of my leg. Sweet, sweet lidocaine began to work, but so did Jake. He stitched with ugly black nylon thread.

"If you hadn't ripped out the sutures, my work would have healed with minimal scarring."

Let him be mad. We'd had one half a date, and he'd seen me without pants twice. I said, "You've only seen the bottom half, wait until you see the rest. I have a scar that looks like a Peruvian desert carving."

"Let's keep this G-rated, please." The nurse glared at the doctor, some voiceless message passing between them over my legs. She threw away suture detritus, pulled off her gloves, and swept out of the room with a harrumph.

"Did I say something?"

"You're not registered." He finished taping a sterile pad over the top of the wound. "We're off books. Otherwise I'd have to file an incident report, in triplicate, and then talk to the police. As half the police are already here, the wait time would be minimal. I haven't filed the last report. I don't plan to, but maybe you should head over to Ninth Street next time you get mugged."

"Some doctor told me they'd send me back here."

"This isn't a joke. What did you accomplish besides getting your friend shot?"

That hit too close to home. "You're outta line, Jake. I appreciate the stitches and the secrecy, but you have no idea what's happened. This wasn't a good deed gone south. This was an act of war." I slid to the floor, and pulled up my pants. "It wasn't our war, but we fought regardless, and we won."

I limped out of the room. So much for a second date. Anyway, he was married. Separated was not single in my book. I possessed few morals, but the few I held were non-negotiable. I would take up a life of herding cats, gardening, and muttering at seagulls before breaking a solemn oath to God. Especially since He gave our Deputy back to us.

16 AFTER THE ALAMO

Max assured me his club maintained a rotating quota of four men minimum on guard at the Ellis home at all times. It included escort service for errands. "The family ain't ever alone. Your friend's mom was wigged out, but then she started leaving coffee and donuts on the back porch."

We spoke no more of the week's festivities. We didn't need to. I finished my morning shift at St. John's, and drove back to the hospital, reeking of disinfectant and sautéed onions. The Navy lifer, to whom we all owed a debt of gratitude, stood at the check-in desk dangling a lanyard from one bony finger. "Hey, hey, are you Jayne Mansfield? Pastor Mansfield?"

I took a deep breath, and turned on a wobbly leg. "I am."

"Well ain't that something. A real life celebrity doing good works here in our little corner of the world." His smile was wide, but his eyebrows were dubious. "Doc Tannenger dropped this here pass off so you don't havta keep sneakin in."

"In a bit of a hurry is all, sir, no disrespect."

"Ah, I ain't worried 'bout you. Doc wanted to make sure you got this." He handed me the badge, commenting that I sure didn't look like any pastor he knew. I nodded in agreement, slipped the lanyard around my neck, saluted, and crossed to the safety of the elevator.

Deputy Ellis would be kept in ICU indefinitely due to the risk of infection, and due to all the non-local cops who kept trying to get past the nurses' station. They failed every time. Everyone feared the nurses of ICU. No court order superseded their protection. Plus, the cops had a lot of ground to cover what with the shootout at Port Bryant, all the bodies, and no identification as of yet. Oscar told me a scholar at Homeland Security had floated the idea of an Al Qaeda attack. Sometimes the systemic stupidity of bureaucracy provided the best cover.

I knocked on Bobby's door and poked my head in. A nurse I didn't recognize checked things off a chart. She looked up and raised an eyebrow. I held up my lanyard for her inspection. Bobby's breathing tube had been removed, but he remained tethered to a half dozen machines that blipped and beeped. I kept telling myself that his heart hadn't actually stopped, that we fractured a couple of ribs as a preventative measure.

"Am I interrupting anything?" I asked.

"Hey Jess, you just missed Lilia. Cherr snuck her up."

The nurse shot me a look. I held my hands up. "I don't have any kids. I promise."

"Deputy, you are not dead, praise Jesus, but you don't need people traipsing in and out of here all day." She walked over, picked up my lanyard, and laughed at the honorarium. "Y'all are gonna need some Jesus if we don't get some quiet up here. We made Cherryl go home, she is no good to any of us if she doesn't get some sleep."

I waited until the nurse left and pulled a chair up next to the bed. "How's it going?"

"They won't let me up. Said they'd tie me down if I tried."

"Bobby ..."

"No. I'm just mad. Nothing hurts, they got me on all sorts of painkillers. That one just left? She likes to poke my toe with a needle. I can feel it, but I can't move it. She said it's a good sign. I don't see how waking me up and poking me with a needle is a good thing."

"Modern medicine."

"Voodoo more like. Bill come in and told me Vincenti is back in the good books, getting credit for the take down."

"An Army of One?"

"Sounds like they mostly shot each other, what with all those foreigners and all those guns. Bill told me a whole lot of other stuff, but I can't remember the half of it. Seems these folks were fighting over a Point of Import – that's what Bill called it. Legal talk. But Bryant ain't in any trouble. Seems Vincenti said the guy at the bank set the whole thing up couple years back, when the marina went bankrupt – the note was too big for all the money this guy loaned the owners. Can you believe that? Money. People getting shot over money."

"I can believe it, but how did you get shot?"

"Oh yeah, Bill said he's gonna quit policing and go into writing. See, I was in the city, checking out a flop house, looking for some tourist kid whose folks called her in missing while they were on island, on vacation. I took the call and went in undercover like. Just a coincidence."

"Maybe we should go into government work because we are all getting very good at lying, Deputy Ellis."

He coughed out a laugh and finished with a groan. "I am in government work, but I ain't that good at the lyin' part."

"Bill's good enough for both of us. How's Cherryl holding up?"

"Aw, you know her, piss and vinegar. You ain't seen her?"

I shook my head. "I'm part of the problem."

"No you ain't. She said you stayed with her til I woke up. Wouldn't leave. She ain't gonna tell you, but I know it made her feel better having a friend here, hold her hand since I couldn't. Cherr said your friends been good to her and the kids. She said they got four on the house round the clock. Get by there soon, she's going crazy with five kids in the house, her folks, and those bikers. The other nurses kicked her out after I woke up, said she needed to sleep. And she ain't letting the kids back to school just yet." He took a deep breath as a wave of pain he claimed did not exist moved through him. He pushed the breath out and asked, "You think we gotta worry about more folks coming?"

"Not likely. This was never about Bear or his marina. That bank agent has got some explaining to do. Bill will get to him soon enough, if one of those cartels haven't already."

"We're keeping those kids, Jess. All they been through? They got nobody. Their own kin doing this. Man, that's just wrong." A breath caught in his throat, and he scrunched his face in pain.

I stood and grabbed the call button. Within seconds, the dubious nurse rushed in with a party favor to knock the pain back. I leaned over and put my cheek to Bobby's forehead. It was clammy.

"Is he okay?" I asked.

She pushed buttons on the I.V. machine and picked up Bobby's wrist. Within seconds his face relaxed in a narcotic haze. "Get outta here before these ladies hurt you," he warned.

I mouthed thank you at the nurse and scurried out the door before she decided she didn't like me. I left the badge with the Navy man and escaped before he could send me on a chaplain run. Avoidance was high on my skill set, and I had items on my to-do list that could not be avoided, like visiting the gang of children and their mom and their body guards.

I drove south from the hospital, and turned onto Jackson. The Ellis clan lived on the west end in a ranch style brick home with plenty of room for the herd to run. Minutes from their church, from the hospital, from their schools. Bobby had a bitch of a drive to work, but he didn't seem to mind as long as his family was happy.

I parked the truck on the berm outside the fence and walked up the drive. No bikes in evidence, but I felt eyes on me. I hope someone gave the guards my description. Xavier came tearing around the corner of the house with Theresa on his tail. The boy stopped abruptly when he saw me and was tackled from behind.

"Hey, where's the football?" I asked.

Theresa helped her new brother to his feet and said, "We're playing tag."

Xavier took a slow step toward me, broke into a run, and jumped on me. I held him in a bear hug for several moments. He leaned back and looked at me, a small smile crossed his lips. "Thank you, Ahulane."

What the hell was I supposed to do with that? "No, Xavier, I'm plain old Jess, or Auntie Jess, nothing else. Got it?" He shrugged. I took that as an agreement and swung the boy to the ground, chasing both of them to the back yard. No sign of the sentries, but I didn't need one. Steady was not a man to filch on his word. I chased the three younger children around the trees in the back yard until Cherryl yelled the word food. I followed them in the house. She'd laid out grilled cheese sandwiches, slightly charred, and made with real processed cheese. I hadn't had one since service, and those were stone cold, soggy, and I didn't like to think about whatever was in that alleged cheese.

"Wash up now. Nobody touches a thing until hands are inspected. Lilia, Bobby, come on." Cherryl said.

I closed the door and leaned back against it. My leg throbbed from chasing the taggers around the yard. Lilia, a shadow of the beautiful young woman she would grow into spoke softly, "You've come."

"Scoot now, go wash up." Cherryl said to Lilia. "Bobby, make sure those heathens' hands are clean before feeding them, okay?"

"You bet, mom."

She gestured toward the door and followed me out. We walked a distance into the yard, away from little or big ears. I lit a cigarette and waited some more. Cherryl held her hand out for my smoke. I passed it to her. She took a drag, held it, then chuffed it out. "Blech, I am glad I quit those things."

"Me, too. I only have four left."

"Gonna quit?"

I shrugged. "Maybe next year."

She turned toward me, hands on hip. "Bill told me what you did."

That was a loaded statement. I smoked my cigarette and waited for punishment or commendation.

"You kept my husband alive. You kept him breathing."

"We all did."

"Yeah, Billy said he might have cracked a couple of ribs pumping on him."

"He'd lost a lot of blood, he was in shock."

"He lost enough to make his damn heart stop. I know it did."

"Cherryl, it didn't, he got close, but it didn't stop."

"How the hell do you know that?"

"Training. Field medic. We all had to learn basic skills, the boys and the girls. Trauma team did a blood draw, right? Did any of those, what do you call them, enzyme markers, did they show up?"

"No, but the doctor said he thought his heart had stopped."

"Did you see it in his chart?"

She harrumphed at me, and shook her head.

I finished my cigarette, stubbed the fire out, and stuffed it in my pocket.

"That's gonna stink." She scuffed a dirty tennis shoe in the grass. "Jess, I gotta tell you, I am so sorry I yelled at you. It wasn't your fault. Bobby was doing what was right. They took our children. I mean, they're not ours, but by God, we got plans to make them ours."

"Don't apologize to me. We should have seen it coming. Those people wanted those kids. The savageness they'd already shown, we messed up. This is on us."

"I asked Lilia if she wanted to talk about, you know, what happened. God, it's only been, what, four days, five? Seems like a year. I took her for a walk, just me and her. I asked if anyone hurt her. You know, hurt her." Cherryl bent her quotie fingers to emphasize the word hurt. "Did those bastards hurt my children? Oh God, please tell me they didn't. Xavier keeps raving on about a black faced warrior killing the cyclops. And Lilia will only say that Boolook is satisfied. What the hell happened to my kids?"

Some secrets were better left buried. No purpose would be served by the truth. I plastered on a poker face, and engaged my ability to lie like a rug.

"Cherryl, you know how kids are. Lilia seems older, but she's just a girl. Remember yourself at that age. We thought we were so sophisticated, but inside she's just a kid. My hand on a bible, the kids were roughed up, the hell scared out of them, but they were not molested in any way. Please, let it go."

"So what about this blue jack or blue-luke? What the hell is that?"

"Make believe, mythology from their homeland. We have the Greeks, they have the Maya. Think about it. Who fought the cyclops? Who was the black faced warrior? You said the kids were tearing through adventure books your mom had dropped by. The Odyssey, Call of the Wild? What are some of the other titles? You read, the kids read, you have more books than dust bunnies. Kids use stories to make sense of things they don't understand."

"And you are an expert on child psychology."

"It's what I did when I lost my parents. No shrink. No therapy. I had decent people who looked out for me. Bill was one of them. And Hannah, and Sarah."

"Sarah was a good woman." I nodded in agreement. Bill's late wife was sorely missed by anyone who had had the good fortune of meeting her. And I used that love to sidetrack the course of this conversation.

She sighed and smiled, remembering our friend. "You know, my folks weren't happy about us taking on two unexplained children outta the blue, but they came to stay as soon as I called. Did you see those biker guys? My mother thought she was losing her mind until she caught one of them out and made him talk. Dad's already asking if the kids might like something besides turkey for Thanksgiving, you know, since they aren't from here. Since they – they – they're orphans."

She fell apart, shaking with days of pent up terror. I held her until the worst had passed. She wiped at her eyes. "I'm not much good right now."

"You're wrong. You're a rock. But you need new mascara."

Her laugh sounded good in the fall air. I sent her off to clean up, issue instructions to the children, and go see her husband, alone. "I'll be fine here, we've got the guards."

"Unless the little ones tie you up playing Cowboys and Indians."

The thought of fending off a gang of sugar-crazed children was terrifying. It would not be a fair fight. I found the remote for the television and punched buttons until that crazy talking sponge made an appearance. It smothered all thoughts of mutiny. I can't say I wasn't relieved when Cherryl's folks showed up with pizza and ice cream.

17 BLESSED ARE THE POOR IN SPIRIT

I soldiered past the roadhouse, splashing west through the surf, arriving at land's end, my mind blank. It felt as if the earth were breathing easy while the gulf rolled slowly toward high tide. Beach traffic was light, save for surf fishers dotting the shore. They were a hardy people and fished year round. I peeked in each bucket as I turned east in the sandy roundabout, promising myself to get a license, a bucket, a pole, and a guide. Maybe I'd get a bucket, fill it with beer, and offer to trade for fish.

I wiped the sand off my feet, and let the cat out. He shot down the stairs, disappearing beneath the jungle of erosion canopy. Purslane, sea oats, morning glories, and rosemary, which all had to be thinned periodically. Hannah loved the vegetation so I planted it and weeded it and replaced it when necessary. We were environmentally aware of the effect of hurricanes and tidal flow on our coast.

I poured a drink, and enjoyed the late afternoon sun on the deck, clicking at the cat pouncing in his habitat. The only things Ralphie had caught these many months were a cigarette wrapper, a small stick of driftwood, and a napkin from the Shrimp Basket. Life forms were in no danger. Trilling of the house phone annoyed me out of the deck chair.

"Can you come over, like in an hour? I'll feed you before we leave." Cherryl instructed me to bring a suit, valid identification, my DD214, and a toothbrush. "Just wear regular clothes. I'm not sure when we'll get in to see the judge."

"Of course."

I grabbed my funeral suit, found hose and shoes, grabbed a purse out of Hannah's closet and changed into the cleanest clothes I owned. I pulled the copy of my military discharge out of the now empty gun safe and slipped it in the purse to keep company with my driver's license and Florida firearms card. That piece of plastic proved I had not been convicted of a felony. With room to spare, I dropped in toothbrush, toothpaste, and a hair brush.

I collected the cat, filled extra food and water bowls, and locked up the house. Orders had been issued and I was in no position to disobey. Bill may have lo-jacked the escape van, but I failed to connect the dots. Abandoned children, dead parents, barbaric criminal activity, and south of El Paso actors. The list of 'should-haves' was long and dark, as was the list of the damned and the dead. We were thunderous gods last Sunday, we extracted our vengeance, but it was the Ellis family who paid the price. Cherryl must have a damned good reason for telling me to pack for an overnight. She rarely left Bobby's side except when threatened by her co-workers.

Cherryl's mother was laying plates around the table, and I could hear a man's deep voice from the family room reading a story out loud.

Cherryl announced, "Spaghetti for dinner."

Service was fast yet far more polite than mess hall. I scraped and rinsed dishes while Cherryl issued instructions to Bob Junior. She pulled me into what passed for her private office, the laundry room on the back porch. She stuffed clothing into a garbage bag.

"Mom and Dad are cleared to stay. They're talking about pulling the fifth wheel to Tate's Hell and camping. They'll have an escort. Mom has grown fond of our guards. It defies belief. She's been feeding them. Your Doctor Tannenger gave me a note for the schools, saying we've been trading the flu, and I'm keeping everyone home since Bobby is in the hospital."

"He's not my anything."

"Funny, that, he's asked after you several times."

She handed me a manila envelope that had been sealed with security tape. Eight dollars of cancelled stamps covered the top, and it was addressed to Mrs. Robert Ellis, hand written in block letters. No return address.

I slid the contents out on the lid of the washer. On top of the stack of papers were two crisp birth certificates signed and imprinted by the clerk of Webb County, city of Laredo, dated May of this year. I didn't recognize the mother's name and the paternal box contained the word Unknown. Months earlier Vincenti had created a history for Xavier and Lilia out of his love for their mother. He had planned to extract the family.

The third official document bore the seal of Webb County as well. A death certificate stapled to letterhead of a judge. The name of the deceased was Joy Denise Tamarak. The letter itself was addressed to Whomever It May Concern.

Joy Denise was an third cousin, twice removed, formerly living in a trailer parked on an unincorporated patch of desert off US-59 called Ranchitos Las Lomas in Webb County, Texas. Ms. Tamarak had died tragically, but not unexpectedly due to complications stemming from her use of narcotics, leaving behind two children, a girl and a boy. The note advised Whomever to present a birth certificate, marriage license, recent tax return, and proof of employment to apply for custody of the children who had been living alone in the trailer until the good Samaritans of Santa Teresita Mission discovered them. The Mission would continue to house, feed, and cloth the children until such time a suitable relative could be located. In spidery handwriting, the judge concluded with the hope that this request would find Mr. and Mrs. Robert Ellis in a position to be suitable relatives. An illegible signature finished the request for Whomever.

Cherryl arranged for Bobby's care while I mapped out a route to the Webb County courthouse in Laredo. I printed four sheets of paper and wiped the history and cache from their aged desktop computer. She packed provisions, kissed her children goodbye and told her mother not to worry. "I'll be back tomorrow night or early Tuesday."

Her mother stood at the back door watching in wonder while we packed the new children into the Ellis family mini-van, and covered them with blankets.

Cherryl chauffeured as we set forth after sunset for the thirteen hour drive to the Laredo courthouse so Cherryl could present herself as the hoped-for suitable legal guardian. The kids emerged from hiding as soon as we hit the I-10. Cherryl and I traded seats at midnight.

At 0800, a thousand miles from nowhere, I pulled into the dusty lot of the church listed on the note attached to the death certificate. I stepped out blinking in the sharp morning light, stretching and yawning. Cherryl hopped out, smoothed her clothing, and led the children into the church. I harbored few superstitions, but I checked the sky for lighting before entering the sanctuary.

We were expected. A young woman led us into the sanctuary where an old priest awaited our arrival. He sped through the baptism in Spanish. I stood as godparent to both children. I recognized the word Satan and said I do when the priest asked if I renounced his works. No thunder shook the skies, no hole opened in the floor. The old man anointed the children, then Cherryl, then me, and pronounced us reborn.

I asked no questions while the priest pecked letters on an ancient typewriter. He offered me a pen and pointed at a blank line at the bottom of the document. I signed. Cherryl spoke Spanish with the old man in hushed tones. She thanked him for the role he played in this mission. He kissed both her cheeks, and motioned for the young woman to escort us to the door.

We sped past cattle ranches fuzzed with green, interspersed among the desert hard pan. Ranch houses sprinkled the landscape in the vast nothingness. I breathed a sigh of relief when I spotted a billboard for an upcoming Aggie football alumni weekend.

Cherryl left me with the children at the corner of Clark and Tilden with explicit instructions not to leave the area. She pointed at a café and said she would pick us up right there when she was done at the clerk's office. She was hoping for an expedited judgment.

We walked around the neighborhood in the midday heat. The children took turns translating words and signs, amused at my lack of language skills. No one bothered us. No one questioned why these beautiful children were wandering around with a road hard gringa wearing scuffed cowboy boots. Maybe people like me were babysitters in this part of town. The streets were quiet, not much traffic. It was a school day, a work day. The few people we encountered were pleasant and uninterested.

My phone beeped. Cherryl was on her way to the cafe. I was to change clothes, and all three of us must be ready to roll. Xavier was hungry again. I sent Lilia to the counter with cash to order what her brother needed. I wanted a cold drink. Beer preferably, but she brought me a soda. The cafe mixed their own drinks with syrup sweet enough to rattle my fillings.

I exchanged dirty jeans for my funeral suit and heels in the restroom, and ran a brush through my hair while we waited outside in the dry sunshine. Cherryl drove us to a modern municipal building flavored with southwestern flair. We sat in a tiled hallway until a bailiff waved us in. The children fidgeted not at all, but I was ready to jump out of my skin. I suffered no remorse committing violent felonies when warranted, but this paperwork nonsense was worrisome. My real name committed forever to some government functionary, and then exiled to a filing cabinet in dusty catacombs where all paperwork went to molder.

I stood in front of a judge in my official capacity as a decorated Marine and current business owner, vouching for the fitness of Mr. and Mrs. Ellis. I attested that Mr. Ellis could not attend the hearing today having been injured in the line of duty, but he was progressing well. I had been called up to stand as their godmother, and expressed pleasure that both sets of grandparents were alive and well and looking forward to spoiling their new grandchildren.

The judge either through goodness or expediency found a plausible way to remove the cost of two children from the county budget. With no hesitation, he signed temporary guardianship pending formal petition in the county in which the children would permanently reside. He also wrote a separate note, in his official capacity, that no one had applied for guardianship, and he felt that the children would benefit greatly by adoption into the Ellis family. They would have siblings, school, religious training, and extended family.

I stopped in El Campo to fill the gas tank and refill my coffee. The pot had been warming on the burner longer than it should have, but with bitterness came wakefulness. Cherryl woke up grumpy as we sped through Baton Rouge.

Without preamble she asked, "Do you know why I abandoned my family to drive to Texas, why I dragged these two refugees halfway across the country?"

"No. I did as ordered without question. If you want to tell me, great, if not, stop yelling." I pulled the rearview mirror down, centering it on the back seat. The children slept on undisturbed.

"When those people fled Guatemala, only two people knew where they were, right? Vincenti said it was an emergency evacuation. Just him and his partner. I accepted that premise. The family we met as Reyes escaped the DEA and arrived in Pensacola. Why here?"

"Don't know."

"For God's sake, think. How did those killers find the family? Were their bank accounts being monitored? Do drug dealers have an APB system?"

I pulled the rearview mirror down again. Xavier had slipped off his seat belt and curled up in his sister's lap. She leaned against the window with her free arm wrapped around her brother. Back and forth the voices in my head argued for and against giving Cherryl this last piece of the puzzle. Cherryl lived in a world of family and church, of duty and responsibility. She lived in the world, but not of the world. I dug inside for the words to warn her of the world where her new children had lived and damn near died.

"Most of what I know is conjecture. Tell me what you know first.

"Alex, their father, was laundering money for some drug organization in Guatemala. Then another gang wanted in, that's when they ran." Cherryl said.

I checked the rearview again. I would explain what I could only once. "Guatemala is almost incidental. New opium fields are being carved out of the rain forest and the farmers, any farmer, will sow and harvest whatever makes the most money. Understand that the money from drug trafficking is billions upon billions of billions. Cartels control whole branches of government from Mexico, down through the tip of South America. Makes production and distribution a whole lot easier. The cartel known as Chiapas is the strongest, they control the means of production, the routes of export, the courts, the police. A splinter broke off and grew fast. In less than a decade, this new group calling themselves Leon Nuevo was challenging the largest cartel in the world for supremacy. And it's ugly. They don't bargain, they don't blackmail, they destroy, without mercy." I paused, checking the children again. "The children's maternal grandmother is – was – the wife of the man who heads this upcoming cartel."

Cherryl struggled with her safety belt until she was facing me. "This isn't real."

I nudged my head toward her new children. "Their grandmother was seriously into some Mayan mythology business. Blood sacrifice, celestial patterns, all that. She told Lilia's mother that she was free to go wherever she wanted, but when the girl reached puberty, she would be used to reignite the empire. She put word out to Chiapas that if they brought her the children, she would broker a truce with her husband's cartel."

"Mayan empire? Are you kidding? They were Catholic."

"Really." I laughed. "That's your concern. Maybe that woman found a way to assure utmost loyalty in her husband's organization by invoking a long dead empire with all their gods and mysticism. I don't know. But I know the woman you knew as

Isobel Reyes loved her children enough to risk her life getting them to the United States. Where she thought they'd be safe. As to why Pensacola? I think it was just dumb luck."

I could give up Vincenti or chalk it up to fate. The hatred Cherryl harbored for the agent was already too strong, it served no purpose to the future of those children. "The Reyes's used cash to buy identities burying the connection between grandmother and granddaughter. Unfortunately, Isobel and the agent who died at the marina were having an affair. Isobel contacted him when they settled in. The agent broke cover to meet her, and somebody found out. It's damned hard to buy our agents, but over the border? Those guys barely make enough to feed their families. Someone somewhere leaked."

The chanting of Cherryl's prayers softly rose over the noise of the tires on the asphalt.

I waited until she finished and said, "The kids have a legal and unbreakable identity now. Nothing is left tying them to anyone in Guatemala or Mexico. Vincenti finished the paperwork his partner started."

"You can't make me like him."

"You don't have to."

"What about Bear's marina? The firefight? Bobby said an awful lot of stuff while they had him drugged up."

"The feds will bury every last thread. They let this filth into our country, and now they gotta stop it. Maybe. Finally."

"Thank you for the commentary on your faith in our democracy."

"I have faith in God, but the Republic is in jeopardy."

She yawned hugely and knuckled a fist to cover her mouth. "Get off my lawn, right? You sound like a grumpy old man, but what you are now is godmother to those children, in charge of their education spiritual and otherwise should something happen to Bobby or me. You think about that while I go back to sleep."

18 THANKS GIVING

Attention seeking do-gooders ran us regulars out of St. John's so they could signal their virtues on television, mugging with local celebrities, while actively avoiding the disadvantaged, downtrodden, and smelly. I spent the morning dragging around the house. I considered driving into the nursery. Maybe other sad sacks would wander in to shop away their blues, but that required an effort of will I lacked. Without work, without my Thursday morning service, without my aunt, I was aimless. I planned to drink myself into liver failure with the cat. Ralphie wasn't drinking. He was the designated driver.

Bobby's surgery was scheduled for Monday morning. Cherryl assured us the very best cutters would suit up for the big game. Even if successful, Bobby would require months of painful and expensive rehabilitation. With two more kids to feed, it was time to consider fundraising. Or maybe an anonymous donation.

The mailman had tired of stuffing our mail into the overflowing box. He shoveled everything into a Wynn-Dixie bag and left it on the porch, tied to the door handle.

I dumped the bag on the table, and sorted the mail into piles of garbage, bills, and personal correspondence until I ran across a thick manila envelope, return address listed a 606 zip code.

I carefully placed the envelope on the counter and stared at it. While I played War Games, a cashier's check for a stupid amount of money had squatted in the mailbox like a big fat toad.

Without Hannah to advise me, I asked the stupid cat what to do with the money. The cat licked his paws and blinked lazily at me. I had no one else to ask.

Oscar had flown to Grenada for the long holiday weekend to liberate the local lasses from their propriety. Bear was off with the cute deputy from Haynes Street. Angela had invited me to dine with her parents and forty or so of their relations and friends at a foo-foo Sushi joint around the corner from the Saenger

Theatre. I thanked Mrs. Kimball for the invitation, but declined politely. The thought of shopping for suitable attire gave me heartburn.

I walked the morning away up and down the beach, avoiding family units. Not out of malice, but self-pity. I fed the cat, pulled on boots, and brushed my hair in preparation for dinner at the Waffle House. The phone rang. Cherryl wanted to know where the heck I was, dinner was darn near ready, and she needed a quart of heavy cream.

I showered, located clean blue jeans, and found a blouse that wasn't too wrinkled. Tom Thumb provided the requested cream. I thanked the violet haired clerk for taking a holiday shift. She said it was safer here than at dinner with her family. They didn't like her hair. I told her it looked festive.

The gravel turnabout was crowded with assorted passenger vehicles and motorcycles. With all the bikes in plain view, Cherryl's mother must have invited most of the biker club. Chirps and squeals and the clanking of dishes flowed out the back door. I stood outside, wondering why in the hell I answered the phone. I hated crowds and noise and small talk and paper plates and candied yams. And I felt the irrational need not to be around all this fragile happiness.

I was an adult, and I would behave as such. I slipped a smile on my face and stepped into the house.

Risking injury, I put the cream in the refrigerator and backed out of the kitchen. Cherryl was sweating and yelling at what had to be a sister. They shared the same hair color.

"Get the kids out from the kitchen or I won't be responsible for their injuries." The sister shooed a half a dozen children from underfoot with a towel and yelled for Bobby Junior. "I thought you said you'd corral these ponies." She swept past, favoring me with a vague party smile.

"Hiya, come on in, they're not quite housebroken, but most of 'em don't bite."

If she only knew …

The cooks did not need my help and no one was bleeding or shooting. I wandered through the house and found a dozen siblings, cousins, and assorted friends yelling at a television. Tiny men ran scattershot around an unnaturally green field covered in white stripes. I didn't get close enough to determine who was playing, but judging by the comments, nobody liked anybody.

The front door stood open. I stepped outside and found Bobby Junior and Lilia explaining the finer points of Ghost in the Graveyard to a motley assortment of children, including their own brother and sisters. The huddle broke and the younger children scattered for hiding places. Lilia counted to ten slowly, in Spanish, then yelled, "I come to get you." She shot past me with a huge grin on her face. Bobby slowed long enough to say hey and followed in the girl's wake.

How much longer would the big kids play with the little ones, I wondered, grateful they were doing so now. How much longer would the angst of oncoming adulthood be kept at bay? I walked around the yard and scuffled through the leaves of early turning oaks. I crossed to the picnic table and smoked a cigarette, then a second, pouting like the ugly girl at a party. So why the self pity? The feds were cleaning up their mess and pointing so many fingers at each other for the breach of security that they forgot all about us. Bobby's recovery had progressed far enough for the surgeons to schedule removal of the last bullet fragment. I asked God to replace this gloom with gratitude, but He must have been out to lunch.

A late model sedan pocked with door dinks pulled into the drive as I was about to light a third cigarette. Jake stepped out and smiled over the top of the hood. "Didn't think you'd come."

"I had to bring the whipping cream."

"I brought the beer. Cherryl said her people don't drink a lot so she didn't get anything."

"Bullshit. They're running low. Don't let her kid you."

He opened the trunk and pulled out three cases of beer. "It's cold, but I brought a couple of coolers just in case." I lifted a cooler full of ice out of the trunk, pretending not to strain under the weight. My vanity refused all assistance. I was woman, hear me groan. I let him shift the second cooler.

Silently, except for my grunting, we toted the wares to the back porch and nestled cans into the ice. He handed me a beer. "You can wash down those damned cigarettes with some alcohol."

We clinked tin and drank. "An intern at the med center in Foley removed the stitches. He asked if I'd done the sewing myself."

"And you threw me under the bus."

"No, sir. I told him I'd watched a video and it seemed simple enough."

Jake laughed. "At least you're walking without a limp."

"Every day, up and down the beach."

"I thought you lived at that nursery."

"I have a secret lair. With a gulf view."

Our witty conversation was interrupted by a southern twang at full volume. Cherryl pushed out the screen door laden with grocery bags. "I'm taking Bobby dinner. Who all's cars are blocking me in?"

It was a mad scramble to get the Ellis family mini-van unblocked without being injured by the woman who wanted to serve her husband a hot home cooked meal for Thanksgiving.

I wandered around the house, eventually meeting everyone, including the honor guard assigned to Chez Ellis. Dinner was a buffet service piled high on disposable plates. Shrapnel from plastic cutlery flew through the air. The laughter was louder than the football game. I skipped the yams. I noticed Jake didn't take any either. Only thing we agreed on since we met.

19 ON HATING THE IRISH

Hannah returned the morning of Christmas Eve full of stories of how lovely Ireland had been, everyone so welcoming and friendly and healthy. The troubles were over but the Celtic Tiger had been house broken. London was dirtier than she remembered. I gritted my teeth and oohed and aahed in all the right places. She showed me several lovely pieces of hand-tatted lace and produced a bottle of Jameson, which she opened immediately. As she'd brought it all the way from the verdant fields of my forefathers, she suggested I choke down a glass or wear one, my choice.

I toted her luggage into the bedroom, shooed the cat out, and tossed a sheet over the bed so travel cooties could not soil her personal bedding. Ralphie was curled around her neck and up into her chin as she was poured tumblers of whiskey.

"Ralphie is no worse for wear." She said.

"He's been suffering happy feet at all hours since you left, regardless of the position of the sun."

She sipped at her glass staring at a gray cardboard box tied with twine. It had magically appeared on the counter while I attended her luggage.

"I brought you a sweater."

I made no move to touch it.

"I also found this." She slid an envelope out of her purse and laid it on top of the box.

I shot the whiskey back and stared at her. I loved the hell out of her and worried when she was away even if she weren't in the land of giants and ghosts.

I chuckled. "Only you, Hannah dear, would risk my wrath."

"It is not your wrath that gives me pause."

I held my glass out for a refill knowing something wicked this way was coming.

The envelope was new and stiff. I flipped the lid and a single picture fell out. Yellowed with age, its colors flattened as the emulsion faded. Three people in the photograph squinting in the late morning sunlight. Standing in front of a bakery. Dad was laughing and looking at mother, who stood a half foot taller than me. Sandwiched in the middle, I had my arms around their waists.

It took several moments to speak. "How did you get this?"

"The woman who gave me the photograph was a child herself when her Mother took that picture."

My temperature plunged to zero. "Tell me you didn't – "

"Not everyone on that island hates. Most did not want the wars. It was a small faction that caused so much bloodshed, on all sides."

"Hannah, the statute of limitations – "

"The woman gave me the picture because I told her it was my brother and his family that had been killed. She was away at school or she would have been there. Several shops had to close their doors for weeks. And when they reopened, no one spoke of the incident again. To anyone."

I poured more whiskey for us both.

"No one knows of your existence, Jessica."

"I'm sorry. I know you wouldn't – not even accidentally."

"I rarely do anything accidentally." The corner of her mouth tried to turn up, yet a tear leaked out of a cornflower blue eye.

"Forgive me. We have nothing left of your parents. When I found out the bakery was still operated by the same family, I took a chance."

I came around the counter and hugged her tight, thanked her for the sweater, and wiped my eyes on a dish towel.

We toasted my green Aran sweater, loose and soft, large enough to fit over my holster. The crisis had passed and the smiles came more freely as the whiskey of my forebears loosened our tongues.

I shared an abridged version of the exciting adventures at Chico Bayou, omitting my personal body count. She was glad to hear Port Bryant was open for business again, and horrified at the news of Deputy Ellis's injury.

Hannah was most interested in the newest members of the Family Ellis and how they were fairing as New Americans. She especially liked the story of the Child Services agent assigned to Cherryl and Bobby's adoption petition.

According to legend, upon inspection of the happy Ellis home, the agent expressed disbelief that the third cousin twice removed, given her living conditions, had never contacted the Ellis family before now. And my, weren't the children exotic looking. Were they perhaps Mexican?

Cherryl's reaction to the repugnant woman was so violent that the agent was forced into retirement. A nice lady was assigned the case and expedited the documentation. She had no opinion as to who the children resembled. They were registered at school under their forever names within days.

The secretary at the elementary school had taken the news of Bobby's injuries personally and proceeded to organize bake sales, car washes, and extorted every family at both the elementary and high school for donations. Then she went after the diocese.

An anonymous donation disguised as a large chocolate sampler had been dropped on the secretary's desk while she was at lunch. A note taped inside the lid read Deputy Ellis.

I didn't tell Aunt Hannah about the money I'd received. Not yet. I wanted it to be a surprise. Later perhaps, when she least suspected it, maybe a box of cash would show up on her doorstep with no return address, dressed as a sampler of imported Swiss chocolates.

On New Year's Eve, armed with half a dozen bottles of sparkling cider and disposable champagne flutes, Hannah and I drove into the city and snuck our way into St. Katherine's. Bobby had been in residence since recovering from surgery. Prognosis guarded, but optimistic. The whole family, and most of the floor staff, toasted to a happy and prosperous New Year.

Back home, we rang in our new year with a bottle of imported champagne. We were too old to brave the crowds. I awoke without a hangover. My new year was off to an adult-like start.

20 TOSSING DEAD FISH

The crowd parted around Deputy Bobby Ellis as he clomped his way into the sacred circle. The kids had jammed rubber balls on the feet of his crutches so he wouldn't sink in the sand. The clapping started somewhere in the middle of the crowd and rose until the noise overwhelmed the senses.

Bobby Junior was allowed to select a fish out of the bucket for his father. Bobby Senior dropped his crutches and inspected it. He nodded at his oldest, folded the fish over, reared his arm back, and launched the mullet sixty feet into Alabama.

In recognition of Bobby's big damn hero status, he had been tapped by management to open the Annual Interstate Mullet Toss. For decades, the event, attended by tossers from around the globe at the end of every April, heralded in summer season on the island. Revelers roared and complete strangers reached out to clap Bobby on the back. Bouncers disguised as deputies parted the crowd so the family had room to escape the circle safely.

A small warm hand crept into mine. Lilia had grown an inch over the long spring, not quite looking me straight in the eye, but it wouldn't be long. She smiled at me, happy and healthy. The shadow of her mother's sacrifice was losing its strength. My other hand grabbed and squeezed by a boy far less pale and far more outgoing than the one I'd met in November. He had become a sun bunny like his brother and sisters. "Come on, Aunt Jess, a whole picnic your Miss Hannah makes. We eat at the sea."

Cherryl made her way toward us, pushing Elizabeth and Theresa ahead, a hand on each of their shoulders. "Would you all get these four down the beach? Bobby Junior is showing his dad off. It's going to take a while getting them to the car." While Deputy Bob had made great strides in his recovery, he was not ready to dodge twenty thousand partiers to walk a mile down the beach to our own picnic.

Jake caught my eye and smiled, reaching out for the girls. His marital status had changed legally in late January, but my track record with men was short and fraught with danger.

Throughout the winter, Jake and I met for coffee regularly. Neither of us ready for dinner quite yet.

On a warm March afternoon, I decided to act like a damned adult and give our friendship a chance. I ran into town and bought a family sized meal of smoked pork from Parker Grocer and Meats. I tracked Jake down at the hospital. We sat on a bench outside the hospital and ate ourselves silly.

We became honorary aunt and uncle to the Ellis clan, babysitting the brood when Cherryl wanted to spend time alone with her husband. Not dates so much as play dates with kids neither one of us owned.

Lilia led our pack east, at times stretching my arm painfully, winding through a half mile of partiers oiled and bronzed, some burnt to a crisp. Old, young, and in between. The Mullet Toss drew a diverse crowd. All were clad in shorts and swim gear, costumes or wetsuits. The number of people we dodged around dwindled as we drew farther away from the nucleus. Sure enough, I spotted the pop-up tent I'd anchored above the high tide line this morning. My hands were dropped as Xavier challenged his sisters to a race through the surf.

The kids made a game of seeing who could kick water the highest. By the time we arrived at the tent, we were all were soaked. I ordered everyone to wipe down lest Hannah beat us for tracking sand in her house. A chorus of giggles rose at the thought of my silver haired, blue-eyed impish Auntie chasing them about with a stick.

Jake lifted a cooler lid and frowned. "I was promised food and drink for my babysitting efforts."

I kicked the red cooler. "This one is for the grown-ups."

Jake lifted the lid and laughed. "Damn, your auntie knows how to stock a cooler."

I reached past him and grabbed an ice cold bottle of bubbly. I held it out for inspection. "Will this do?"

He grabbed glasses from the table and nodded toward the surf line. I peeled the foil, shoving it in my pocket. The Grande Dame herself stared imperiously over my shoulder, refusing to meet my gaze. I pocketed the cage and traded his glasses for the bottle. He aimed the bottle neck toward the horizon and eased the cork out with his thumbs.

The pop was exceptional, the cork arced over the water. "Fifteen feet, maybe. I can't beat the deputy's distance with a cork." He filled our glasses.

I linked my arm through his and held my glass out for a toast, smiling into those tired brown eyes. I didn't know what would come tomorrow, but everything had to start somewhere.

§ 918. Art. 118. Murder

Any person subject to this chapter who, without justification or excuse, unlawfully kills a human being, when he—

(1) has a premeditated design to kill;

(2) intends to kill or inflict great bodily harm;

(3) is engaged in an act which is inherently dangerous to another and evinces a wanton disregard of human life; or

(4) is engaged in the perpetration or attempted perpetration of burglary, sodomy, rape, rape of a child, aggravated sexual assault, aggravated sexual assault of a child, aggravated sexual contact, aggravated sexual abuse of a child, aggravated sexual contact with a child, robbery, or aggravated arson;

is guilty of murder, and shall suffer such punishment as a court-martial may direct, except that if found guilty under clause (1) or (4), he shall suffer death or imprisonment for life as a court-martial may direct.

(Aug. 10, 1956, ch. 1041, 70A Stat. 72; Pub. L. 102–484, div. A, title X, § 1066(b), Oct. 23, 1992, 106 Stat. 2506; Pub. L. 109–163, div. A, title V, § 552(d), Jan. 6, 2006, 119 Stat. 3263.)

HISTORICAL AND REVISION NOTES

Revised section	Source (U.S. Code)	Source (Statutes at Large)
918	50:712.	May 5, 1950, ch. 169, § 1 (Art. 118), 64 Stat. 140.

The words "of this section" are omitted as surplusage.

After spending more than three decades generating non-fictional layers of ones and zeroes to create elaborate information systems for the enrichment of mankind, I stopped to write in my native tongue for my own enrichment. In all endeavors, I seek knowledge outside of my own. I've met heroes and villains. It is hard to tell the difference, unless of course, they put ice in their bourbon. In which case, the bodies are never found. There are some offenses even God cannot abide.

Thank you for coming on this ride. I don't know when it will end, as none of us know the hour of our death, but damn, that's half the fun.

"Courage is doing what you're afraid to do. There can be no courage unless you're scared." ~ Eddie Rickenbacker

Folks here in the Middle Kingdom remember his name.

RKFADAMS.com for more of Jess Archer's Island Adventures.

www.ingramcontent.com/pod-product-compliance
Lightning Source LLC
Chambersburg PA
CBHW071137170626
46809CB00002B/661